A Killer Came Knocking

About the Author

S. B. Caves was born and raised in London. He loves crime and thriller novels, classic horror movies, Korean/Japanese thriller films and true crime documentaries.

A KILLER CAME KNOCKING

S.B. CAVES

CANELO

First published in the United Kingdom in 2019 by Canelo

This edition published in the United Kingdom in 2020 by

Canelo Digital Publishing Limited
Third Floor, 20 Mortimer Street
London W1T 3JW
United Kingdom

A CIP catalogue record for this book is available from the British Library.

Print ISBN 978 1 78863 765 7
Ebook ISBN 978 1 78863 662 9

Look for more great books at www.canelo.co

Printed and bound in Great Britain by Clays Ltd, Elcograf S.p.A.

For Benicio. Love you, son.

Things will go wrong in any given situation, if
you give them a chance.

—*Murphy's Law*

Chapter One

The boy had grown into an ugly man.

He lumbered along with the shopping trolley, a creased, too-small polo shirt pulled tight over his rounded shoulders and gut. Patchy stubble sprouted over his face, as coarse as Velcro. A chunky gold bracelet hung from his thick wrist; a gaudy contrast to the dull, illegible tattoos that crawled up his arms.

Jack might not have recognised him at all were it not for the eyes. Those speckled green eyes were like emeralds thumbed into a lump of unbaked dough, his stare piercing and effortlessly intimidating. The man had only glanced at him in passing, but it had been long enough. Beads of sweat burst through Jack's pores.

Placing his basket on the ground, Jack reached out to the nearest shelving unit for support. The supermarket swam around him, his throat closing. He couldn't seem to take the gulp of air that he needed and his heart thumped angrily in his chest. *My god, I'm going to have a stroke,* he thought wildly, as the pressure built up inside his head.

Gradually, the dizziness dissipated, and the supermarket snapped back into focus. He picked up his basket, inhaling as deeply as his lungs would permit, and staggered on after the man with the green eyes.

He caught up with him in the pasta aisle. Jack touched the bulge on the breast of his jacket, feeling for the folding knife he kept handy for slashing boxes open at the warehouse.

The man stopped, and ten feet behind him, Jack did the same. The man scanned the range of pastas, idly handling a few packets before settling for fusilli. As he tossed the packet in his trolley, he abruptly turned and stared directly at Jack, frowning.

Jack whipped his head toward the sauces on the shelves in front of him, making a pantomime of choosing before picking something at random. The glass felt slippery in his hand and he nearly dropped it, but the weight of the knife in his jacket pocket reassured him. He looked back over at the man, but he was gone.

Jack hurried down the aisle and emerged near the busy checkouts into oncoming traffic. His thighs crashed into a woman's trolley with a clang, and she yelped in fright as he muttered an apology, stepping around her. It was almost five in the afternoon and the supermarket was bustling with mums and school kids, the aisles clogged. Jack spun around, scanning the herd, but couldn't find his man. He picked his way through the congestion, relieved when he found him again a few aisles down.

The boy who had ruined Jack's life was hiding somewhere in the blubber of this grotesque man. A single drop of sweat trickled down the trail of Jack's spine, and he shuddered. The supermarket lights were too bright, the music too loud. Jack's fist tightened around the handle on the basket until the plastic dug into his calloused palm.

I could kill you now, Jack thought, transfixed by the fold of flesh that spilled out from the man's shirt as he reached for something on the top shelf. He stared at the shiny stretch marks on the man's love handle and thought, *I could walk up to you and stab my knife into your neck, twist the blade, and you'd be dead before anyone could staunch the wound.*

There was something vaguely disappointing in seeing what the boy had become. Killing this pitiful man would almost be doing him a favour. He owed him a debt, and Jack had waited twelve years for repayment. He intended to savour every last ounce of misery that he could squeeze out of him, even if he went to jail for the rest of his life.

The man rounded the corner and grunted as he waddled down toward the tills. The queues were long and sprawled into the aisles. The man with the green eyes said, 'Fucking hell,' loud enough to earn a glare from the woman waiting in front of him.

Jack lingered by the magazines, submerged in the cacophony of beeps from the scanners. He was hot all over, and his stomach felt watery, as though a surge of vomit might rise up his throat at any moment.

Over the hubbub of the supermarket, Jack saw the man mouth something to the checkout lady. It was probably a complaint if his facial expression was anything to go by. The grooves of his furrowed brow looked deep enough to plant crops in, and the crescents of tiredness carved beneath his eyes aged him another decade. If Jack's maths was correct, the man would be pushing thirty by now, and yet he looked closer to Jack's age.

At forty-five years old, Jack Bracket was physically stronger than he had been in his twenties, but of course he'd never so much as lifted a dumb-bell before that night when the boy came knocking. Now Jack could bench-press over a hundred kilos if his back was co-operating.

Years of hauling boxes had played havoc with his sciatic nerve. He might be strong, but one sneeze or cough at the wrong moment and he'd be laid up for a week.

Still, he stood trembling at the sight of this oafish, ungainly man who looked as though he'd struggle to tie his own laces. But no, that wasn't quite correct. The man may have been overweight and uncoordinated, but he *did* look strong – not gym strong perhaps, but he had the kind of natural, rugged strength that you could only inherit.

The ground felt spongy beneath Jack's feet as he followed the man through the automatic doors and out of the supermarket. He gave him a few yards of slack, but wanted to be closer, close enough to pick up his scent, to hear him breathing. A low throb of panic tingled through him for fear that he might lose his target again, that the man would evaporate among the other shoppers. All those years of fruitless searching, harassing the police for updates, pleading with them to widen and extend their efforts, all for nothing. Then, by chance, he literally bumps into the boy in broad daylight and it was all too convenient. The unreality of it clung to him like a fever.

Jack's footsteps echoed through the basement-level car park. He blinked sweat out of his eyes, fumbled for his keys, and made a beeline for his van. From his vantage point behind the pillar, he watched the man shuffling up to a spotless black Mercedes that looked as though it had just rolled out of the showroom.

Jack waited for the man to pull out of his spot and then drove after him.

Chapter Two

As soon as Jack got home, he retrieved his address book from the bottom of his sock drawer and thumbed it open to Emily's number. The ink on the page was faded, the paper slightly crinkled. He returned downstairs and located the house phone. How long had it been since he'd made a call on this thing? He couldn't remember. May always called him, but that was the only time his phone ever rang. He'd had a mobile once upon a time, but he couldn't get on with it; didn't like the ritual of buying credit, charging it. Too much hassle.

With the receiver nestled between his head and shoulder, he squinted at the number and stabbed the buttons with his finger. In the seconds before the call connected, he tried to remember the last time he had spoken to Emily. She'd called him to see what his Christmas plans were. She and her housemates were having a little gathering for Christmas lunch and, knowing he'd probably spend the day alone, invited him to come over. He'd told her that he might, but as they said their goodbyes, they both knew he wouldn't make an appearance. That had to be at least five, maybe six years ago. Definitely before he met May.

'Hello?' Emily's painfully familiar voice answered, and in that instant, Jack forgot why he was phoning.

'Hello, is that Emily?'

A pause. 'Yes. Can I ask who's calling please?'

'It's Jack.' He switched the receiver to his other ear and wiped his hands on his jeans.

He was about to narrow down the list of Jacks by offering his surname when she said, 'Jack? Oh my goodness. How are you? It's been so long.'

'Yes, yes it has,' he said, surprised at how easily a smile now came to his face. Christ, it was so nice speaking to Emily. Why on earth had he not kept in touch? 'I hope I'm not disturbing you, am I?'

'No, definitely not.' It sounded like she was smiling too. 'This is a very welcome reprieve from the dishes.'

'Oh good...' He trailed off to silence, could hear her TV on in the background. 'I... um, well, I was wondering if we might be able to meet up.'

'Yes, that sounds great,' she replied eagerly. There had been no lingering moment of uncertainty, no pause to dredge up an excuse. 'What's your schedule like? What are you up to these days?'

'I'm still at the warehouse, but I sort of make my own hours, so I'm flexible.'

'Great.' But now there was a pause. The TV in the background muted. 'Is everything OK, Jack?'

He allowed a couple of breaths before replying. He regretted not rehearsing the call beforehand, but knew that if he had, he probably wouldn't have picked up the phone in the first place. He would've found some way to talk himself out of it, to convince himself that he was wrong about the man at the supermarket.

'I have something I need you to see. Are you around tomorrow at all?'

6

Emily was waiting for him on the doorstep. To Jack, it looked as though she had hardly aged, but then again, he was well overdue a visit to the optician. And the dentist. And the doctor, ignoring their letters about a prostate examination. May was right; he really did need to start taking better care of himself.

He brought the van to a halt and gave her a wave. Emily's face brightened. She shoved her hands into her jacket pockets and made her way to the passenger side. She opened the door, inviting a gust of bitter cold wind into the van.

'You look well,' she said, leaning over for a hug.

'You too. I was literally just thinking that you haven't changed a bit.'

'You must be joking,' she laughed and touched her hair self-consciously.

'No, seriously. You look just like—' He stopped. It was too difficult to say what he had wanted to. She'd picked up on it too, and her eyes darted away from his. 'You look good. So? What're you up to these days?' He pulled away from the kerb. The lavender sky was darkening to plum. It'd be full dark in less than an hour.

'I'm working for a charity at the minute. It's only temp work, but' – she shrugged – 'the money's good. It's an eight-month contract, so I'll be looking for something else soon. Other than that, just more of the same really.'

He nodded. 'I've got the heating on. Let me know if you're too hot.'

'No, it's lovely, thank you.' She touched the heater. 'It's been freezing lately.'

'Oh, I know. The mornings are the worst.'

They slipped into silence. It didn't feel awkward the way it probably should have. When he pulled up at a traffic light, Emily said, 'Where are we going?'

'Not far. It shouldn't take more than half an hour, forty-five minutes at the most. That OK?'

'Yeah, sure. I'm allowed to stay out late tonight.'

Jack wasn't sure what she meant. When she didn't elaborate, he said, 'Are you seeing anyone at the moment?'

'Roger. Been about two years now. We're thinking of getting engaged, then maybe moving in together after Christmas.'

'Really? That's nice. You going to buy in London, or…'

'No, we're not buying,' she laughed. 'I'd need to win the Lottery before I could think about doing that. We live together at the minute, but you know, housemates and things, it gets crowded. How about you?'

'No plans to move.'

'No. I meant, are you seeing anyone?'

'Oh, sorry. Yes. Her name's May, but she was born in June. I always mention that to her and she hates it. She has a sister called April who was born in January, if you can believe that.'

Emily laughed. It was a nice, musical sound. 'You been together long?'

'Going on four years,' he said, nodding. 'She's a good woman. You'd like her.'

They filled in the gaps for the rest of the journey. Emily hadn't really settled in a career these past few years, but instead just bounced around from job to job, doing enough to pay her share of the rent. The minute she truly started to resent a job, she jacked it in without a second's hesitation. He admired that about her; she didn't get tied down to something she didn't like, which he supposed was why she'd never been married. She broke off her last engagement, to Doug (a name Jack remembered because she'd signed a couple of Christmas cards from the two of them), about eight years prior because they ran out of things to say to each other. 'And to be honest,' she added, 'I'm not completely sold on the idea of moving in with Roger, just in case things go pear-shaped. But I have to grow up some time, don't I?'

'Don't be so hard on yourself.'

'It's true though, isn't it? I mean, I'm thirty-eight soon, unmarried, no children, renting with a bunch of stragglers. The house is like a hippy commune. It's like I never moved on from student life. Not exactly a picture of success.'

'But are you happy?' Jack glanced at her briefly.

Emily made a clicking noise with her tongue, mulling it over. 'I'm not *unhappy*, let's put it like that.'

'I guess that's fair enough.'

'What about you? Are you happy?'

'I'm…' He was about to say something convoluted but stopped himself. 'I don't know. I don't think it's an easy question to answer really. Let's just say I have my good days and I have my not so good days.'

Jack turned into the road leading to the Frazier Avenue estate. Street lights lined the walkways, bleaching the pavement with their ghostly glow. Jack parked in front of a tall, grim tower block barnacled with satellite dishes, and shut off the engine. The sound of a dog barking somewhere in the distance bounced off the buildings.

'This it?'

9

'Yeah,' Jack said over the ticking of the cooling engine.

'OK. So what are we doing here?'

Jack reached into the glove compartment and withdrew a bottle of dark rum that he'd bought specially for this outing. He handed it to her. 'You still drink, don't you?'

'Rum? Are we going to a party?'

'No. But take a few sips anyway. Trust me.'

She eyed him quizzically and then uncapped the bottle and took a large gulp without grimacing. When she tried to hand the bottle to him, he shook his head. 'No. Keep hold of it.'

'All right. What's this all about?'

Jack flexed his fingers. He struggled to swallow before saying, 'Yesterday when I was shopping, I saw a man I recognised. He had these green eyes, these unmistakeable green eyes.'

'Jack...'

'Please, let me finish. I recognised the man because he was the one that killed Kate.' It sounded strange coming from his lips, a thought that'd brewed in his mind like a storm cloud for over twenty-four hours. He expected to be interrupted again, and when he wasn't, he continued. 'As soon as I saw his face I knew it was him. He's older now, obviously, but except for a bit of weight and a beard, he's exactly the same. Same green eyes. Same pig nose.'

Emily took another nip from the rum and left the cap off.

'I watched him go to his car, and then tailed him to that building.' Jack pointed through the windscreen toward the tower block. 'The man who killed your sister lives there. I followed him into the building and kept behind him when he went up the stairs. He went to the eighth floor and that's where I left him, but I held the landing door open so I could see which flat he was going to.' He exhaled, suddenly breathless from the tale. 'Emily, I know where he lives.'

She didn't speak for a long time. She just sat there, chewing it over, sipping from the bottle.

'How can you be sure it's him?'

'The eyes. I could never forget those eyes, Emily.'

'That doesn't mean it's him. There are a lot of people with green eyes.'

Yes, there are, Jack thought absently. 'I could never forget his face. If he was standing in a crowd of a thousand people that all looked similar, I'd be able to pick him out. Ever since that day, it's all I've ever thought about. It's him, Emily.'

Emily's expression hardened, her chest noticeably rising and falling with every breath she took. 'It's been so long. Your memory might've tricked you. I mean, I can't even remember people I met five years ago, let alone twelve.'

'I hear what you're saying, believe me I do. But you have to trust me. There's no way I'd get something like this mixed up, and I wouldn't have even mentioned it to you if I wasn't a hundred percent sure. I will never forget that moment, Emily. It is the worst thing that's ever happened to me and I still re-live it each day. I wish I could forget, but I can't. If you'd been there, you'd understand. I know this is the man.'

Emily's eyes sparkled. She knuckled the tears away, rubbed her palms down her face and said, 'Do you ever watch any crime shows, Jack?'

'Crime shows?'

'Documentaries. You know, how they catch the serial killers. That sort of thing.' Jack shook his head. 'Well, I do. And sometimes, when someone's been through an ordeal, like you did, they get confused. Like they might say the killer had black hair when he was actually blond, or that he had green eyes when they were actually blue. Do you know what I'm getting at?'

'Yes,' Jack replied. He wanted to barge in and persuade her that his memory of that night was crystal-clear, but he resisted the urge and let her finish.

'So how certain can you really be that he's the one that killed Kate? If he was a boy then and now he's a man he could've changed so much.'

'He *has* changed an awful lot. But the one thing that hasn't changed is the eyes. I know I keep going on about it, but, well, like I said, I won't ever forget them. It *is* him, Emily. You have to believe me. Don't you think I know how crazy this is, me bringing you here? I wouldn't put either of us through this if I had even a hint of doubt. This isn't some gut feeling or me just acting on a whim here. I wouldn't do that. I wouldn't be so... *irresponsible*.'

She sniffed. 'Do you have any tissues in here?'

He opened the glovebox again and handed her a packet of Kleenex. She dabbed her eyes and then wiped her nose. 'OK. So let's say that's him. What do you want to do?'

Jack reached into her lap and claimed the bottle, and then took a long slug. It was cheap stuff and burned on the way down, but it gave him the kick in the head that he needed.

'I want to kill him,' Jack said. 'I was wondering if you wanted to help me.'

Chapter Three

Two cups of black coffee from the bakery hadn't even tickled him. Jack got out of the van and walked around toward the warehouse door, his eyes aching in their sockets. He never got more than four or five hours' sleep a night anyway, but today he was running on fumes. He hadn't been able to sleep after how things ended with Emily. But what had he been expecting? The best-case scenario would've been a conversation about his proposal, but all he got was stony silence. She hadn't even said goodbye when she got out of the van. But she hadn't exactly told him to fuck off either.

All Emily needed was some time to think it over.

'Oh? And what time do you call this?' Colin said, sitting on a box with a smirk on his face.

'You want me to start counting up all the time you spend on your phone when you should be unpacking boxes?'

'Touché.' Colin stood up. 'Perhaps I can get you a cup of tea, boss?'

'Coffee, black.'

'I'm on it.' He walked up the steel steps, his footfall clanging through the warehouse.

'Be snappy about it too, we have a lot of drops today,' Jack said, consulting the clipboard.

Colin saluted him from the top of the staircase.

Jack started heaving some of the more manageable boxes to the back of his van. He couldn't help thinking about the way Emily had stared at him. Had it just been shock or was she frightened of him? Jack wasn't talking about giving the man a stern telling off, he was talking about murder. Maybe she thought Jack had lost his marbles.

Maybe she was right.

'*I could rip that fucker apart with my bare hands. With my bare hands!*' That had always stayed with him. Jack had actually believed her capable of it. That was when the pain was still raw, a couple of months after Kate was killed. Jack knew for a fact that kind of fury never really went away. It just learned how to hide.

–

'Do me a favour, will you? Get off that phone for a minute.'

Colin flung his iPhone onto the dashboard but immediately began drumming a rhythm on his thigh with his hands. The boy had the attention span of a gnat. 'What's up?'

'How long have you been here now? Two years?'

'It'll be four in June.'

'Four?' Jack scratched his beard. He remembered the day Colin started; he wouldn't say boo to a goose. Jack turned down the radio. 'You happy?'

'Happy? Yeah, sure. I mean, I'd like more money obviously. I have my performance review in March, so I'm hoping…'

'I can't guarantee you a raise, but I think you're a good guy. You piss around a lot, but you pull your weight. I'll see what I can do about getting you up a bit. Probably won't be much, and it's not for certain, but you know, every little bit helps, doesn't it?'

Colin's grin widened. 'I'd appreciate that, Jack. I really would.'

'I know. Which brings me on to my second bit of business.'

A text alert popped up on Colin's iPhone, snagging his attention. Colin's eyes shot to the screen instinctively, then back to Jack. 'I'm listening, I'm listening.'

'Do you wanna earn some extra beer money for the weekend?'

'Extra money? Yep, of course. What do I have to do?'

—

Colin saw a pair of women leaving the building and grabbed the door before it closed. He pressed the call button for the lift but there were no signs of life. Looked like a death trap anyway. He picked up the box and shouldered through the door leading to the stairwell, where he was met with the stink of fermented piss, mingled with something vaguely chemical.

Bottles, crushed cans and twisted cigarette ends littered the stairs. The graffiti-camouflaged walls in the stairwell were slick with condensation, and there were puddles on the uneven concrete landings. Colin was extra vigilant about where he trod. One of his best friends was a bin man and he said that a dirty needle pricked him through a rubbish bag he was handling once. Thank god it had only been an insulin needle, but still.

When he reached the eighth floor, he wrapped the sleeve of his fleece around his hand and pulled open the landing door. The windowless hallway stretched forever, its eggshell walls reflecting yellow fluorescent tube lights. The box felt heavy as an anvil in his arms now as he approached number 83. Music pulsed from behind the door and set his heart racing. He'd asked Jack what this was all about, but Jack told him not to worry about it. The fifty pounds he offered Colin soon put a stop to any more questions.

Colin pressed the doorbell but the music swallowed the sound. He pressed again, and when he still didn't get an answer, banged on the door with his fist. The music died.

From behind the door: 'Who is it?'

'Strident Homeware. I have a delivery.'

'Delivery for who?'

'Ah, that's the thing.' Colin released a nervous laugh. 'I'm not exactly sure.'

The door opened. A large man filled the doorway, dressed in a T-shirt, boxer shorts and a tatty dressing gown. He stared at Colin blankly. Colin felt the hairs on the nape of his neck rise.

'What delivery?' the man said, unblinking.

Colin stroked sweat away from his neck. 'There was a slip-up at the warehouse.' He pointed at the box, unable to meet the man's piercing eyes any longer. They were so green they almost looked neon. They creeped Colin out big time. 'This box has an address but some idiot in the office left the name off it. It's for a "mister" but that's about all I know. This is number 83, isn't it?'

Ignoring his question, the man said, 'What is it?'

'I don't know that either. If I had to guess, judging by the size and weight, probably a microwave?'

The man stepped out of his flat and nudged the box with his toe. 'I didn't order a microwave.'

'You didn't?'

The man looked at him, and for a second Colin thought the man was going to slap him. 'No.'

'Shit, it happened again. Well look, this box has your address, so as far as I'm concerned, it's yours.' The man's eyebrows pinched together suspiciously. 'You'd be doing me a favour if I didn't have to carry it back down those stairs.' He tittered again, shifting from foot to foot. The man just continued staring at him. 'If it's a microwave in there, like I think it is, then it'll be a good one. You're looking at a hundred and fifty quid for a Strident microwave.'

'All right. I'll take it. But if you try and come back and want me to pay for it, you ain't getting shit. Got it?'

'That's not going to happen,' Colin said. He was so nervous he nearly patted the man on his shoulder just to occupy his hands. 'It's got your address on it, so it's accounted for.'

The man eyed Colin again, and then picked the box up and took it inside the flat.

'Oh, one last thing,' Colin said before the man closed the door. 'I've to get a signature just to say it's been delivered.'

Colin handed the man a folded invoice and a biro and pointed at the X on the paper. The man scribbled on the line and handed it back to Colin.

'Just for my records, what's your name, mate?' Colin tried to make it sound casual, hoping that the man wouldn't pick up on the anxiety in his voice.

'Craig Morley,' the man mumbled, and closed the door.

Chapter Four

May slid into the booth and shrugged out of her faux-fur coat. She'd glammed herself up with blusher, dark eyeliner and fire-engine red lipstick, and was wearing half a bottle of perfume by the smell of it. 'Look at this decor. It's so trendy, isn't it, hun?'

Jack smiled, nodded. 'It's great,' he said, reaching for the laminated menu. He had no appetite for a hamburger or a milkshake, and he was too tired to put on much of a show for appearances. He'd already planned to blow off date night and spend the evening researching Craig Morley, but when he pulled up to the warehouse at the end of the day, May was already parked there, waiting for him. It was a surprise, she said. It was a trap, he thought.

'Look at this, Jackie – they do Cajun chicken burgers. That's just what I'm in the mood for. What are you going to have?'

Enthusiasm jumped off her in sparks, and it made him feel even heavier. She was so excited about a burger and all he could think about was getting away from her and obsessing over Craig Morley. Craig Morley, Craig fucking Morley. He couldn't get the name out of his head.

Be nice, he reminded himself. *Even if you don't feel like it, be nice.* He reached across and patted her hand. 'You get anything you want.'

'Starters too?'

'Go for it,' he said. She gave him a look of such sincere gratitude that he felt genuinely sorry for her. 'Get a cocktail too if you want.' *Why not?* he thought. He was stuck there for at least an hour. Might as well show her a good time.

After dinner, he drove May back to her house. She raved about the food all the way home, the two Cosmopolitans she'd drunk causing her to trip over her words. When he pulled up to the kerb, she leaned over and gave him a wet, breathy kiss, clutching his face with both hands. 'I can fix us some drinks inside. I've got all the ingredients for a screaming orgasm if you want one,' she said, rubbing his inner thigh.

He braced himself, stroked her cheek with his knuckle, and said, 'I can't, love. Not tonight.'

Her lipstick-smeared mouth slackened. Her eyes shimmered with drunkenness. 'You're not coming in?'

'No.' He had to look away. He liked May a lot; she was talkative where he was contemplative. She was interested in things where he was indifferent. She was a petite little thing and made him feel like a giant when he held her. But she was clingy and used her tears to get her way and that manipulation made him resent her. In a selfish way, he'd come to depend on her, so that he didn't spend all his time alone in the house brooding, or looking at pictures of Kate and crying himself to sleep like he'd done in the years before. Soon, he knew, he would come to depend on her even more. Maybe one day he would open up to her, show her who he really was, warts and all. But she wasn't ready for that yet.

'May, I've not been feeling well. I'm run-down.'

'I don't understand this, Jack.' She shook her head slowly, the confusion contorting her face. 'We were having a nice evening. The dinner was lovely... I'm all dressed up and I thought...' She shook her head again. 'Is it me? Have I done something? Just tell me if I've done something wrong.'

'No, no, of course not.' He rested a large hand on her shoulder and gave it a squeeze. 'I'm not feeling very well, that's all.'

'Well, what's wrong with you?' she whined, screwing her face up. The storm had broken and the first tears squeezed from her eyes, trailing mascara down her powdery cheeks.

'I don't know. I'm going to make a doctor's appointment first thing Monday.'

She wiped her eyes with the heels of her hands, smearing the makeup. 'How about you just come inside? We don't have to have sex if you don't want to. You can just go to sleep and I'll look after you.' She clutched at his shirt, grabbing two handfuls of collar. 'I'll give you a massage or... or I can just leave you alone and cook for you. Soup! I can make you soup.'

She was blubbering and babbling and Jack was too tired to listen to it. 'May,' he said firmly, 'I need to go home and rest. We've had a nice night, and I just want to...'

'It's another woman, isn't it?' She was sour now, the pouting replaced with a sneer. She looked a little crazy with her smudged raccoon eyes. 'Don't treat me like a fucking idiot. Just be straight with me and tell me. You owe me that much at least.'

He took a deep breath. The tiredness was chiselling away on the inside of his skull. He pinched the bridge of his nose, trying to stem the oncoming headache.

'May, I'm going home. I'll call you tomorrow.'

'Fine. Fine.' She fumbled with the lock and eventually got the door open. She climbed out of the van, arse first, and stumbled in her heels. Jack reached across and closed the door. 'Go on, drive off and do what you want. I don't care.'

'I'll call you tomorrow,' Jack said again.

'Piss off,' she shouted from the kerb.

Jack started the engine. When he looked at the wing mirror in preparation to pull out, May reached out to the van, slapping the window with both hands.

'I'm sorry, Jackie. Please, I'm sorry! Don't be mad. Are you cross with me?'

He knew if he stopped the engine now she'd guilt him into the house. Either that or she'd turn nasty again, slagging him off, accusing him of nonsense. He wound down the window, blew her a kiss and said, 'It's all right, May. Go to bed and I'll—'

'You'll call me tomorrow? But I want you tonight!' She almost screamed it, her reedy voice cutting through the silence of the street.

Jack put his foot down and watched her shrink in the rear-view mirror. He hoped that once she sobered up she'd see sense, but he doubted it. It wasn't the first time she'd accused him of ditching her to see other women, but it was the first time she was right.

It was just after eleven when he reached Emily's house. She lived in an attractive, three-storey Victorian build on a nice middle-class street. It was the kind of place where people took the time to separate their rubbish from their recycling, kept their lawns clipped, and had a rapport with their neighbours. She'd moved there with some friends in her early twenties and the landlord hadn't ever given her a good enough reason to leave. The last time Jack was here was a year or so after Kate's murder. Emily had invited him round for tea and cake and he had agreed. They needed to prop each other up, to talk about Kate and keep her memory alive. Ever since then, they had settled for the occasional phone call, a cordial 'how are you?' every two or three years, which eventually tapered off.

It took him a long time to walk up the path. He knew he shouldn't be here, especially not this late, but the name Craig Morley was stuttering in his head like a stuck record. He had to speak to her about it.

He caught sight of his blurred reflection in the frosted glass window of the front door. He looked like a shaggy bear. He pressed the bell and stepped back, keeping at a non-threatening distance as he waited. A silhouette appeared on the other side of the glass, and then the door opened.

'Hello?' said a tall, slim man with salt and pepper hair and glasses. He hadn't asked 'Who is it?' before he opened the door, and that bothered Jack. It bothered him badly.

'Hi, I'm sorry to be calling at such a late hour. My name's Jack. I was wondering if I could speak with Emily please, if she's available.'

'Sure, just a moment.' He closed the door and walked off. A minute later Emily appeared, dressed in a faded cotton T-shirt and leggings.

'I thought you'd be calling,' she said, lighting up a cigarette.

'Sorry, I know it's late. I haven't disturbed you, have I?'

'I was just watching Netflix, nothing important.'

'Can I come in?'

She exhaled smoke, squinting. 'Probably not a good idea. I haven't really spoken to Roger about you.'

'Oh. Right, of course.' He forgot that she had her own life. 'Tell you what, if you're free at all this weekend, I'd like to see you again. To talk about, you know, that thing we were talking about.'

She looked down the street. 'I don't know if I want to.'

He nodded. 'I understand that. I know it's been a long time. I'm sorry to have come by. I'll let you get back on with your evening.' He had begun walking down the path when she called out to him.

'You think I don't want to get him? She was my twin sister, Jack. When she died it was like—'

'Like a part of *you* died,' he finished. 'You're not the only one.'

She looked at him a moment, chewing the inside of her lip. 'I miss her, and I know you do too. But what you're talking about isn't right.'

'Why not?' he asked. It wasn't a challenge. He was genuinely interested.

'Because it doesn't work like that. You can't just go around—' She stopped herself, looked down at her toes. Maybe she was counting to ten before she said something she'd regret. 'You don't even know it's him, Jack.'

'Craig Morley.'

'What?'

'Craig Morley. That's his name. I had one of my colleagues do a dummy delivery to his flat. So that's the name of the man that ruined our lives.'

She opened her mouth to say something when a figure appeared behind her. He was younger than her, had his ears and nose pierced, and was scruffy in a deliberate way that irritated Jack.

'What's going on?' he said gently.

Emily pointed her cigarette at Jack. 'This is my brother-in-law, Jack. Jack, this is Roger.'

'Brother-in-law?' His brow creased for a moment and then smoothed over when the penny dropped. 'Oh, your... I see.' The defensiveness melted away and he was suddenly all smiles. He turned to Jack and gave him a sheepish wave.

Jack nodded. Roger waved again, and then said quietly to Emily, 'When are you coming in? I've got it on pause.'

'Just watch it and let me know what happens,' she said irritably.

'All right. How long are you going to be, though?'

'For fuck's sake, Roger, I don't know, I don't have an egg timer on me.'

Roger flinched, visibly wounded, and slunk back into the house without another word. When he was gone, Emily laughed humourlessly, shaking her head. 'And that's Roger.'

'Seems like a nice guy.'

Ignoring him, she said, 'Jack, listen to me. If you think this Craig person is the one that killed Kate,' she gulped, 'then you should go to the police.'

Jack eyed the surroundings, searching for curtain-twitchers. 'Maybe we shouldn't talk about it out in the open like this.'

'Stop being paranoid. Nobody's listening to us. Look, if you think it's him you should go to the police and let them handle it.'

'Oh yeah? So he can get some fancy solicitor to talk his way out of it? Too much time's passed. If they couldn't pin him down then, then there's no way they'll get him now. It wouldn't even go to trial. And let's say it did. What's he gonna get? Twenty years and be out in ten? No, not a chance.'

Emily took a drag on her cigarette. She was silent for a long time, tapping her thumb on her lip, thinking.

'You shouldn't do anything stupid,' she eventually said. 'Not until you know for sure.'

'I do know for sure.'

'No, you don't. You think you do, but you don't.'

Slowly, he said, 'I was there, Emily. You weren't. I saw him.'

'That's not enough,' she hissed. 'That's not enough to do what you're thinking of doing.'

'All right,' he relented, rubbing his face with his hands. His mouth was so dry he could've struck a match on his tongue. 'What about if I can prove it's him?'

'How?'

'I don't know yet, but let's say I can prove it. Would you want to help me then?'

She considered the question for what seemed like a very long time before answering. 'You need to understand where I'm coming from. I think about the boy that killed Kate every single day. I think about him probably more than I think about her. If I knew for certain where he was right now, I'd buy a gun and I'd shoot him dead.'

A gust of breath bellowed out of Jack. 'He deserves it, Emily. He...' the words evaporated from his mouth. He felt himself welling up, remembering Kate's face, that beautiful smile, the way her cheeks would flame red when she was embarrassed. He gritted his teeth together, the muscles tightening in his jaw. 'I don't want him to think he got away with it. I want him to suffer. The way we've suffered. I just think...' He broke off, turned his back on her and wiped the sleeve of his coat across his eyes. 'I don't know, maybe I'm being an idiot, but I just want her back.'

Quietly, almost in a whisper, Emily said, 'But that won't bring her back. I wish it would, but it won't.' She saw his shoulders shrugging, heard him sniffle, and then watched him walk away with his hands balled into fists. 'Jack?'

He didn't answer. When he reached the van, Emily heard a strangled moan escape him, and knew that he had given himself permission to cry. That sound, so despairing, so defeated, made her want to cry too.

'Jack? Let's have dinner tomorrow. How about it?'

He raised a hand in a wave, got into the van, and drove away without another word.

Chapter Five

Emily jerked awake, her leg tangled in the quilt, a pillow clutched tightly in her fists. She had been locked in a nightmare where she was lost in the woods and could hear Kate calling her name from the darkness. The calls turned into horrible, jagged screams, and that's when she forced herself out of the dream with her heart galloping. She sucked in air, cringing against the memory of her sister's screams.

'What's wrong with you?'

Reality clicked back into place. The tinny sound of dialogue through the laptop speakers, the bluish glow on the walls from the screen, the smell of grease and barbecue sauce. What the hell was that? She looked over at Roger, who was lying on his side, turned away from her.

'Are you eating?'

'Hmm?'

She pulled his shoulder back, saw the plate of sausages next to the laptop, a brown smear of sauce on the sheet. It was so bizarre that for a moment she thought she'd woken up in another dream. 'Are you eating sausages in bed?'

'What?' he said, almost outraged. 'I got hungry.'

'You got sauce on the sheet!' She reached down on the floor for her phone, checked the time. 'It's two in the morning.'

'So what am I supposed to do? Starve until breakfast?'

'They *were* for breakfast,' she said, lying back down, the anger raising her temperature.

'They were? Well, I'll have toast or something,' he said through a mouthful of meat. 'Hey, don't be like that. I didn't know you'd get mad, did I? You think I would have eaten them if I knew you'd get all pissy about it?'

She scrunched her eyes closed and curled into a tight ball. Her heart was still thudding and the smell of the sausages was making her queasy.

'Hey.' She felt his greasy fingers touch her shoulder and cringed. 'I'm sorry, OK?'

It wasn't OK. *She* wasn't OK. She thought she had beaten the nightmares and finally escaped the awful sound of her sister's screams. But they were back, ringing through her head like a fucking siren. Jesus Christ, those screams – like no sound she had ever heard before. She wasn't sure if she could cope with them again. Not after the last time nearly landed her in the nuthouse. The insomnia, the boozing, crying so much she would become dehydrated and give herself a migraine. Six years of therapy undone with one visit from Jack.

If only there had been an arrest or a reason for the murder that she could understand, then maybe her life would be completely different. She might have been married with children by now. If there had just been some sense of justice, then she might have even learned how to be happy.

That eternal, unsolvable conundrum had thrown her own life into limbo. *Who would want Kate dead, and why hadn't they been found by now?*

Could Jack really have found him?

She did not fall back asleep that night.

–

'You know, when you called, I thought to myself, to what do I owe this pleasure?' Bernard laughed with his mouth closed, a habit he'd developed from all the years of teasing he got about his teeth. He shook his head good-naturedly, 'My lucky day. It's been what? At least a year?'

'Something like that,' Emily said, sipping her latte. It had actually been about three years since they last saw each other, and she suspected he knew that too.

'Did you change your number? I tried to call you a few times but…' He let the question linger, warming his hands around his mug.

'You know what happened? I changed phones and they gave me a new SIM, but I had your number written down, thankfully. God, you know what I'm like. I'd lose my head if it wasn't screwed on.'

He rolled his eyes. 'Yeah, I remember. Like that time we were supposed to meet for the cinema and you got the day wrong.' He stared at her, one of his crooked front teeth resting on his bottom lip. He looked down into his cup. 'I waited for ages.'

'Well, I got it right today,' she said, sticking her thumb up.

'And remember when we were supposed to go to dinner and you cancelled just as I left my house?'

She shifted in the seat. Why had he picked the world's quietest coffee shop to meet up? The airy jazz music was too low and there were only a handful of customers dotted around. If they'd gone to a Starbucks or a Caffè Nero the noise would've helped buffer these awkward stretches of silence.

'Then,' he said, loud enough so that the barista looked over, 'you just give me the silent treatment for all this time. I must've really done something terrible to offend you so bad.'

'Oh don't be silly, Bernard. People lose touch. You know how it is.'

'No, not really. That day you made me dinner at your house and then… nothing.'

She gulped the last of the coffee. 'All right, I get it, I'm a bitch. Come on then, let's have it.'

'Have what?'

'Everything you've wanted to say to me after all this time. Tell me what's on your mind.'

He smiled, revealing a row of chipped wall-tile teeth, then quickly covered his mouth with his hand. 'I don't have anything to say. I was just happy to see you is all.'

'You sure? I'll give you a five-minute window.'

He opened his mouth to say something, then blushed and shook his head. 'I was just a bit disappointed. I thought we liked each other.'

'Bernard, we went on two dates.'

'Three dates. Four if you include that time you cooked for me. Maybe you don't count that, though.'

This was more difficult than she'd anticipated. She hadn't thought he'd make her feel so rotten, but she supposed she deserved it. In the years that she was single, after Doug and before Roger, Emily signed up with half a dozen different dating apps. She must've gone on over fifty dates, all of them duds. Bernard wasn't exactly handsome – he was overweight and had bad acne scars, but his profile said he had a great sense of humour, and well, if she had a laugh but didn't find love, was that such a bad thing?

'Well, I guess I owe you an apology,' she said, tearing a strip from the napkin. 'You know, in my defence, you have about ten years on me. You were just a bit too old for me is all.'

'Age ain't nothing but a number, babe.'

She gave him one of her good fake laughs, even though the comment creeped her out. There was something slithery about him that she didn't like; his greasy dandruff scalp, the fingernails chewed to the quick. And there was something else that bothered her about him but she couldn't quite remember what it was.

'So, you still working at the station?'

He nodded. 'Yeah. Pain in the arse. Had some nutter in the other night. Took his trousers off and tried to flush them down the toilet. Flooded his cell.'

'Christ, what a headache.'

'That's not so bad. He just had mental health issues. It's the alcoholics that are the worst.'

'Right,' she said, cutting him short. If she gave him the chance he'd talk her ear off about how shit his job was, just as he had on the three dates that she showed up for. 'I was thinking about something the other day. You know when you're booking a prisoner in…'

He sniggered. 'It's not jail. They're not prisoners. *Detainees*.'

'Oh, OK. Anyway, you know when one of these guys comes in, you have all their info on a system, don't you?'

He slurped his cappuccino. A chocolate-flecked foam moustache coated his upper lip. 'Yeah. Anyone who has been in custody is on the system.'

'Interesting.'

'Why's that interesting?'

She leaned in over the table. 'Can you keep a secret?'

His eyes almost glowed with excitement. 'Secret? Yeah, of course.'

'I have a friend and she's dating someone, but I have my suspicions about him. I get a weird vibe off him and I just know he's dodgy. You know when you get a dodgy vibe off someone?' He nodded, his jowls wobbling. 'Well, I tried to tell her that and she got all angry with me. Anyway, she always gets involved with the crazy guys, so I thought...'

'You thought you'd use me to check out his history, to help your friend's love life. Is that it?'

She shrugged. 'Well, I also wanted to see how you were doing too.'

'Oh, I just bet you did.'

'You really think I'm that much of a bitch, Bernard? I just thought I'd ask because we're talking, that's all.' She tutted and looked out the window at a group of tourists posing for a group selfie by a bubble tea place. 'Maybe we should call it a day. This has all seemed a bit awkward from the get go.'

'No, don't go.' Bernard held up his palm, his face pained. 'Sometimes I say things without thinking and I regret them later. I'm an idiot like that. I'm sorry.'

'So, do you want another coffee? Croissant?'

'No. Relax, please. I've put you on the back foot, haven't I?' He raked his sausage fingers through his thin, shiny hair. 'I actually think it's rather admirable, you wanting to help your friend out. If you can help her avoid a scumbag before she gets too invested, then that's a good thing.'

'That's what I was thinking.'

'I'll check it out for you,' he said, lowering his eyes. He gave her a half-smile, making a conscious effort to keep his lips closed. 'Is he black? I'll bet he is.'

'Sorry?'

'This boyfriend. Is he a spade?'

The question unbalanced Emily. She now remembered the other reason why he bothered her so much. On more than one instance, he had let loose a casual racial slur, sliding it so effortlessly into the conversation that it was almost subliminal. Whenever he recalled something about his job, he would mention this coon that got done for shoplifting, or a sneaky chink that had been involved in an insurance scam.

She cleared her throat and smiled. 'Look, Bernard, you don't have to do this. I don't want you to put your job at risk or anything.'

He waved her off. 'It won't. I'd be glad to help. Really I would.'

Emily smiled and saw his face redden. The guilt fell on her like a hammer.

'I never understood that,' he said. 'Why is it the bad guys get all the good girls?'

Chapter Six

Jack pecked at the keys with his index fingers, looking up at the screen after every word to ensure there weren't any squiggly red lines under them. He sat at his workbench with his cranky old laptop that squealed and whirred every time he pressed enter. Between this ancient laptop and the spyware-infested work computer, Jack was just about ready to pull his hair out. He'd been scanning Google with a fine-tooth comb since he'd got back from seeing Emily, sitting in the cold garage with the hideous luminescence of the bare light bulb dangling above his head. He hadn't moved to eat or go to the toilet in a very long time, and when he finally opened the garage door to get a glass of water, he was confused to be greeted with darkness. He checked his watch, saw that it was just after eight in the evening, and realised he'd been cyberstalking Craig Morley on and off for almost twenty hours straight.

In the kitchen, he ran the cold tap, filled a glass and gulped the water down. He did this a couple more times until the beating in his head began to ebb, and then splashed his face with water to chase away the grogginess. All that time staring at the screen had numbed his brain and his eyes burned when he blinked. He leaned against the counter looking out at the garden that he had let go to seed. He had never really had much interest in a garden beyond the patio where he could sit and have a cold beer on a hot day, but Kate was the complete opposite. 'You don't get it,' she'd say whenever he questioned why she spent so long toiling under the sun in her floppy hat. 'If you have a nice garden, it's like having another room in your house.' Whenever her vegetables began to show or her fruit started to ripen, she always took great pride in showing him. 'It's crazy to think, isn't it, we can eat these for dinner and we didn't even buy them in the shops.' And when she did throw the potatoes and carrots together in a casserole, he'd say how lovely it all tasted, much better than anything you could get at the supermarket, although he couldn't really tell the difference.

In the last couple of years, the garden had begun to bother him more and more. He would take his coffee out into the misty morning air to assess how much work was needed to get it back on track. Wild flowers grew amidst the jungle of weeds, and thorny vines snaked their way through the foliage, culminating in a snarled mass around the base of a pear tree that no longer bore fruit. A bird feeder swayed in the breeze; it had once attracted blue tits but was now nothing more than a rotten reminder of his wife's smile.

Craig Morley. He concentrated on the name until the shame of his unkempt garden dissolved into anger and he could feel the vein throbbing in his neck. He hadn't been able to find much on the man beyond an archived local news article from 2006 detailing Morley's sentencing for robbery, for which he received six months in Feltham Young Offenders Institution. The article showed a mugshot of Morley that almost knocked Jack off his stool. *That* was the face he remembered: the upturned, piggish nose, the long black hair tied into a bun, the peach fuzz moustache, and of course, the eyes. He looked exactly the same as when Jack saw him smiling out of the car window.

He'd opened up the fridge, unsure as to whether he was hungry or not, when the doorbell rang. The sound jarred him out of his stupor and stirred an image in his mind: May dolled up to the nines, smiling as though their argument had never occurred. He pressed his forehead against the fridge door and sighed deeply, wondering what to do. He didn't have the tenacity or the emotional dexterity to deal with her tonight, and yet the doorbell would keep ringing, of that much he was certain.

He knew there was no way she would ever understand this business with Morley, especially considering she didn't know that his wife had been murdered. May knew that Jack had been married once a long time ago, but she never seemed particularly interested in his life before they became a couple. She had been married once too, but all she ever said about her ex-husband was that he was a bastard, and Jack always assumed that to mean he either beat her or cheated on her, or both.

He waded through his dark, silent house and answered the door.

Emily was standing there, not May.

'Hey,' she said, holding up a bottle of wine. 'Can I come in?'

'Sure, of course.' He held the door open for her, his brain struggling to process the surprise.

'What're you doing sitting in the dark?' she asked, moving through the front room and planting herself down on the couch.

'I was sleeping,' he lied, switching on the lamp, stirring up a tornado of dust motes beneath its shade. His house was simple and Spartan. May called it soulless, but he didn't care. He wasn't into films, he didn't read or have any hobbies, and he had successfully resisted all her attempts to clutter his house with ornaments and pictures. It was the husk of what it had once been – a place of light and laughter – and yet he had never really thought of it that way until he saw Emily glancing around, trying to spot something that she recognised from years before.

'You have any glasses?' she asked, holding up the wine bottle. Perhaps he was reading too much into it, but Jack thought she seemed unsettled by the house, as though somewhere among the faded wallpaper and tatty old furniture, she could still sense her sister's presence.

'I do,' he said, and fetched the only two wine glasses he owned. They were wedding presents, dusty from years of neglect. When May came over, they drank their Shiraz out of short Ikea glasses.

He rinsed them out and Emily filled them up. They didn't say cheers. He sat in the armchair opposite her and sipped the wine. It went down with a sharp bite that started to revive his headache before it reached his stomach.

'Morley served prison time in 2006,' Jack said, swirling the wine absently. 'He robbed a woman on a train with a knife. Only got six months.'

'I know,' she said.

'Oh?' He leaned forward in the chair. 'You saw the article?'

'No.' She reached into her jacket pocket, removed a scrap of paper and unfolded it. 'Should've brought my reading glasses.'

'What's that?'

'Sitting comfortably?' she asked dully, and then drained her glass. 'Craig Jacob Morley, aka Flashy Menace aka Flashy, born March 2nd, 1989. In February 2005, he was arrested for robbing a boy on a train with a seven-inch knife. In August 2005, he was arrested again for criminal damage; says here he broke a pawnshop window, tried to do a smash and grab, but ended up breaking his hand and severing some tendons. Idiot almost bled to death.'

'What is this?' Jack asked, setting his glass down on the coffee table. 'This is Craig Morley? The one from Frazier Avenue? The same one?'

'The very same. Let me finish. It gets better. He closes 2005 with a drunk and disorderly, but he starts 2006 with a bang. In January, he's arrested for TDA.'

'TDA? What's TDA?' Jack asked frantically.

'Um, hold on…' She paused to remember. 'It's stealing a car. Um… taking and… taking and driving away, that's it. The little bastard steals a car, speeds down the street doing eighty, and wraps it around a lamp post. It doesn't say here whether he was injured or anything.'

Jack was on his feet, pacing the living room. 'I don't believe this. I don't believe this. Keep reading.'

'OK, where was I? Right, again in 2006, he pulls a knife on a woman on a bus, and gets caught a couple of days later from the CCTV. It says here he threatened to slit the woman's throat if she didn't hand over her phone.'

'That's when he did his stretch in Feltham,' Jack said eagerly.

'Where'd you hear that?' she asked.

'Online, there's an article. They wrote about him in the *Weekly Chronicle*,' he said impatiently. 'What about 2007?'

She looked up at him. 'Nothing in 2007.'

'What does that mean?' He was shouting now, breathless from his own enthusiasm. 'So he didn't get arrested in 2007?'

'Jack, calm down.'

'I am calm,' he said dismissively. 'What is that paper? Where'd you get it?'

'A friend of mine works as a detention officer. They have a computer system that shows all the people that go through custody all over London.' She waved the paper. 'He said that when he checked Morley's name on the system there's a warning marker, because he's known to carry knives. So anyone that goes to book him into a cell has to be extra careful.' She tried to get a read on Jack, but his face now seemed unusually vacant, his eyes staring through her. 'But the thing is, this isn't Morley's criminal record. This is just a list of the times he was booked into the various holding cells before they shipped him off to court. It doesn't tell you where he's done time, only what he was booked in for.'

'But there's nothing for 2007?'

She shook her head slowly. 'No.'

Jack sat back down, his knees trembling convulsively. 'Nothing in 2007,' he murmured. 'And 2008?'

'Nothing until 2009. He got arrested for driving without a licence.'

Jack clapped his hands together. The sound reverberated around the room. 'That's it! That proves it, then. It's him.'

'How does that prove it?'

'He did the stretch in Feltham in 2005 but he didn't get arrested again. That has to mean that he was on the streets, not locked up somewhere. If he had an arrest anywhere near July 2007, we could assume he'd be in jail during that time, couldn't we?'

'Maybe. But my friend said these records can be spotty. He could've been booked in and it might not be recorded. He said it's only really accurate back to about five or six years ago.'

'He wasn't locked up anywhere in 2007,' Jack said defiantly. 'He was roaming around, free as a fucking bird, and on July eighth, he came to this house and killed Kate.'

Emily gasped as though he'd smacked her. She hadn't been braced for that kind of bluntness. She sat there, panting quietly, fingering the neck of her jumper, pulling it away from her throat for air.

'It's him, Emily. Go on Google and type his name in. There's an article that shows his face. You're asking me for more proof? How's this – I saw the picture of Morley and I nearly vomited. Now I'm telling you,' he said, his voice rising again, 'that Craig Morley is the one that killed your sister – my wife!'

Emily cradled her head in her hands. Memories rushed through her mind like a speeding train: going to the funfair on their tenth birthday; the argument they had over the broken *Madonna* CD; sneaking downstairs to watch *Fatal Attraction* when their parents went to bed, only to be caught when Emily screamed in fright during the film's climax.

'Emily, I'm sorry I shouted. But every day it's like a weight sitting on my chest, crushing me. Sometimes I dream about her, and I'll wake up, and for a second I truly believe she'll be lying right there beside me.'

'I believe you,' she said, the grief strangling her voice to a whisper. 'If you tell me it's him, then I believe you. After all, you were the only one that saw him, so you're the only one that would know what he looked like now.'

Jack licked his lips, suddenly thirsty again. He began to feel faintly dizzy. With a blink, two tears rolled down her cheeks, and she looked away.

'Let me refill you,' he mumbled, groping for the wine bottle.

'Thanks,' she said, her slick cheeks reddening. 'And you're sure you don't want to go to the police,' she asked, catching a stray tear on the knuckle of her index finger.

'If I knew for certain that they would charge him and he'd get a lengthy sentence then maybe I would.'

'Would that be enough for you, though?' She leaned forward, elbows on her knees. 'Knowing that he's in jail, still socialising, still eating three square meals a day. Would that be justice?'

'What do you think?'

Her expression became bitter. 'He'd get adjusted to it, wouldn't he? I mean, it's not like a South American or Russian prison like you see on the documentaries. It'd be a nice comfy cell, probably with TV and a PlayStation and god knows what else. It'd be more than he deserves.'

'That's what I think too.'

Chapter Seven

Emily took a gulp of wine and laughed drily. 'Jack, are you saying you really think you could kill him?'

'Yes. I think I could.'

'But could you live with yourself afterwards, knowing what you'd done?'

'If you mean would I feel any guilt, then the answer is no, absolutely not.'

She exhaled. 'But do you think killing him would make you feel any better?'

'It couldn't make me feel any worse.'

She drank a mouthful of wine, placed the glass on the table and stood up. She laced her fingers together and cracked her knuckles. A ghost of memory whispered through him. Kate used to crack her knuckles the exact same way and it drove him nuts. Every time he heard that concerto of pops, he would berate her about arthritis.

'All right, so how would you do it?'

'A knife, probably. But I wouldn't do it quickly. I wouldn't just cut his throat.' When he said this, Emily's forehead crinkled. 'What I mean is, I have a process. I want him to know who I am, who Kate was, and I want to know why. Why did he knock on our door that night? And why did he...?' His mouth became a tight line. The leather armrests creaked where he gripped them. 'Why did he do what he did? What was it all about? That's what I'd want to find out. And when I had all my answers, I'd put him out of his misery.'

Emily shook her head. She exhaled and said, 'This is insane. This is absolutely insane.'

'What're you talking about?'

'Everything you've just said. It's just some twisted fantasy, isn't it?'

'Huh?' Confusion fogged his mind. 'No, of course not.'

'You said you wanted to kill him. Now you're talking about becoming his biographer.'

'Interrogator,' Jack corrected.

'Yeah? I thought you were just going to catch him somewhere and do it, in and out.'

'No.' Jack shook his head. 'That's not what I meant at all. And I never said that.'

'So let me get this straight,' she began, rolling her shoulders. 'You're going to *kidnap* him, *interrogate* him, and *then* murder him. Am I right so far?'

'Yes,' he replied flatly, 'and you don't have to sound so condescending about it either.'

'In fairness, maybe I do, Jack. When you told me you wanted to kill him, I assumed your plan was to get away with it.'

He shrugged. 'Of course it is.'

'So explain to me how you plan to carry all this out, without attracting any attention to yourself.'

He stared at her for a few seconds. There was nothing but steel in his gaze. 'What's your tone like that for?'

'My tone?' She cocked her head, lips pursed, and just that gesture reminded him of arguing with Kate. It was like looking at a very good imitation of his wife.

44

'You're talking to me like I'm an idiot.'

'No, I'm not. What I'm trying to do is understand your plan, because by the sound of it, there's a lot of kinks we're going to need to iron out.'

He leaned back, the muscles in his neck bunching painfully. His sciatica was playing up and his thigh was becoming numb.

'He has a brand new Mercedes parked on that shitty estate. I'd wait until dark and smash one of the windows, setting off the alarm. When he came down to investigate, I'd hit him, bundle him in the back of the van and take him to Cheshunt.'

'Cheshunt? What's in Cheshunt?'

Jack scratched his beard, went into his wallet, removed a business card and handed it to her. 'Just got these printed the other day with the new warehouse's details on it. What do you think of the design? I did it myself on the computer.'

The font was awkward and the logo appeared squashed, as though he'd shrunk the image down to fit the card.

'My boss is expanding the business and we're shifting stock to a new warehouse in Cheshunt. I'm mostly going to be working out of there in the next few months, but I'm overseeing the transition of stock from the Dagenham warehouse. It's half empty now, right at the end of an industrial estate.'

She stuffed the card in her pocket, leaned against the wall and tilted her head up toward the ceiling, studying it as though it were a Magic Eye puzzle. He could almost hear the cogs turning in her head. 'And after?'

'After? You mean when I kill him?'

'Yeah,' she said in a tired sigh. 'What're you gonna do with him?'

'Bury him.'

'Just like that?' she said, the words tinged in sarcasm.

He nodded. 'Yeah. I'll bury him in a field somewhere. Nobody'll find him.'

She looked at him hard for a moment, her tongue clicking. 'You really think you have the nerve to do all that?'

Jack picked up the wine and gulped thirstily from the bottle. He could feel the gentle tug of inebriation sluicing through his system.

'She was pregnant,' he said, wiping his lips on the back of his hand. 'What do you want me to do, Emily? This man stole my whole life, any kind of future I ever had.'

Mine too, she thought.

They were silent for a long time. Eventually Emily said, 'OK.'

'OK what?'

Her face was as cold and blank as slate. 'Let's talk about your plan some more.'

Chapter Eight

It was breakfast time and the woman sat on the couch eating crisps. Craig could smell the smoky bacon flavouring from the other side of the room.

'Where'd you find this fucking lump?' he asked, disgusted.

'She comes recommended,' Dillon said, biting his lip in an effort to stifle his laughter. 'Black Sally says he uses her all the time.'

'Looks like you just hauled her out of the ocean. The fucking size of her.'

The woman wasn't listening; she was glued to the TV, where a talk-show host was berating some unfortunate-looking bastard about the responsibility a father has to his child.

'That's the point, though, isn't it?' Dillon said, stirring his tea. 'Wouldn't work if she was thin as a rake, would it? Anyway, don't let her looks put you off. She's a pro.'

'Put me off? She's already put me off my breakfast,' Craig muttered.

'She's well padded. Won't be much of a problem,' Dillon offered.

'Yeah, we just have to make sure she doesn't get caught up in McDonald's and miss the flight.' He slid his plate aside. 'Valerie,' he called into the front room.

'Veronica,' Dillon corrected.

'Whatever. Get in here.'

She left the crisps on the sofa and padded over to the table. She looked bored.

'Dillon tells me that you've done this sort of thing before. He says you're a pro.'

'Mmm,' she grunted, nodding.

'How much?'

'Ten grand,' she said.

'No, I mean how much did you take over?'

'Six keys.'

'Six?' Craig couldn't believe it. Six kilos wasn't a lot of weight if you were carrying it, but concealing it was a different ball game entirely.

'Mmm,' she grunted, exhaling noisily through her nostrils.

'Tell him how,' Dillon urged.

'Three kilos in the case, sewn into the lining. One kilo packed into the heels of my platforms.'

'Bullshit,' Craig interrupted. 'How'd you get a kilo in your heels?'

'I'm a size ten,' she said, hoisting her leg up so that he could see the length and width of her foot. 'Three hundred grams inside,' she pointed to her stomach. 'Another seven hundred in a cane I use to walk.'

'That's five kilos,' Craig muttered. 'You said six.'

'One kilo in my hair.'

Dillon burst out laughing. Craig looked at him coldly. 'I'm sorry,' Dillon said, smothering his laughter.

Craig looked back at Veronica. 'You're going to have to explain,' he said.

48

Veronica laced her fingers into her scalp and removed her bushy wig. Underneath it she was bald as a bowling ball. 'They made a packet in the lining of the wig, smoothed it out, glued it on my head. No problem.'

'I don't fucking believe this.' Craig glanced at Dillon. 'If I didn't know any better, I'd say this sounds like a wind-up.'

'It's not a wind-up,' Veronica said. 'I've done it lots of times.'

'And you've never been picked up?' Craig asked.

'I'm here, aren't I?'

'I want to take eight kilos across. How're you gonna deal with another two kilos?'

She shrugged again, a vacant expression on her face. 'Strap to my arse,' she said, so matter-of-factly that it even made Craig smile. 'Strap to my stomach. And some up my vagina.'

'So there you go,' Dillon said, grinning. 'Eight kilos covered.'

'You really think you can do it?' Craig asked her. She shrugged. 'Words, you fucking idiot. Start using words when I ask you a question.'

She didn't get riled up, but instead said, 'I don't see why not.'

'What about dogs?'

'Airport dogs?' she asked.

'No. Pluto and Goofy. Of course airport dogs. What if they sniff you out?'

'No, they don't sniff me out. No chance.'

'Why no chance?'

'Packages are dog-proof. I don't touch the drugs and we don't pack them in the same room as me. No smell

49

transfer. We use Mylar to wrap everything, make it airtight.'

'Mylar? What the fuck is mylar?'

It was the one and only time she conveyed an expression other than blank indifference. Her brow pinched in apparent confusion as she looked from Craig to Dillon, and then back to Craig again. 'Like plastic. Airtight. No smell gets out. As long as I don't touch it beforehand we have no problem.'

Craig rested his hands atop the mound of his stomach and twiddled his thumbs in contemplation. 'You have four kids?'

'Mmm.'

'You love 'em?'

'Course.'

'How old are they?'

'Fifteen, twelve, nine, four.'

'And you know what happens if you fuck this up? If you try and do a runner, you get caught?'

'I can imagine.'

'And you're willing to risk that for ten grand?'

'I'm not an idiot. I don't draw attention to myself. I'm quiet. I don't make no fuss.' She burped into the back of her hand. 'Nothing'll go wrong.'

Craig considered her a while longer, tapping his finger against his lip. The woman was enormous, twenty stone at a guess, but that was being generous. Her skin was oily and blotchy, and that vacant expression on her face disturbed him. It didn't look as though she had two brain cells bouncing around in that skull, and yet, as legend would have it, she was one of the most successful smugglers in the UK. How could this woman mule eight kilos to

Amsterdam without attracting attention to herself? Her size alone made her stand out.

'All right,' he said. 'You're going to fly out early next Saturday morning. Someone'll be on the flight watching you, just in case you decide to get quick on your feet, though I doubt that's going to happen, is it?'

'I won't run,' she said.

'I'm going to buy two tickets for you. You have any friends?'

'Mmm.'

'Good. Take one you trust. They don't have to do anything except go with you. If they stop you at customs you can say you're sightseeing, going to see the windmills, whatever.'

'Mmm.'

'OK. I'll see you on Friday night then and we'll get you strapped up.'

She wheezed. There was a thick rattling in her throat. 'That's it? I can go now?'

'Yeah,' he said. 'And take your crisps with you.'

–

Craig pinched the joint and sucked it down to the roach, then flicked it out the window. He thought about asking Dillon to bill up another spliff, but he didn't want to be too high, just relaxed enough to walk into the meeting without his legs turning to jelly.

They bombed down the motorway, weaving through the lanes. Dillon drove like a psycho at the best of times, and after a bump of coke – which he swore he hadn't done, but his red-rimmed eyes told Craig different – the car seemed to be approaching warp speed. Cool air blew on him from the air conditioner, but Craig was still sweating. The seat of his jeans felt damp against the leather, and his armpits were moist and swampy.

'I hope you're right about her,' he said to Dillon.

'She's done it dozens of times. She's lucky as a rabbit's foot.'

'That's what worries me. She's done it dozens of times and hasn't been caught. What if this is her time?'

'It won't be.'

'But what if it is?'

'We can talk about what-ifs all day long,' Dillon said nonchalantly as the world turned into a colourless blur outside the car. 'No reason to jinx it.'

–

The tyres kicked up gravel as Craig rolled to a stop in front of the town house. A golem of a man waited by the door to escort him in. Craig grabbed the rear-view mirror and checked his face, his teeth, his hair. Then he looked at Dillon.

'Why'd you wear trainers?'

'Hmm?' Dillon was sending a text on an ancient Nokia that had masking tape down one side of it, holding the battery in place.

'You'll show me up going in there with your fucking trainers on.'

'What does it matter?'

'We don't want him to think we're a couple of rude boys, do we?'

'If you're that bothered, why didn't you say anything before we left?'

'Because I was thinking about other things, getting my mind right.'

Dillon gave him a dismissive tut and waved his hand. 'You're overanalysing it. He won't give a fuck what we look like.'

And that there, Craig thought, was the quintessential difference between them. Yesterday afternoon Craig had gone to the barbers, had his beard shaped up, bought a new shirt. He looked smart, and the freshness of his appearance lent him a bit of confidence, because god knew he needed it. Dillon, on the other hand, was almost thirty and looked as though he'd just modelled for a high-street sports shop: a Nike cap, sovereign rings on his fingers, Air Force trainers on his feet.

'You wait in the car,' Craig said, kicking himself for not bringing a towel to wipe the sweat away from his armpits.

'You're overthinking this. He's not our boss,' Dillon said contemptuously, the sun glinting off his gold front tooth. 'We're here to do business with him. It's mutually beneficial.'

'Shut up, you fucking moron. Don't try and talk intelligent. Just stay here and try not to make a fucking nuisance of yourself.'

Craig got out of the car with a groan, his knees popping, his back crackling. The golem gave Craig a look of acknowledgement but said nothing. He opened the front door and led Craig through the town house and into a musty smelling back office. Behind a shiny oak table sat Edward Dekkers, looking at a stack of papers, some of which had pink highlighter through them.

'Sit down,' Dekkers said in his thick Dutch accent, without looking at Craig. Dekkers took the highlighter pen, made another pink streak along one of the rows of numbers, and then scribbled something down in a notepad. 'Do you want a cup of tea or coffee?' he asked in a tone that suggested Craig should decline his offer.

'No, thank you. I had a cup of tea before I left.'

Dekkers set his pen down and regarded Craig sternly. Dekkers was in his fifties and had hair white as untouched snow. Faint scars lined his rugged face and the flesh above his eyes was so hooded it was like two black hollows staring back at Craig.

'So. You have news for me?' Dekkers said, disinterested.

'Yeah. I mean yes.' Craig nodded. 'I've found someone. She comes recommended.'

Dekkers studied Craig. 'And she can take five kilos?'

'She can take eight,' Craig said, his voice quavering. Dekkers' face betrayed the slightest hint of interest.

'That's a lot,' he said.

Yes it is, Craig thought. But he wanted to go above and beyond expectations, show these jumped-up Dutch fucks that he wasn't some two-bit villain but a bold, intelligent criminal.

'She's a professional. She's done long-haul before – Argentina, Chile…'

Dekkers silenced him with a wave of the hand. 'Fine. You have it.'

'Thank you, Edward,' he replied, surprised at how easily Dekkers relented, and even more surprised at the speed with which they had negotiated the deal. Maybe the old bastard was a pushover. 'Honestly, thank you for this opportunity.' When he received no acknowledgement, he said, 'I want you to know that you can depend on me.'

'I should hope so,' Dekkers said, rising from his chair. He extended his hand. Craig patted his palms on the thighs of his jeans, the perspiration turning the denim dark blue. They shook hands. Dekkers' grip felt strong enough to bend steel.

'Talk to Mikkel outside, he will get you eight.'

'OK.' He had turned to leave when Dekkers stopped him with a grunt.

'It's a lot of responsibility. No room for error.' Craig nodded and smiled, not trusting himself to speak. 'Don't make me look for you, Craig. It will be very bad for you. You understand this, yes?'

Craig nodded and no more was said.

Chapter Nine

She saw Kate in her dreams again that night.

Kate was sitting at the table with her hands wrapped around a mug, staring out the window. The steam curling out of the mug smelled like chamomile and honey. She had a white scarf knotted loosely around her neck that flowed down over the mound of her pregnant stomach.

'He told you, then?' Kate said, without diverting her attention away from the window. 'About the baby?'

'Yes,' Emily said and began to walk carefully toward the table. She didn't want to move too fast for fear that it would disrupt the framework of the dream. *Things are different now*, Emily wanted to say. *I know who did this to you.*

'I told him it's bad luck,' she said with a sigh. 'He never listens.'

Emily reached the table.

'My neck hurts,' Kate said, turning to face her now. Her skin was sickly pale, the rims of her eyes coppery red.

She doesn't know, Emily thought. *She doesn't know she's dead.*

Kate carefully picked up the mug and sipped delicately. 'Well, now you know about the baby, I guess we can talk about it. Exciting, isn't it?'

'Yes,' Emily said weakly.

Kate smiled and her mouth appeared like a gaping wound in her white face. That terrible grin gave off an eerie draught that sent needlepoints of fear through Emily. This *wasn't* her sister. Immediately, the tenuous link between her waking and sleeping mind snapped, and Emily no longer wanted any part of this dream. She scrunched her eyes closed in an effort to wake herself, but she was paralysed, pinned by the awful weight of Kate's stare.

'Wouldn't it be funny if they were twins?' Kate said, but her lips hadn't moved. She was talking through her teeth, through that slashed grin. 'Imagine that. Two girls. Then they could be best friends, just like us.'

'Kate,' Emily said, her tongue clumsy inside her numb mouth. It was like speaking after a visit to the dentist. 'It's not you,' she mumbled.

'What's not me?' The rest of her features frowned but the smile remained.

'You're d…' The word crumbled. 'You're d…'

'I'm what? You're not making any sense.'

A red dot appeared on the white scarf. Emily's eyes locked onto it, transfixed. The dot began to blossom, growing larger, spreading through the fabric of the scarf, dyeing it.

'You're dead,' Emily finally managed. She wanted very badly to wake up now, because her terror was spreading like the red on that white scarf. Sweet merciful Jesus above, she had never been so scared in all her life and she couldn't take another second of this.

'Dead? What a silly thing to say. I'm sitting right here.'

No, Emily thought, trying to turn her head away, but some invisible vice held it in place. *No you're not. This* isn't *you.*

'Yes, it is,' Kate answered her thoughts. 'What's brought all this on? Why're you acting like this?'

Emily was clenching her teeth together so tightly now that little lightning rods shot through her gums and jaw. 'He... killed... you...' she finally managed, and just like that, the words set her free. She felt the weight drift away, emancipating her limbs. She shot up from the table, spilling the chamomile and honey tea onto Kate's lap. Kate didn't flinch.

'Yes, I know,' she said sadly. 'But I thought we could pretend, just for a little bit.' She reached up and touched the scarf; her fingers coming away crimson as she worked at the knot. Rivulets of blood ran down her pale neck.

'Don't do that, Kate,' Emily shouted. 'Stop it!'

'It hurts,' Kate said, her fingers like albino worms, burrowing into the scarf. 'I need to get it off.'

Emily watched as Kate undid the knot. The scarf was nothing more than a sopping red rag when she pulled it away and let it fall to the floor.

'Is it bad?' Kate asked, tilting her head to the side, offering Emily a better look at the wound. 'You were always the honest one, Em. Tell me how it looks. Is it awful?'

Emily was expecting a gory display of snarled skin, flapping tendons, slivers of yellow fat. But there was only a hole, a bit larger than a cigarette burn. She was about to say as much when the hole ripped wider and spewed a geyser of blood.

The scream left her mouth before she was fully awake. She pushed herself up from the mattress, mewling like an injured animal.

'What're you doing?' Roger moaned, tugging the quilt back over him. 'You scared the life out of me.'

Emily couldn't speak. She was crying and her jaw hurt from grinding her teeth. Her pillow was damp with sweat, tears and saliva. She could hear her blood roaring in her ears.

She swung her legs over the side of the mattress and sat there, weeping into the palms of her hands. *Kate... my poor Kate... why couldn't it have been me?*

In the black tide of grief that followed in the years after Kate's murder, Emily had often asked herself this question. She was, after all, the failure of the family. Kate had left university with dazzling honours, fought for a job in the banking sector and soared through the ranks, bought a nice house and married a good, honest man. She had done everything right. And then you had Emily, who had dropped out of uni after dismally failing her first year. She had hopped from one low-paid job to another, shuffling her career paths almost as quickly as she shuffled her men. And that just wasn't the trajectory their parents had set for them. They were both expected to graduate in the same year, then go on to mirror each other's achievements in their chosen fields. They were supposed to be the success story that their parents could brag about, and yet Emily could never fulfil her end of the bargain. She just wasn't made like Kate. They were twins, yes, but they were two separate people for god's sake. Kate was born with all the brains, Emily would often say, a trademark bit of self-deprecating humour, but she believed it with all her heart. Kate was the smart one. Emily was the... she didn't know. The one that didn't finish things. The one that had no ambition. Kate never made Emily feel shitty about failing the semester, nor did she lord her engagement over her, even when Emily's inability to sustain a relationship provoked concern in their parents.

Kate was the only constant in Emily's life and then she was gone. No warning, no last goodbye.

The police had failed to catch her killer. Rather than going after the boy who'd knocked on her door and plunged a knife into Kate's neck, they chose to focus their investigation on Jack. Jack, who hadn't gone to university, who had worked in a warehouse since leaving school and earned less than half of what his wife did. For a little while they toyed with the theory that Jack, who had struck gold when he found this beautiful, intelligent and successful career woman, hired a hitman to kill Kate. Even after his teary television appeals that were far too harrowing to be anything other than genuine, the police still had him down as suspect number one. But when they realised she had no life insurance, no will, no savings great enough to warrant a motive, they were stumped. No forensic evidence, no CCTV of the car as described by Jack, no other witnesses that could offer anything of use.

So why her? What could she have ever done to deserve such a horrific death?

Why Kate and not me? It should have been me. It should have been...

Emily stood up and felt the room sway around her. She had to get out of the house. She had to do something.

She had to see Craig Morley for herself.

Chapter Ten

She called in sick, said she was coming down with the flu, but her boss's dull voice on the other end of the line told her exactly what he was thinking: she was taking Monday off, a nice three-day weekend for her. Emily couldn't have cared less.

While she was jostled about on the train heading to Morley's estate, her mind flashed back to a conversation she'd had with her mother a few years before. They had been sitting in the conservatory overlooking the garden, with a teapot and a plate of biscuits between them. During these occasional visits, where the sound of crunching custard creams usually outweighed their dialogue, her mother had asked, 'Do you ever hear much from Jack?'

'Jack? Every now and then. He sends cards at Christmas, that sort of thing. You?'

'He still remembers my birthday. And your father's.'

A pregnant pause followed, but Emily could almost feel her mother's need to discuss him further, to pick at the scab without reopening the wound. It was dangerous territory, of course. If either one of them dropped their defences and began down memory lane, they would both be in floods of tears before long.

Eventually, Emily relented. 'I don't think he ever got over what happened.'

. Her mother's lips unglued with a small, wet sound. 'How could he? How could any of us? It wasn't like she was sick or had an accident. How can you properly begin to grieve knowing that someone out there got away with murder? You know, some days I just sit down and turn that over in my head, or I wake up wondering what that person is doing, whether they ever think about her.' She turned her head slightly toward Emily and then regarded her from the corner of her eye. Casually, as though discussing an increase in the price of bread rather than her daughter's murder, she asked, 'What do you think?'

It was the most her mother had said in a very long time. Had she been waiting for Emily to poke the elephant in the room after all these years?

Emily sighed, looked down at her lap, her hair hanging across her face. 'I used to have these horrible dreams about it. At first it was every night, and I would wake up just… bawling in my sleep because they would seem too real. I used to think she was' – Emily paused, bit down hard on her bottom lip, swallowed a sob that threatened to make its way up her throat – 'I used to think she was angry with me, because I was still alive. Like it should have been me that died. So I had to train myself to stop thinking about, because if I didn't, I knew it would drive me—'

'Crazy?' her mother finished for her. 'Yes. I know the feeling.' She chipped off a piece of custard cream and crumbled it between her fingers. Fine yellow dust flittered to the carpet.

'In a way,' Emily began hesitantly, 'I think it might be worse for Jack. He saw who did it. I can't imagine what that would be like, walking around, always looking for that face. The torment…'

Her mother crushed the biscuit in her hand and ground it up. 'That's the only thing keeping me going,' she said as chunks of custard cream cascaded from her clenched fist. 'I'd be in my grave now if it wasn't for the hope that one day Jack somehow sees him again. But I'm not sure that's ever going to happen, and anyway' – her birdlike shoulders shrugged – 'I think I'm about ready to be planted.'

'Don't say that, Mum.' Absently, Emily bent down and began scooping up the shattered pieces of biscuit.

'Well, it's true. I think I've had enough. The police don't care about it any more. But I suppose you never know.'

Softly Emily said, 'Jack probably wouldn't recognise him today. He could walk straight past him in the street and not even know it.'

'No,' Renee shook her head. 'You would never forget a thing like that, Em. Not as long as you lived.' She patted Emily's thigh, gave it a gentle squeeze. It was the most loving gesture she had offered in a very long time. 'We just have to stay positive, love. Sometimes God answers prayers.'

When she arrived at the station, Emily used her phone to find Frazier Avenue. It was one of the last tower blocks around for miles, standing defiant like a rotten tooth in a mouthful of bleeding gums. They'd knocked all the other estates down and were redeveloping the area, shuttling the council tenants off here, there and everywhere. Frazier Avenue was one of the last of its kind, a lonely relic with only rubble and cranes to keep it company.

Emily didn't have a game plan. She made her way to the main door and buzzed different buttons, keeping silent until someone got fed up and buzzed her in.

She drifted through the foyer, pressed the call button for the lift and waited.

'It's broken,' a voice said, startling her. It was a young boy, maybe thirteen years old, wheeling a BMX out of the flats.

'Thanks,' she replied.

She took the stairs to the eighth floor, pausing at each landing to catch her breath and palm the beads of perspiration away, and then walked through the hallway until she found number 83. This was it. Behind that door was the man who killed her sister.

Or was it? Jack had seemed so unwavering that it was difficult to disbelieve him, and yet there was still a kernel of doubt. Jack could be wrong. If he was, and if they did what he wanted to do, that would make them no better than the piece of shit that knifed Kate.

But what if Jack was right? Could she really help kill another human being, even one as vile and evil as Morley was supposed to be? She reached out and touched his door, could feel the music inside his flat thrumming through her fingers. *I just need to see you*, she thought. *I just need to get a glimpse of you in the flesh to know that this is real.*

She withdrew her hand and walked to the end of the hallway, where she still had a good view of Morley's door.

She would wait for him to leave. All day if she needed to.

She didn't need to wait long. A short while later, Morley stepped out of the flat, all six-foot-five of him, his back as broad as a barn door. He was speaking to someone on the phone about a 'pickup' and then he stopped dead in the hallway, some sixth sense alerting him to her presence. His head turned, slightly tilted, like a wolf scenting a lamb in the air. She began to walk, her heels clicking down the hallway, the rhythm of her stride unsettled by his sudden odd behaviour. He knew something was wrong. She stared fixedly at the gum-stained floor as she walked, glancing up only once. His eyes jumped out at her, reminding her of something from her childhood. When she was little, Kate had bought an astrology magazine because it came with a free packet of glow-in-the-dark stars. Kate stuck them to the ceiling, all around the lampshade, so at night when they went to sleep they could see the luminous constellation.

She saw his expression change as she passed. He had been vaguely suspicious at first, and then it gave way to something else. His eyes narrowed and his lips curled up in the corners. 'Oi, I'll call you back,' he said into the phone, and then, 'Excuse me, excuse me' – his insistent voice rolling after her. She knew that she had two choices just then: either bolt down the hallway for the stairs, or turn and face him, act normal. Every muscle in her body flooded with adrenaline, preparing for flight. That was silly, though. She was just a woman in the hallway. He didn't know her.

But she knew *him*.

She stopped. As casually as she could, she looked over at him. 'Can I help you?'

'Do *you* need any help? You seem lost,' he said, continuing to smile, his eyes gleaming slyly.

'I'm not lost.'

'Oh? Who are you here to see?'

'That's none of your business,' she said curtly, hoping the edge in her voice would repel him. It seemed to have the opposite effect. He trotted on after her, following her into the stairwell. *Damn these heels*, she thought. *If I was wearing flats I could jet down these stairs in no time. If I try anything fancy in these shoes I'm liable to snap my ankle or go tumbling and break my neck.*

'You don't live in this block,' he said. It came out like an accusation.

'So?'

'So, who are you?'

'Like I said, none of your business.' She walked faster, trying to build up a rhythm. She could hear him behind her, could see his shadow stretching over hers on the stairs.

'It is my business when you're in my building.'

'It's your building, is it? Landlord, are you?' The quip didn't come out anywhere near as confident as she'd hoped.

He snorted laughter. 'You've got jokes.' In her haste, her heel clipped the top of a step and she lost her footing, her hand whipping out for the banister. 'Careful now. Don't want to trip.'

'Can you stop following me?' she said shakily, her voice reverberating through the stairwell. She didn't stop, didn't look at him, just kept all her focus on her feet.

'Who says I'm following *you*? The lift's broken.'

What floor was she on now? She looked through the gap in the stairwell and saw the spiral of stairs on the way down. It had to be another four or five floors at least.

'I haven't seen your face round here before. You're pretty, you know that?'

'Am I?' The chipped paint on the stairwell banister scraped into her palm.

'Yeah, you are. You have a man?'

Don't answer. Just keep going.

'You must have a man. Pretty little thing like you can't be walking around with no man. Does he treat you well?'

'He does. In fact he's waiting for me right outside this building. So I'd be careful if I were you.' The private schooling in her accent was impossible to mask. The sentence came out about as threatening as a feather pillow.

'Careful of what? I haven't done anything to you.'

She could hear the smile in his voice.

'Good. Keep it that way.'

He gave a low, throaty chuckle. 'You're not from this building. And I don't think you're visiting anyone from this building. And I don't think you're a policewoman. So why would you be hanging around on my floor?'

Panicked, she thought about saying she was from the council but opted out at the last second. That left the door open to too many follow-up questions and he'd see through her in an instant. But she felt like she needed to tell him something, give a reason for being in the building.

'You have nice hair, you know that?'

'Thank you,' she snapped.

'I can't see too well through that jacket, but I bet the rest of you is nice too, isn't it? Course it is, you look like you take good care of yourself.'

She peered down the gap in the stairwell again. Two more floors to go.

As she rounded the corner, she felt the toe of his trainer press down on the back of her shoe. Her foot came loose and she almost buckled forward down the concrete steps. An involuntary scream leapt out of her mouth and sent a jagged echo through the stairwell.

'Sorry,' he said insincerely. 'I have big feet. You know what they say about men with big feet?'

A runaway thought rocketed through her mind just then. Should she just kick her shoes off and sprint out in her bare feet? She'd get further if she did, and maybe he'd find it funny, so funny that he'd let her go.

She took the last set of stairs and zoned in on the door that would lead her outside. If she could get that door open then she could run outside and scream, tell him to back off and leave her the fuck alone; but in the stairwell she was like a fly in a web. This was his lair.

She could hear him wheezing, the descent taking its toll on him. 'It's true what they say, you know. Big feet.'

She scurried to the ground-floor door, grabbed the handle with both hands and yanked as hard as she could. The door didn't open. She pulled again, releasing a scream of frustration when it didn't budge. She felt his shadow envelope her now. He was standing right behind her, his large palm pressed against the door, just above her head. The strong, cloying scent of his aftershave clouded her. Very gently, she felt his crotch press up against her buttocks.

'Don't touch me,' the words wobbled out of her mouth. 'I'm telling you right now. I know where you live. You lay a hand on me and I'll report you.' She wanted to tell him more, tell him that she knew his name, knew his past. She wanted to scare him off her but knew it would only land her in deeper trouble.

'I'm trying to help you open the door,' he said softly, his breath fluttering her hair, tickling her cheek. 'Do you want me to open the door for you? Like a gentleman?'

'Yes!'

'No need to shout. I'm not deaf.'

'Just open the door.'

'Open the door... *please?*'

The pit of her stomach fell away. He pushed his crotch harder against her.

'Open... the door... *please*,' she said. It sounded like she was begging and she hated him for it. A scream was winding up inside her, ready to spring out of her mouth, but she had the sick feeling it wouldn't come.

'You're not a policewoman and you're not here to see anyone on the eighth floor. That makes me a little bit anxious,' he said in a low, blunt voice that made her cheeks break out in gooseflesh. 'I know every face in this building, but I don't know you. It's a mystery, isn't it? But you do remind me of someone and I just can't think who. You look so familiar.'

'I just want to go,' she told him, pulling the door. It still didn't move.

'Then go. I'm not keeping you here against your will.'

She pulled the door. It made a defiant clunking sound.

'It won't open,' she whispered coarsely.

'It helps when you press this.'

She saw his finger push the exit button by the side of the door that unlocked it. She flung the door open and raced out into the frosty daylight, fleeing from the sound of his laughter.

Chapter Eleven

Jack spent most of his Sunday and almost all of his Monday at the new warehouse in Cheshunt. It had once been home to a company that made bespoke furniture, but now, save for a few scraps of cloth left behind by the previous occupants, it was almost completely bare. Toward the far end of the warehouse was a small room, which Jack had taken great care in soundproofing by lining the cinderblock walls with boxes. On the door of the room was an old, faded sign that read 'Oiling Room'. It would soon be 'Morley's Room'.

The solitude of the warehouse was the perfect place to declutter his mind and focus on the storm ahead. He opened up his laptop and smoothed out the creased sheet of paper that Emily had given him. Then he researched Morley's ridiculous alias, 'Flashy Menace', and was stunned to find results on YouTube. The first video that appeared, titled '*Money Up Front*' – *Flashy Menace feat. Danger*, uploaded in 2007, had 3,465 views. The thumbnail of the video showed a boy wearing a face mask with a skull motif that covered his nose and mouth. Beneath his wiry, conjoined eyebrows was a set of speckled, emerald-green eyes. Jack clicked the play button, his clammy palms leaving a shiny smear over the touchpad. His mouth became bitterly dry, his gums lined with cotton wool.

A confusing jumble of strange-sounding musical notes played as the video began, and Jack could not quite place the instrument. It sounded like pan pipes perhaps, but synthesised over a rapid drumbeat. It was crazy, aggravating music – disorientating almost. The tinny laptop speakers crackled with feedback when the bass kicked in, and Jack felt his face starting to heat up the way it did when he was coming down with a cold.

He watched, disturbed and bewildered, as Morley began rapping over the beat while marching through an estate with about fifty other goons, some of them restraining muscly, aggressive dogs on short leashes. In more than half a dozen shots, the boy wearing the face mask – Morley's alter ego, Flashy Menace – posed with several different weapons, among them a machete, a hand axe, a cleaver and a gun.

The camerawork was as jerky as the music, and by the fifteenth or sixteenth time that Jack watched the video, he began to feel the first stirrings of motion sickness. By the twenty-fifth time he watched it, he felt positively nauseated, but had learned some of the lyrics.

He snapped the laptop closed with the song's chorus rattling around in his head. He had lost a lot of time studying the video, and now he was behind schedule.

–

He drove to May's house, got out of the van and gingerly made his way up the path. The strain of heaving the stock from the van to the oiling room had teased his sciatic nerve, and now electric jolts of pain shot through his lower back. As he reached out to press the bell, the door opened. He could hear a George Michael love ballad sailing out from the living room. May's head poked around from behind the door.

'I'm glad you could make it,' she said sweetly.

'I forgot to bring wine,' he said gruffly.

She laughed. 'I knew you would. Come in.'

When he stepped inside, he saw that May was wearing a black silk gown.

'See something you like?' she asked, with a devilish grin.

'Oh,' he said, unbalanced. 'I didn't realise you were gonna…' He looked down at his own clothes, the stained jumper and jeans he'd worn all day at work. 'I didn't think it was gonna be one of those nights, otherwise I would've showered first and…'

She put a finger on his lips, silencing him awkwardly. 'It's OK. I love you exactly how you are. That's how a man *should* be.' She pursed her lips and kissed him, her tongue sliding in his mouth. She tasted of vodka. 'Take a seat. Dinner's almost ready.'

He plonked himself down on her sofa, relieved to take the burden off his back. His temples still thumped with the music video's bassline, and yet he had a masochistic urge to watch it again, to see Morley's eyes the way he remembered them and fan the flames of his rage.

The smell of dinner wafted out from the kitchen and earned a snarl from his stomach. The last thing he could remember eating was a ham sandwich the night before.

May returned from the kitchen with a glass of whisky. The ice cubes clinked as she handed it to him. 'Get that down you,' she purred.

He accepted it gratefully, took a sip, and said, 'Dinner smells great. What is it?'

'Lasagne,' she replied, but pronounced it 'las-ag-nay', which bothered him. He smiled and sipped the whisky, could already feel it working its magic. 'I know what you're thinking, mister. But you're going to have to wait. Dinner *first*,' she said, stroking his knee. 'Dessert comes later.'

She invited him to the dinner table about ten minutes later. When he stood up from the sofa, his glass was empty except for a couple of nubs of ice, and he no longer felt any pain in his back. His eyes felt raw and dry from staring at the laptop in the dingy warehouse light.

May lit the candles and presented his lasagne to him, garnished with parsley. The aroma flooded his mouth with saliva.

'Go on,' she said, sitting opposite him, her foot rubbing against his leg beneath the table.

'Where's yours?' he asked, forking off a segment of the lasagne and shovelling it in his mouth. It was delicious, maybe the best las-ag-nay he'd ever eaten.

'I'm only hungry for one thing,' she said, lowering her eyes. Her voice had taken on that forced, sultry tone that she used when she decided it was time for intimacy.

He nodded and ate hungrily, opening his mouth to allow the steam to billow out. The food was gone in less than three minutes. May took his plate to the sink and returned with a bottle of champagne and two flutes.

'What's all this in aid of?' he asked as she worked her thumbs into the cork.

She waited for it to pop, foam drooling over her hands, and then said, 'It's two things. First, it's an apology. I've had an awful weekend thinking about how we left things on Friday. I should've been more understanding and it was selfish of me to behave the way I did. I wanted to call you all weekend but I thought I'd let you rest and recover. You look better, by the way.'

'Do I?'

Lyrics from the music video bobbed to the surface of his mind.

Money up front or I'll be at your door with the blade out…
Pay what you owe or I'll carve your face out.

'Yes. Your colour has returned. And secondly,' she said, pouring champagne, 'this is a very special evening.'

He looked at her, confused. It wasn't their anniversary, he knew that for sure. They had met on Valentine's Day at a pub that was hosting a singles-only night. He'd wandered in for a drink after work, not really intending to get involved in any of that Valentine's Day bullshit, but saw lots of people his own age there and that was a nice change from being the old man in the room. May had been alone at one end of the bar, drinking a rum and Coke, looking over at him in between sips through the straw. It was the first and only time he'd sent a drink over to a woman. She was attractive, yes, but pulling a Richard Gere move like that was something they only did in the films and it definitely wasn't his style. He did it because she looked lonely, and because he knew at a glance that she could help him. Maybe not right away, but somewhere down the line, he could open up to her. She was just the thing he needed.

'Why's it special?' he asked.

Ignoring his question, she went into the kitchen and returned with a plate. On top of it was a ring box.

'We've been going together for almost five years now,' she said, and the sexy demeanour she'd maintained all through dinner betrayed her. 'I know it isn't the leap year, but I'm a progressive woman, and I like to think…'

'May, wait a minute,' Jack said, shifting in the chair. The lack of sleep and the stress of Craig Morley had made his thoughts slow and soupy. He had just realised what she was planning on doing when she got down on one knee.

'Don't speak. Please don't speak,' she said softly, shyly almost. He noticed that she was shivering and he wasn't convinced that it was just because she was half-naked. 'Jack, I haven't had a lot of luck with men in my life. I think part of it was probably my own fault. Some of my friends used to say I fall in love too easily, but I can't help that. I'm a hopeless romantic at heart,' she tittered nervously, biting her lower lip. 'When my marriage ended, I thought my life was over. And some nights I wished it was,' she said, the memory visibly paining her. She frowned and bit her lip harder to keep from crying. 'But then I met you, and things were different. I know I can be a bit high-maintenance, but you still treated me nicely. You gave me respect. And for that I'll always love you, Jack.' She took the box from the plate and opened it. A diamond studded gold band winked and sparkled in the candlelight. 'I'd do anything for you, Jack. Will you marry me?'

He looked at her childlike face, the large eyes brimming with hope.

Money up front or I'll be at your door with the blade out…

Craig Morley's face sprung up in his mind, smiling through the rear window of the car.

'May, we shouldn't,' he said, helping her to her feet. He tried to sit her down on his lap but she became rigid as an ironing board in his arms. 'I don't think marriage is a good idea. Not now.'

'Wh–why not?'

'Because I don't want to be married right now. I've got too much to do,' he said, more sternly than he had intended. 'What with the new warehouse and all, I'm run off my feet. Plus, think about how expensive it would be. And this ring – Christ, May, how much did you spend on this thing?'

'Don't worry about the money! And we don't have to have a big wedding. We could just go down to the registry office and—'

'We don't even live together, May.'

'Yes, and that is your choice, not mine,' she stabbed a finger in his direction.

'It's because I need my space. Look, you know how I feel about you, May.'

'Do I? How would I know?' She snapped the ring box closed and threw it on the couch. 'You don't talk to me, you don't tell me anything! You don't give anything in this relationship, Jack. You just take. All these years and you're still so guarded, so secretive. I try my best and you give me nothing.'

He bowed his head, the first painful murmurs of a migraine forming. 'May, there's a lot you don't know about me, and that's deliberate. There's things I'd rather not share with you just yet, and that's just how it is. And that's how it will always be with me. That's who I am.'

'But why? Why can't you just trust me?'

'Maybe I should go,' he said drily.

She blinked, confused. 'What?'

'This isn't doing either one of us any good.'

'You're not… Jack, you can't…'

'Maybe you're right. Maybe all I do is take, and that isn't fair. I don't want to be that person. You do deserve better than that, May, and I can't give it to you right now.'

He got up from the chair, feeling twice as heavy as when he'd entered the house. That soothing feeling of drunkenness that had greased his gears before dinner had evaporated and now the machinery was rusting again.

Money up front or I'll be at your door with the blade out…
Shut up, shut up!

'No, Jack, let's just rewind a little bit, OK? Hold on' – she put her hands up defensively, as though preparing to push him back in the chair – 'I made a mistake. I jumped the gun and I tried to pressure you. Just sit down, please.'

'I have to go,' he said, tired of this constant tug of war with her. 'Let's pick this up in a couple of days or something, how about that?' He trudged toward the door. She turned and ran in front of it, blocking his path.

'No! You're not going anywhere!'

'May…'

'Let's just forget all of this and continue on with our evening like we were doing.' A hopeful smile twitched on her lips. 'Forget about marriage and all that, it was silly. I don't want to get married really. I just thought that was what you wanted.'

'Please move out of the way.'

'No. I'm not letting you go. I won't.' She dropped to her knees and hugged his legs. 'Jack, *please*!'

He reached down and unclasped her hands from around his legs, then manoeuvred her out of the way of the door. She was bawling and wailing incoherently on all fours as he reached for the lock.

'If you go…' she said in a high, strained voice, 'then I'll kill myself!'

He shot her a look that made her stutter on her sobs.

Her face slackened, and there was a second of silent recognition as she read his expression. It had been the wrong thing to say, and the threat of violence crackled in the air between them.

He didn't hit her, though. Instead he exhaled, the migraine exploding in his head. Tiny pitchforks stabbed into the back of his eyeballs. He opened the door and stepped outside.

He hadn't made it halfway down the path when he heard May's bare feet slapping on the concrete behind him. He felt her pummel him in the back with her fists. He turned, caught her at the wrists. 'Go inside, the neighbours will see you.'

Her face was puffy and red with fury. 'I don't care about the fucking neighbours,' she screamed at him, loud enough to pierce his eardrums. 'Don't you dare! Don't you dare walk out on me!'

Jack tried to guide her back to the house but she thrashed in his grasp. 'Get your fucking hands off me!'

He released her.

'Pig! Bastard!'

'Fine,' he muttered, then marched quickly to the driver's side of the van. He saw silhouettes behind her neighbours' windows, watching the drama unfold.

'Who is she?' May screamed, bending over with the effort. She looked possessed. 'Tell me who you're seeing!' He started the van just as May slapped the window with both hands. 'Who is she? Tell me her name!'

'Go inside,' he shouted. She slapped the window again, rattling it in the frame.

'Fuck you! Bastard! Go to your little floozy! You bastard, I fucking hate you!'

He pulled away and left her standing there, shouting and swearing with her nightgown billowing in the breeze.

Chapter Twelve

'It's not going to work,' Emily said, entering Jack's house. He caught a strong waft of alcohol as she walked past him. 'And what's wrong with your phone? I've been calling you for ages.'

'I had to unplug it,' he muttered wearily, rubbing his forehead. 'What's not going to work?'

'Your plan for Morley isn't going to work.'

'Why not?'

She walked through to the kitchen, searched for a glass in the cupboards, found one and filled it with tap water. She gulped it down and took a seat at his kitchen table.

'You didn't tell me he was a fucking giant, Jack.'

'You saw him?'

'Yes. I waited in the hallway on the eighth floor.' She got up from the table restlessly, went back into the cupboard and grabbed two chipped mugs. 'You want tea?'

'Yeah,' he said absently. 'You went to Frazier Avenue by yourself?'

With clumsy hands, she filled the kettle up and flicked it on. Over the burr of the boiling water she said, 'I had to see him for myself. I had to make it real, and I wanted to see what he looked like in the flesh. And now I know none of this is going to work.'

'It'll work,' Jack said darkly, his migraine still echoing with the sound of May screaming. 'Doesn't matter how big he is. If I hit him, he'll go down.'

'It's not the going down part I'm worried about; it's getting him up off the ground and moving him,' she said, opening the fridge. 'Where's your milk?'

'Don't have any,' he said.

'Shit,' she hissed. 'Morley is massive. How are we going to get him into the van and then out again, swiftly, and without attracting attention to ourselves?'

'You leave that to me. I can manage it.'

'With respect, Jack, I'm not sure you can.'

'I lug boxes bigger than him around all day. He won't be a problem.'

'And to get him out of the flat, you're thinking about breaking into his car? That's not going to work either.' The kettle clicked, and she poured, spilling hot water on the counter. 'Jesus!'

'Is everything all right? You seem shaky,' he said, rushing in with a tea towel to mop up the water as it dripped off the counter.

'I'm fine,' she huffed. 'The car park is right in view of all the windows. If we make a fuss then people are going to be looking right down on us. It only takes one nosy neighbour to get the licence plate or a description of the van.'

'It'll be dark, they won't make it out.'

'The car park is lit up with street lights, Jack.'

'I'll change the licence plate. Even if someone sees us, you really think they'll report it to the police? I don't know if you're aware of it, but there was a huge riot on that estate in the eighties because of police brutality. A policeman was murdered and—'

'Will you just stop it?'

'Stop what?'

'Stop trying to paper over the cracks of your plan by being flippant. I don't like this rushed thinking of yours. You're so eager to go in and get him that you aren't thinking things through properly.'

'Believe me, I am. And I'm not being flippant. I'm just saying that I don't think we have to worry about people ratting us out to the police, if it even gets that far.'

'I don't care what you *think*, Jack. I need to feel comfortable that we're going to do this properly. And that means not alerting the whole fucking estate that we're there by setting off Morley's car alarm.'

'OK.' He grabbed his mug, removed the teabag from the scorching water with his fingers and slung it in the bin. He blew on his tea and then took a sip. 'What did you see today?'

She placed a loose strand of hair behind her ear and said, 'I waited in his hallway for him to come out. I was thinking of knocking on his door, pretending to be a Jehovah's Witness, but then I remembered you'd already done that delivery thing, so I left it.'

'And?'

She laced her fingers together and cracked her knuckles. 'At about three o'clock his door opened.' She told him what had happened back in the tower block. When she was finished, Emily held the mug by her chin, the steam rising and warming her face.

Jack's stillness was beginning to frighten her. He listened to her relay the story without interruption, the

82

muscles in his jaw pulsing. He smoothed his beard with the palm of his hand and said, 'Why would he harass you like that? Did you provoke him in any way?'

'No. I just walked past him.'

Jack nodded but the pupils of his eyes seemed to darken. 'He was terrorising you for no reason then. He knew you weren't a policewoman. He didn't care that you might report him to the police either.'

'He did it because he knew I was up to something.'

'How?'

'I don't know. It was weird the way he turned on me. Maybe I was giving off some sort of vibe.'

'No.' Jack shook his head. 'He's made his bread and butter from being able to spot police. He's spent enough time around them, learned from his mistakes. He could probably suss out a plain-clothes policeman in a crowd as though they were holding up a fluorescent sign. He knows the way they move, and he knew you didn't move like a copper. But you were on his floor and you made him jumpy, which means he's hiding something in his flat.'

'What do you think it is?'

'Drugs, probably.' Jack shrugged. 'I can only imagine that he's graduated to selling hard drugs now. It's probably what bought him that Mercedes.'

'You don't think he knows that I'm Kate's sister, do you?'

Jack's eyes narrowed. 'Did you mention her?'

'No. Not at all. But I look like her, don't I? And he said I reminded him of someone.' She placed her cup on the counter. 'I watch a lot of documentaries about serial killers, and a common thread is that they keep souvenirs of their victims. All right, so maybe Morley isn't a serial killer, but I'll fucking bet he has a newspaper clipping or something like that. He has something to remind him that he got away with murder.' She clapped her hands. 'That's it. He recognised Kate in *me*.' She slapped the counter, angry at how pathetic she'd been in the stairwell, angry that she let him bully her. 'All this time and he thinks he got away with it.'

'But he hasn't. And we're going to get him.'

She nodded slowly. Yes, she wanted Morley dead and then maybe the nightmares would go away. *Or maybe killing Morley will make the nightmares worse.* 'Wait,' she said, exasperated. She was beginning to feel headachy and lethargic. Even exhaling seemed to take incredible effort. 'This isn't a game, Jack. This is—'

'Justice,' he finished for her.

'Yes, but... we have to be a hundred percent certain.'

'And aren't you?' Jack asked, his words coming out more aggressive than he had intended.

'I don't know. I think so...'

Without another word, Jack hurried out of the kitchen and returned with a laptop, slamming it on the counter. He opened the lid, the laptop stuttering and whirring as it woke up. The screen was paused on a YouTube video.

'What's this?' Emily asked, but she had already read the title and thought she had a good idea.

Jack pressed play. There was a delay as they waited for the laptop to wake from its stupor, and then they watched the whole three minutes and forty-two seconds in silence. Emily could feel him tensing next to her, and in her peripheral vision saw his shoulders rising and falling.

When it was over, Jack said, '*Money up front or I'll be at your door with the blade out… Pay what you owe or I'll carve your face out.*'

She hadn't even realised that those were the words. The whole song sounded messy to her, and the particulars were difficult to decipher.

Very quietly, almost in a whisper, Jack said, 'He's bragging, He's bragging about Kate.'

Chapter Thirteen

It took May a long time to get ready. Her brain felt like a wrung-out sponge, and her throat was sore and scratchy from vomiting. After Jack drove off and left her sobbing and screaming in the street – *god, what must I have looked like?* – she turned her rage on the house. She became a whirlwind of fury, wrecking the living room, smashing plates and glasses, ripping pictures from the walls. Then, when she had burned up the last of her energy, she collapsed in a pitiful heap, cutting the soles of her feet on the shards of shattered crockery.

She sat there crying miserably, watching blood dribble out of the wounds, wondering what she had done to deserve such terrible treatment. She replayed the evening in her mind, cringing as she recalled Jack's reaction upon seeing the ring. The grey beast of depression reared its head and for the first time in years, since Carl split on her for a younger model, she thought about the sleeping tablets. Why shouldn't she do it? Nobody gave a fuck about her. All anyone ever did was use her up, waste her time. First Carl takes the best years of her life and then ditches her, and now Jack, who she loved more than anyone, takes off on a whim. Her life was just one big fucking joke to them, wasn't it?

Trailing bloody footprints into the kitchen, May picked up the Jack Daniels and sucked it straight from the bottle. The whisky burned her throat and she coughed as it lit a fire in her stomach. She sobbed, gasped, drank.

Before long, she was unconscious on the sofa. She woke somewhere near dawn to the horrible sound of birdsong, and felt the violent urge to vomit rocketing up through her. She stood up and tried to run upstairs to the bathroom but everything was off-kilter like one of those crazy houses at the funfair. She and Jack had gone to a funfair a couple of summers ago, and hadn't they had a great time? More tears, the sponge wringing in her head.

She didn't make it to the bathroom. She was halfway up the stairs when she was sick, puking warm bile onto her bare, bloody feet. When the first wave of nausea had passed, she crawled up the stairs and into the bathroom like a dog – and why not? Isn't that how everyone treated her anyway? – and stayed by the toilet.

It was just before noon when she finally found the courage to leave the bathroom. The inside of her stomach was still a rough tide but she had been dry heaving for the last hour or so, and the hangover wasn't going to get much better than that for a long while. She brushed her teeth, dressed, washed her feet and found plasters for the cuts, then gingerly made her way out into the awful sunshine.

When she got behind the wheel, she wasn't sure she could face driving. At this rate, the way her head was feeling, she'd end up ploughing into another vehicle. She sat there a moment gathering her strength, beads of perspiration dotting her forehead and upper lip. She rolled the window down, welcoming the frigid breeze, and then started the engine.

The traffic was light and she made it to the warehouse in half an hour, driving with a thumping drumbeat in her skull. She parked by the gates of the industrial estate and walked to the door, breathing in through her nose and out through her mouth, and then pressed the buzzer.

'Oh, it's you… sorry, I mean hi,' Colin said, his face breaking out in a friendly smile as he opened the door. 'I thought it was a delivery.'

'Hello Colin,' she said, inviting herself into the warehouse. Her voice was crackly. 'Is the boss man here?'

'Jack?' Colin shook his head. 'No, he's called in some emergency time off.'

She suppressed a smile and said, 'Oh really? Did he say why?'

'No. He just said he had to take the rest of the week off, but he'd be popping in for a few bits and pieces.'

'How did he sound?'

'Funny.' Colin shrugged, scratching the back of his head. 'He didn't sound himself. Actually, I tried to call him back because one of his regular customers popped by and had a question about an order, but the call wouldn't go through. Is he OK?'

'Well,' she began shakily, 'we had a bit of a fight yesterday.' She paused for Colin's condolences. When he didn't offer them, she said, 'I think he was a bit upset. You know what he's like. He just bottles everything up.'

'Yeah,' Colin said, biting his thumbnail uncomfortably.

'I thought we might have to break up and he took it really badly,' she said, studying Colin's reaction. The boy was as thick as two planks. He was avoiding eye contact and chewing his thumb as though it was the first thing he'd eaten all week. 'You know we've been thinking about getting married, don't you?'

'Um, no, I don't think so.' May didn't say anything, just stared at him with her bloodshot eyes until he felt obliged to add, 'Actually he might have said something about it. You know, he doesn't talk very much.'

'Well, I expect he did. He was *very* excited.' She leaned close and said in a low voice, 'Between you and me, the wedding probably will go ahead but don't go spreading it around.' She waved her hand, gesturing to the warehouse.

'Oh no, I won't. So, do you want me to tell him you came by, or…?'

She shook her head and nails drove through her skull. She winced, swallowed and said, 'No, he'll only grumble. Honestly, he's so silly sometimes. Don't mention I came by. I'll catch him at home and we'll patch things up.' She smiled and rolled her eyes. 'All right, hun, well, don't work too hard.'

'Don't worry, I never do,' he said, laughing nervously.

She headed back to the car. In the sober light of day, she could see just how stupid this whole thing really was. After replaying it in her mind, she realised that he was probably just frightened. They had both failed at marriage before, so she could understand his fears; they weren't completely irrational. They had both survived the plane crash of divorce and here she was trying to book tickets for their next flight. He had every right to be apprehensive. God, she could be such a bubble brain sometimes.

On the way to his house, she thought about stopping at a florist to pick him up a bunch of roses to say sorry, but knew they'd probably just make him uncomfortable. Most presents she got him usually did. Instead, she just continued with a renewed sense of determination, and the closer she got to his house, the more excited she became. She turned the CD player on, skipped to track 6, and belted out 'Edge of Heaven' for motivation. Their love really was just like a George Michael song, wasn't it? It was emotional, it was timeless, and it was perfect. Well, now she was going to roll her sleeves up and get her man back. She was singing along with the stereo, almost screaming out *Yeah, yeah, yeah!* on the chorus with George, thumping the steering wheel triumphantly. A hangover couldn't stop her now, oh no, she was flying.

Just as she turned onto his road, she saw Jack leaving his house and walking toward his van. She caught her breath at the sight of him, felt a low current of electricity tingle in her stomach. That initial jolt of excitement quickly transformed into a nervous, jagged pain in her guts.

He wasn't dressed like he usually would be for work. He was wearing black jeans, a black jacket and black boots – the same black suede boots she had bought him for a birthday present just this last September. He looked like he was on his way to burgle a house.

'And just where the fuck do you think you're going?' she said aloud, her nails digging into the steering wheel. She thumbed the volume down and felt the moisture evaporate in her mouth. A brutal thirst gripped her throat so suddenly that it almost trigged a panic attack. She fought against her tongue to swallow, rolled the window down and took a large gulp of air.

Her initial confusion transformed into a complicated alloy of emotions. There was fear, oh there was always fear somewhere, and then there was scalding hot anger. She resisted the very tempting urge to scream and stomp down on the accelerator. She wanted to ram the car into his legs, pin him beneath the tyres and question him. Instead, she idled at the end of his road, her eyes unblinking, and waited for him to pull away from his parking spot.

It didn't take long to realise that he wasn't on his way to the warehouse, and he wasn't on the way to her house either. She started to sweat and gasp and the hysteria escalated with each street she passed. She could not remember a point in her life when she'd had to exercise this much self-restraint. Every impulse in her body wanted to accelerate straight into the back of his van, but she somehow kept her composure and her distance.

She was so blind with rage by the time he finally pulled over that she wasn't even sure what area she was in. She'd followed him onto a dual carriageway and off it a few miles later, then tailed him into a nice, posh neighbourhood. When he parked up, she reversed and slotted her car into a space where she had a clear vantage point of his van. Normally she had trouble with reverse parking on her left, but she performed the manoeuvre so slickly her tyres didn't even touch the kerb. It was then she noticed the licence plate. Why would Jack change it?

He was getting out of the van.

'Jack, please. Just turn back,' she whispered as the first notes of 'Careless Whisper' played.

He was walking up a path, approaching a house. Whose fucking house was this?

He was knocking on the door and…

'No,' she said. She could feel the hairs on her forearms prickle as the anger boiled her blood. She wanted to scream, to punch straight through her windscreen, to walk over to him and rip his head off. Her hand went to the door handle. She thought about getting out, but she couldn't. All she could do was watch.

The front door of the house opened and she saw a woman answer. May became boneless. She raised her hand to her mouth and bit down on it until she could feel the bones grinding against her teeth.

The woman followed Jack to his van. When the woman got into the passenger side, May tasted blood.

Chapter Fourteen

Very few things made Dillon as uncomfortable as these special errands that Craig sent him on. That was surprising when he stopped to think about it, because over the years the two of them had taken some insane and unnecessary risks together. They had driven all around the country with enough cocaine packed into a spare tyre to put them both away for a quarter of a century apiece. Even rolling up to the Dutchman's house hadn't set his stomach squirming the way it was now.

Dillon leaned against his car, fidgeting with his phone, which was no good because he had to keep his focus on the school gate. He pocketed the phone but kept his hand on it, tapping the screen with his thumbnail, clearing his throat every few seconds. At once, the gentle calm of the neighbourhood was abruptly broken by the clamour of excited chatter, yelps, squeals, peels of manic laughter. The pupils of Blair Academy were funnelling out of the buildings and scurrying across the schoolyard in disorganised clusters. Dillon was dimly aware that there were a few other adults by the gate, parents awaiting their children. Dillon, who was visibly too young to be a parent of any secondary school child, hoped that he looked like an uncle, or someone's older brother, but wasn't confident that he did.

A teacher made it to the school gate ahead of the children to stand sentry. Dillon looked at her, and saw that she was inspecting him the way she might a pupil who made some minor deviation from their school uniform. She had a stern, pinched face and an awful haircut, and there was something strangely intimidating about her. Perhaps it was because Dillon couldn't imagine her ever smiling, or having fun, or wearing something other than those dreary clothes, as though she were not even a real person but a piece of property that belonged to the school.

For his own part, he had dressed as conservatively as he could, swapping out the tracksuit for a pair of jeans and a plain jumper, but he knew the disguise did little to mask his intentions. And he knew that the teacher, whose glances he caught in his peripheral vision as he watched the chaos of children nearing the gate, had him figured out. He supposed it was difficult not to look like a creepy older guy trying to pick up impressionable girls, because that's exactly what he was doing. If the teacher came over and began an interrogation, he'd put her in her place with as much mock outrage as he could muster. He was there to collect his little cousin to give her a lift home; that was his story and he was sticking to it.

The more he overthought things, the hotter he seemed to become. The kids were making a racket and the volley of sounds made him jittery. That, combined with the different music from a dozen or more mobile phones, was giving him a headache.

The pupils bottlenecked through the gate and lingered around, packing the pavement. Dillon caught the smell of body odour baked inside the boys' blazers, pungent and unmistakeable. Losing the battle to that was the light and unobtrusive fragrance of female body spray and bubblegum. He watched the girls particularly, trying to avoid the smooth, bare skin of their legs or the confident heave of their budding breasts, and trained his attention on the faces. He could barely remember what this Tara girl looked like, and thought she might appear a damn sight different in her uniform. He removed his phone, his thumb nimbly sliding across the screen as he wrote her a message: *I'm by the gate. Where are u?*

The teacher craned her neck over the crowd to get a better lock on Dillon. She wasn't interested in the little game of push-and-pull two boys were engaged in over a football, nor did her concentration waver when a nearby group of girls screamed before breaking into gales of hysterical laughter. The children were invisible to her now. There was only Dillon, and the threat she instinctively knew he posed.

When he saw the teacher's eyes narrow, Dillon thought about getting in the car and driving off. Common sense had told him to park a few streets away to avoid suspicion, but as usual he ignored it for the sake of convenience. His patience wouldn't have stretched long enough to play a game of text message tennis in order for her to find him.

'Come on, where are you, for fuck's sake?' he said under his breath, his fingers curling tightly around the phone. His eyes flicked toward the teacher, who now had her chin angled slightly upward like an animal scenting danger in the air. Dillon knew she was a few seconds away from cutting through the throng to begin questioning him. He felt for the car door handle, ready to back down the instant she made her move. He didn't even want to be there, let alone endure the embarrassment of any veiled accusations that she would undoubtedly throw at him. After all, *he* wasn't the one that wanted to fuck some underage girl – so why did *he* have to feel like the pervert?

The teacher began to walk, her lips parting in preparation for speech. Dillon opened the car door casually. In his other hand, the phone vibrated. He looked at the screen and saw a message that read: *I'm by the gate.*

His jaw tightened. She had basically batted the exact same message back to him, which was of no use to anyone. For the life of him, Dillon would never understand what Craig liked about these young girls. What kind of conversation could you have with someone that wasn't even old enough to buy cigarettes? Of course, maybe that was the attraction: less talk, more action. Whatever it was, the whole thing made Dillon embarrassed and uncomfortable. He had a daughter who would one day be old enough to attend secondary school. Would some fucking monster be waiting by the gates, to…? He pushed the thought away angrily. Fuck this, he didn't need it.

He got into the car, started the engine. In the wing mirror, he saw the teacher hustle around a row of over-animated boys in an attempt to keep up with him. Some juvenile part of Dillon wanted to wind the window down and give her the finger, to embarrass her in front of all her students, but instead he drove. He looked down the road in preparation to make a U-turn, and saw Tara on her phone, waving an arm in the air. His phone began vibrating, but instead of answering it, he cruised on over to where she was standing.

The stupid girl hadn't even realised he was parked beside her. He honked the horn once. She jumped, almost dropping her phone, and then laughed. Dillon checked the rear-view mirror, saw the teacher talking to another member of staff and pointing at his car.

'Hurry up,' he told her.

Tara opened the door, yelled something to another girl on the other side of the road, and then got in.

'You all right?' she asked with casual ease, as though talking to someone she'd known forever, as opposed to a man she'd bumped into a week before. The top two buttons of her shirt were undone, her tie hanging loosely over a hint of bra. 'Where's Jerome?'

Jerome was the alias that Craig gave all these nitwits that he picked up. It was his pet name, he said, although Dillon had no idea what that meant. They had been at a petrol station, filling up, when Tara and a couple of other girls were leaving with sweets and cans of pop. She was wearing leggings and a hooded jacket, not particularly provocative, but she had the confidence to make a beeline over to the car where she saw Craig staring. She had asked, in the assured voice of someone much older, whether Craig wouldn't mind buying her some cigarettes. Craig had obliged, taken down her number and said he would give her a call.

And here she was. Craig never liked to pick the girls up from school himself, said he had too much of a profile. The truth was, he had been sniffed out once by a vigilant headmaster, and had never wanted to chance his luck again. From then on, it became one of Dillon's duties by default.

'Jerome's waiting for you at home.'

'OK,' Tara said, reaching out to turn the music up without asking. This wasn't her first time at the rodeo, he knew, and that made Dillon anxious.

Dillon wasn't sure why, but his stomach was twisting into knots. All his instincts screamed at him to pull over and kick her out, to let Craig know that now wasn't the time to be messing around with young girls, not with everything going on. He should have trusted his gut.

Chapter Fifteen

Craig Morley had already made two rather serious errors. Three if you included the age of the girl that was currently in his bedroom.

The first error was bringing the heroin back to his flat. He knew it was a stupid, irresponsible thing to do, but he shrugged it off, told himself he had no other choice, which he supposed was true. Was he to entrust it to that fucking dildo, Dillon? He'd probably fall asleep and leave it on the train and cause a bomb scare. No, he had to keep an eye on it, be close enough to reach out and touch it at any time.

The second error, while not as serious as the first, was still careless of him. Letting people know his location was a bad move. Because he couldn't be bothered to drive to her house, he had told Veronica to come to him for the initial smuggling interview. And now he had this sixteen-year-old girl naked in his bed. Well, she *said* she was sixteen, but his experience told him otherwise. She was fifteen at a push, but as long as she maintained the façade, he wasn't going to ask for a passport to prove it. He had spent the majority of his day drinking brandy and smoking weed, and now his rational mind was struggling to fight through the chemicals. He was just starting to realise that sleeping with this girl in his flat would be a terrible thing to do

– who knew what she'd seen? – but she was already out of her school uniform and he was stiffening; nothing he could do now. Young girls had big mouths. It was trouble no matter how he chopped it up.

He began to unbuckle his belt, thinking that as soon as he was finished with the girl he was going to move the duffel bag somewhere else, maybe stash it in a storage facility, when he heard the crash of broken glass outside. His hands froze instinctively. Then, when he heard the oop-oop-oop of a car alarm, *his* car alarm, he knew he'd made another mistake in parking the Merc on the estate. It was a robbery waiting to happen.

He hurried to the kitchen window, which gave him the clearest view of the car park. He couldn't tell from this height but it looked as though his windscreen was shattered and the lights of the Merc were flashing. Why would someone smash the windscreen if they were trying to steal his car? He raced back to the bedroom, snatched the cover off the girl and said, 'Up! Now!'

'What's wrong?' she asked, all sexiness escaping her. She covered herself with her arms, cowering. 'What's going—?'

He grabbed a handful of her hair and dragged her off the bed. She screamed and hit the floor with a thump.

'What have you done?' he yelled into the girl's face. 'You think you can trick me?'

'Wha—'

He slapped her hard across the face and then kicked her clothes toward her. 'Dressed. Now!'

He stormed through the flat, pulled back the carpet in the living room, wiggled the lino free and retrieved the revolver. If that stupid fucking girl wasn't in his room he could already be down there now, but here he was, waiting for her to get dressed because he couldn't chance leaving her alone in the flat. He went back to the kitchen window, still didn't see anyone in the car park. His indicator lights winked in time with the wailing alarm.

This girl, Tanya, Tina, whatever, had set him up. She'd lured him to bed to occupy him while one of her other boyfriends stole his car. Was that it? He stomped to the bedroom, the pistol cold and oily in his clenched fist. His brain fired off paranoid theories that told him to do one thing: raise the gun, cock the hammer, and blow this bitch's head off. Who cares if the neighbours hear it? He could shoot her, call Dillon, and have the body disposed of within the hour. It's not like anyone would know where she was. Her parents probably thought she was at a GCSE study group.

The girl had her skirt on and her blouse halfway buttoned up when he aimed the gun at her face. She froze like a deer in the headlights, her cheek blushed red where he had struck her. 'I didn't do anything, I swear,' she said, with a terrified sort of defiance. 'I just came here to have sex!'

'Who's down there?'

'Down *where*? I don't even know what's going on!'

Morley didn't have many skills. If he was honest with himself, he was an average criminal, more of a brutish thug than the mastermind he aspired to be. He'd had the clichéd sort of life one would expect from a common crook – abusive household, experimenting with drugs from a young age, crime, in and out of detention centres, prison. Yet woven into the depressing patchwork of his past was an ingrained ability to read people. It was a talent he'd developed while maturing among liars, both on the streets and behind concrete walls. Body language became a kind of telepathy to him, and he knew that most times, when a person was scared, their body would tell you what their mouth wouldn't.

She was telling the truth. That realisation didn't immediately dampen his desire to shoot her in the face, but it realigned his thoughts. *Who the fuck is down there messing with my car?*

'Hurry up,' he said, distracted, waving the gun toward the door.

'I'm going,' she said, darting away from him, slipping her feet into her shoes and snatching her backpack off the floor. He grabbed his keys and followed her out, slamming his door behind him, the sound bouncing down the hallway.

'Do you want me to wait?' the girl asked, her arms poised to protect herself in case he lashed out again. She had acted like such a big woman when he saw her at the petrol station that day. She had a sort of edgy maturity about her that he liked. But now she was nothing more than a dumb fucking girl and he wanted to kick her teeth down her throat.

'Go home,' he snarled, and bolted past her.

Chapter Sixteen

Darkness came to Frazier Avenue.

The rain tattooed against the roof. Next to the driver's side door was Morley's Mercedes. Jack's face was expressionless as he examined the car's exterior, his eyes tracing every curve and contour.

Emily felt nothing but fear. It wasn't the thought of getting caught that frightened her, it was Morley himself. What if they bungled this? What if Morley carried a knife or a gun? She thought about that a lot. There seemed to be so many ways for this to go wrong, and very few ways for it to go right. Try as she might, she couldn't shake the notion from her head. They weren't accustomed to this kind of thing, weren't built for it. They had their flaws but when everything was said and done, it came down to this: she and Jack were good, decent people. They weren't like Morley. He was a hyena. He lived for trouble, was accustomed to the effects of adrenaline on the body, knew how to manage the negative emotions that came with a life of crime.

He was a killer and they were not.

Not yet, anyway.

They sat in silence for an hour, peering through the windscreen at the tower block. Silhouettes scuttled in and out of the shadows surrounding the building, a seamless flow of nocturnal activity. So far she'd seen three young men, their faces shrouded by hoods, standing sentry. They talked among themselves for maybe ten minutes, and then dispersed, each going in a different direction.

'All right,' Jack said, his growly voice severing the silence. He reached down into the van door's compartment and picked up a claw hammer. 'I'm going to pop his windscreen, get his attention. When I do, scoot over to the driver's side and duck down.'

His composure only added to her unease. In the darkness of the van, his craggy face looked as though it belonged to a much older man. She could have been sitting next to a total stranger in that instant. He reached for the lock on the door when she said, 'You sure you know what you're doing?'

'I guess we're going to find out.'

'What if someone interferes?' She couldn't help it; she just blurted it out. She'd cooked up another disastrous scenario in her head, and it had gained weight in the silence that followed.

'If anyone interferes, they're probably going to regret it,' he said, so coolly that it instantly allayed her worries. He put on his balaclava, and then he got out of the van.

Chapter Seventeen

Morley tucked the revolver in his waistband and chugged down the stairwell. The exertion filled his lungs with what felt like crushed glass and made his heart bounce painfully against his ribcage. His breath was leaving him in short, sharp gasps as he burst through the door and into the rain.

The car alarm pulsed urgently. As he neared the Merc, he saw that there was a single, jagged hole in his windscreen, the epicentre to a network of cracks. When he got closer, his eyes detected something etched into the bonnet. He squinted and saw the word KILLER keyed diagonally in foot-high letters.

Killer?

He came to a halt suddenly and pressed the button on his car keys to quiet the alarm. He stood there a moment, his breath visible as he scanned the car park.

'Someone's in trouble,' he told the darkness. Slowly he dropped down to one knee and peered under the vehicles, looking for feet. He saw none, but still didn't want to go any closer to his car. Just because he couldn't see anyone lurking, it didn't mean they weren't there. He stood back up and began walking around the perimeter of the car park, his focus and his gun trained on the darkness between the street lights.

He was alone, he was almost sure of it, and yet the flesh at the nape of his neck burned. He flirted with the idea that some little bastard had popped his windscreen for a laugh, but the writing on his bonnet seemed too specific. A kid would smash the windscreen and run off laughing. They wouldn't have the bottle to stand there keying words into the body with the risk of getting spotted at any moment.

Whose van is that? He'd smoked too much and now his mind was turning against itself. Or maybe not. He couldn't remember ever seeing a van like that in this car park. But did he ever take notice of things like that? Yes, of course he did. He was a stickler for details.

Raising the gun, Morley aimed his voice toward the van and said, 'Why'd you fuck with my car?' He tried to sound conversational, as though his casual tone might coax the perpetrator out of his hiding place. The howling wind was the only response he received. He tried again. 'I said, why'd you fuck with my car? You cowardly piece of shit.' He did a three-sixty, and then added, 'I know you're still here.'

Nothing stirred. He approached the Mercedes from the rear. There were no crowbar marks on the boot's lock; nobody had tried to break into it. Morley tapped the barrel of his revolver on the van windows. The tink-tink-tink sound unsettled something within the van. He heard movement, and maybe a yelp of fright, he wasn't sure.

'Listen to me carefully,' he said. 'I'm going to count to three, and if you're not out of there by then, I'm going to put a bullet through this door. You hear me in there?' There was another tiny sound amplified in the silence, a rustle. He thumbed the hammer on the revolver back. 'Here we go, you ready? One. Two. Thr—'

Morley's head exploded. Or at least, that's what it felt like as he began to plummet. He hit the concrete like timber, the bulk of his frame pillowing the impact. His first thought was that he had been shot, and as the hot blood dribbled into his eyes, he became more and more certain of it. His body was completely numb, paralysed. A solitary thought floated through his mind like an autumn leaf caught in the breeze: *So... this is what dying feels like.*

Then his hands flew up to his face of their own accord, scooping blood away from his eyes. The numbness became feeling, and he was rolling onto his side, his equilibrium like a spinning top. He reached out for the van's bumper for support, no longer thinking anything, just trying to move, to get away. Where was the gun? Gone. He was on his own.

He felt hands grab him from behind and pull at him roughly. His ears felt like they were stuffed with cotton wool. An arm wrapped around his neck and squeezed, trying to cut off his air supply. Morley managed to twist away, breaking the hold, and then flailed his arms blindly.

Morley had been pounced upon more times than he cared to remember. Once, as a teenager, he was ambushed on the street by a group of boys, and woke up from a coma three days later, handcuffed to a hospital bed with a gunshot wound in his back. He knew that if there was a rule to surviving a gang beating, it was this: don't let them get you on the ground. Too many times in the past he'd seen, and participated in, someone getting floored and then having their head turned into a trampoline. All he had to do was get to his feet, and then he could deal with whatever fucking idiot was mad enough to trouble him.

Through blood and blurred vision, Morley saw the shape of a man – not a teenager like he had originally thought. He felt something hit him in the nose, heard the bone crunch as it broke. *Don't go down.* He slammed against the van door, his hands held out limply in front of him in a parody of defence. He saw the shuddering shape swing for him, and on instinct Morley turned his back. Something hard struck his shoulder and a flare of white-hot pain shot through him. *What the fuck is he hitting me with?* Morley balled his hands into fists and walked backwards. He thought that he might pass out – he couldn't even feel his legs beneath him. He wiped the blood out of his eyes, but more dripped off the curve of his brow.

'What do you want?' Morley said, but couldn't hear his own voice. *Oh, Craig, you are so fucked. This nutcase is going to kill you in this car park if you don't—*

The shape in front of him struck out again, and this time Morley ducked and charged the man. His shoulder crashed into the man's midsection and the momentum took them to the floor. Morley didn't know what was up and what was down, but he could feel the man beneath him and knew the rough location of his face even though he couldn't see it. Morley mounted the man, wrapped his hands around his throat and squeezed with all his energy. The man bucked and clawed at Morley's eyes, but that didn't bother him; he couldn't see anyway. Morley turned his head away and found the strength to squeeze harder, and this time he heard the man gargle. He felt the man's struggles weaken, the strength pouring out of his body the way blood was pouring out of Morley's skull. The hands fell away from Morley's face and he heard them hit the concrete with a wet slap.

'That's it!' Morley said triumphantly, even though the effort of speaking made the pain and disorientation swell within him. 'That's it, you fucking piece of shit. Go to bed.'

The man's neck was still in Morley's hands. He gave one last squeeze and then—

Black.

–

The hammer dropped from Emily's grasp. She could still feel the tingle running up her arm from the impact of the blow against Morley's skull.

That was it. She'd killed him.

She covered her mouth with her hands, all sense and rational thought scattering. She could smell the coppery tang of Morley's blood – blood she had helped spill – and now he was lying limp and lifeless. She was sure that at any moment the wind would carry her away back to her bed and she would wake up. Another nightmare, nothing new.

A cough. She looked down, saw Jack struggling to sit up. She dropped to his side and clutched his arm.

'Don't worry about me,' he said weakly. 'Grab his feet.'

She looked over at Morley. Blood was pooling out of his head, painting a crimson halo on the concrete.

Jack stood up, coughing violently. He stumbled and staggered, opened the back of the van, and then wobbled toward Morley's body.

'Is he dead?' Emily asked, trembling like a tuning fork.

'Get his legs,' Jack croaked.

'Jack, is he…?'

'Get his fucking legs!'

She snapped to attention and looped her arms around Morley's feet. Jack went to his head, secured him by the waist and hoisted him up. He grunted as he sidled around to the back of the van, his face shiny with sweat. He threw the top half of Morley's body into the van like a bag of sand, and then relieved Emily from the burden of his legs. Then Jack entered the van and dragged Morley deeper into the darkness.

'Close the door,' Jack said from the back of the van, and Emily obeyed.

In a daze, she rushed to the driver's side of the van and got in. She could hear Jack moving around back there, bumping and banging. He was hacking and coughing, cursing vehemently under his breath.

The keys jangled in Emily's grasp as she started the engine. The van roared to life, startling her. Her heart felt as though it was about to kick straight out of her chest. It seemed like every muscle in her body had melted to jelly and now she could not stop her knees and thighs from shaking. She was too anxious to drive. She sat there, looking at the glowing dials and the rain dotting the windscreen, and wondered what to do next. *Drive, you idiot*, her mind screamed, and some reflexive muscle memory took over. She put her foot down on the clutch and… something was wrong. With her right foot, she felt the pedals. There were only two. Where was the clutch? She turned on the interior light and looked down at the gearstick.

'Why aren't we moving?' Jack yelled gruffly.

'This van is an automatic!'

'So what?'

'I've never driven an automatic,' she said weakly, thinking that at any second she was just going to collapse from the stress. She looked at the letters around the gear-stick as though they were hieroglyphs.

'Just put it into Drive and go,' he said.

'OK, OK,' she said, exhaling shakily. She could do this, no problem. Driving an automatic was supposed to be easier than driving a manual, wasn't it? She'd failed her driving test four times before she finally scraped through. She moved the gear stick into Drive and pressed the accel-erator. The van shunted into the railing surrounding the car park. She jerked forward, almost smashing her face on the steering wheel. A loud bang echoed from the back of the van, followed by Jack yelling out. She put the van into reverse and stepped on the accelerator again. This time the van reeled back, scraping Morley's Mercedes with a long, ugly screech.

'What are you doing?' Jack growled.

'Shut up! Stop shouting at me!' The pedals were too sensitive, especially the brake. Her feet were confused by the lack of a clutch, and she dealt with this confusion by overcompensating on the other pedals. She looked in the wing mirror, did a looping three-point turn, and sped out of the car park.

Chapter Eighteen

May sat behind the wheel, stunned. Her jaw hung agape and she was breathing very heavily, the confusion and shock welding her to the car seat. A pressure built up in her throat and she realised she hadn't swallowed in a very long time.

What had she just witnessed?

She replayed the scene in her head. What was it all about? Was it some kinky sex thing? Who was that woman? She was the one that got Jack mixed up in all this trouble. Yes, that made sense, didn't it? Jack was having an affair with that tart, but she had a husband. They wanted the husband out the way, so they planned to kill him! That had to be it.

She leaned against the steering wheel, hugging it for support. What on earth was happening? She looked over at the spot where the van had been and saw blood, bright red like paint, on the ground. There was something else too. May got out of the car and walked toward the blood, intrigued and repelled by it in equal measures.

Then she saw the hammer. And the gun.

It was like a real crime scene. The hammer wasn't of much interest to her, although it had been used to crack a man's skull open, and that was sort of exhilarating. But it was the gun that mesmerised her. It was small and dull-looking, cumbersome almost; nothing quite so exciting as you saw on TV. Yet presumably it was a real firearm. She bent down, and with the sleeve of her coat over her hand, picked the gun up and put it in her bag without really thinking about what she was doing. She could feel its weight, its power, and her body flushed with heat.

She turned her attention to the hammer. The head gleamed with blood and had a tangle of hair caught up in the claw. Again, careful not to let her fingers touch the weapon, she picked it up and placed it in her bag. Did removing them from the scene of the crime make her an accessory to murder? She didn't know if that was just something from the TV, but what she did know was that it gave her the tools to win Jack back. A crime of passion – so what? They could lock her up and throw away the key.

A sound distracted her. Snuffling, hitched breath, moaning. May spun around and saw a girl wandering toward her somnolently, holding her blouse together with her hand. One side of her pretty face was swollen and red. Immediately, May knew what had happened. Some cowardly piece of shit had put their paws on her. When May was fifteen her first boyfriend, and subsequently the first boy she ever slept with, had slapped her once for embarrassing him in front of his friends. At the time, she told herself she had deserved it. All he had done was squeeze her boobs in front of them, and she was embarrassed so she told him to fuck off. That only made his friends laugh, saying that she wore the trousers, he was under the thumb, all that schoolboy shit. But that single moment had set a precedent, one that would follow her through to adulthood.

'Are you all right?' May said, the timbre of her voice wavering madly.

'I'm… my boyfriend…'

'It's OK. What's your name?'

'T-Tara.'

'All right Tara, what's wrong?' May walked toward the girl. 'Has someone hurt you?'

'No, nobody h-hurt m-me,' she said. 'They… they…' The sobs racked her and she shook her head, crying like a child in denial. 'My boyfriend, he… they took him!'

Boyfriend? May looked at this young girl. How old was she? Fourteen? Fifteen? She could see the girl's pimples beneath her powdery foundation, the clots of mascara in the corners of her eyes. This was a little girl trying to look older, probably had tissues stuffed down her bra to pad it out.

'We need to call the police,' Tara said. 'Can I use your phone? I… I left mine in his flat.'

'Wait, hold on a second,' May said, suddenly conscious of the fact she was carrying two of the weapons involved in the crime this girl wanted to report. 'Why don't we get out of this cold and sit in my car, how about that?'

'The p… police…'

'We'll call them,' May said, 'but we don't have to catch pneumonia while we do it.' She smiled at the girl, but the girl was not ready to smile back. 'Come on.'

May walked to the back of her car and put her bag in the boot. Then she opened the door for the girl and they both got inside.

'Did you see what happened?' Tara asked.

114

'No, I was just…' She tried to think of an alibi, and when none came she said, 'I didn't see anything. What happened?'

'They beat up Jerome and took him! They beat him and… they took him. I went back inside to try and get help and…' Her face crumpled, her bottom lip sticking out childishly. 'Nobody would help me!'

May was relieved: she hadn't been seen picking up the hammer and the gun.

'Don't worry,' May said, giving her a reassuring pat on the leg. 'You just calm down. We'll figure this out.'

Chapter Nineteen

Relief washed over Emily when she finally found the warehouse. Not because they had completed the first part of their objective, but rather because they had made the journey without getting into a fatal collision. Emily could not get the hang of driving the automatic and kept slamming them to a screeching halt every time she so much as touched the brake pedal. There were hardly any cars on the road that time of night, which was lucky considering she'd had to go on the motorway.

She turned the ignition off and got out, feeling weightless. *Boneless*. The sky was brightening; lavender clouds scudded across a sliver of sunlight. It would have been a beautiful morning were it not for the carnage waiting in the back of the van. She looked around; nobody was there at this early hour, so she opened the back door of the van. Jack got out, handed her a set of keys and said, 'Unlock the grille with this one, then open the door with that one. When you go inside the alarm will beep. The code is two–seven–zero–eight. Got it?'

'Yeah, I got it.'

'What's the code?'

'Two–seven… um…'

He bent his head down so that he was face-to-face with her. 'Emily,' he began in a soft voice. 'We've done it. You can calm down. Just relax. The code is two-seven-zero-eight.' He smiled. It didn't touch his eyes.

'Got it,' she said. She unlocked the grille and the door, went inside, and keyed the code into the alarm system with trembling fingers. The beeping stopped. Jack got into the driving seat, turned the van around, and reversed so that the back doors were facing the entrance of the warehouse.

He stepped inside the warehouse and flicked the light switch on. Cold white light washed over a kingdom of boxes and crates. The musty smell of damp cardboard hung in the chilly air. He walked over to a large, square pallet trolley that they used to unload and move boxes, and set it by the door.

'Come on. I need your help for this part,' he said, and climbed into the back of the van. Emily followed him in. Morley's hands were tied in front of him with duct tape and he had a bandage turbaned around his head. Blood was seeping through the bandage, and the sight of it reminded her of the dream with Kate and the scarf. She closed her eyes against the sight of it and pushed the thought away.

They awkwardly push-pulled Morley out of the van and placed him on the trolley. His face was streaked with dried blood and his complexion was ashen beneath the warehouse lights.

'What're we going to do with him?' Emily asked.

'Oiling room is down there,' Jack said, pointing with his chin. 'That's where we're taking him.'

'Aren't we going to' – she swallowed, sucked in air – 'bury him?'

'He isn't dead,' Jack said grimly. 'He started to stir again when I was tying his hands up, so I had to give him another dig. He's as strong as an ox, that's why we need to get him in his room before he starts to regain consciousness.'

Emily moaned. She was relieved, but couldn't understand why. This is what she wanted, wasn't it? She wanted justice for Kate. No, not justice, revenge. So why did she still feel so queasy about the whole thing, so... guilty?

Jack grabbed the handle on the trolley and began to wheel Morley down one of the aisles. She followed him through the labyrinth of shelving units and up to the entrance of the oiling room. It was about the size of her bedroom at home, yet the confines had been made smaller by the boxes lining the walls. At the far end of the room was a large thick pipe that ran into the floor. Jack dragged Morley off the trolley and pulled him into the room, stopping halfway to regain his breath.

'He weighs a tonne,' Jack said, palming sweat from his face before dragging Morley the last three or four feet to the pipe. He sat Morley against the pipe, spat on the floor, and then walked out of the room.

'Keep an eye on him for a sec. Shout if he starts to wake up.'

'Where are you going?' she asked, the urgency causing her voice to echo off the corrugated roof.

'To get the rope from the van,' he said over his shoulder.

She stayed by the door, ready to slam it closed if Morley suddenly woke up. The man was somehow even more intimidating when he was unconscious than he had been when he was awake. For all she knew, Morley could be playing possum, waiting to snap alive and make his exit when she least expected. She looked at the pipe and wondered whether it would hold him. She wasn't sure. The pipe was sturdy enough, but Morley was a bear of a man, and if he was determined then maybe he might just be able to break free. She remembered coming home from a club on the night bus when she was eighteen or nineteen and seeing half a dozen police officers trying to subdue a man in the road. The man wasn't as big as Morley but he still managed to give the police hell, thrashing like a shark out of water, bucking the police off him as though they were children. They must've sprayed a gallon of CS gas in his face and still he had a defiant and ungodly strength that made them call for backup.

Jack returned with the rope. 'Did you put the hammer in the van?'

'The hammer?'

'When you hit him. Did you put it in the van? I couldn't find it.'

She had no idea what she'd done with the hammer.

'I don't know,' she said. 'Was I supposed to?' His eyes bore through her. She cringed away from his gaze. 'Everything happened so fast. I didn't know what to do.'

His face softened. He wiped the sweat from his forehead with the crook of his arm and nodded. 'Yeah, I know. It wasn't exactly a smooth transition, I admit. Don't worry about the hammer.'

He walked over to Morley, looped a length of the rope around his neck, and then tied the remaining rope around his feet. To Emily, the rope didn't look thick enough, and she suddenly had a vision of Morley waking up and snapping free of the bonds. Her thoughts shifted back to the hammer.

'*Should* I be worried about the hammer?' she asked.

'Nothing we can do about it now, is there?' he said, standing. He appraised his work, tested a couple of the knots to make sure they were tight. He picked up Morley's hands, which were cocooned in duct tape, and seemed satisfied. 'We can't go back for it.'

She bit her lip. 'You think they could link it back to us?'

He looked at her hands. 'You're wearing gloves.'

'Yes, but you're not.'

'I've never been arrested. My prints aren't on any databases. Anyway, you seem to forget he had a gun. I'm sure that would be of a lot more interest than the hammer.' He gave Morley one last glance and then began to walk out of the oiling room, closing and locking the door behind him. 'Let's go and get a cup of tea.'

'Wait. Do you think we should put something over his eyes?'

'What for?'

'So that the next time you open the door he doesn't see you.'

'Doesn't matter if he sees me or not. He's not going to live long enough to give anyone a description.'

Emily's stomach rolled over. *So this* is *real then*, she thought, and became aware of a heaviness in her bladder that hadn't been there a few minutes ago.

He led her up the stairs into a large open space, at the end of which was a kitchenette area with a sink, a kettle and a fridge. He began to make the tea. A couple of packets of biscuits were on the counter, along with bottles of water and a loaf of bread.

'Sorry, Em, how do you take your tea again?'

'I don't want any,' she said, plopping down on a moulded plastic chair. What she wanted to do was use the toilet, but even more than that she wanted to get away from this place.

'You sure? It's freezing in here.'

'Jack,' Emily said, holding her head in her hands, trying to still the cyclonic shift of her thoughts. The last few hours had been so surreal that she no longer felt like herself. It was as if some inner part of her had separated and she was a remote viewer of her own life. 'What happens now?'

Jack leaned on the counter and folded his arms. 'Now I'm going to have a cup of tea, and then I'll go down to see our mutual friend and give his head a proper dressing in a couple of hours. I don't think I fractured his skull when I hit him. What about you?'

'How on earth would I know? I'm not a doctor.'

'Are you first-aid trained?'

'No.'

'Well, I am,' he said. 'Have to take health and safety courses every few years, working with machinery and that. But I'm not a doctor either, so at best I can clean his wounds, maybe superglue his cuts back up, do enough to keep him alive for as long as we need him. But if he has a fractured skull or something worse, then I guess that's it.'

She rested her elbows on her knees and bowed her head. She had never been this exhausted in her entire life, not even when she was maid of honour at Kate's wedding and they were up from five getting ready, rushing around, dressing up the venue. Nor had she been this drained on the day that they buried Kate, even after she'd been weeping pretty much non-stop in the week preceding the funeral. Now, she wanted nothing more than to climb into a bed by herself, pull the cover up over her head, and fall asleep forever.

'Why don't you go home,' he said. 'I can do the first shift with him.'

'First shift?'

'Yeah. We can't afford to leave him here alone, not while he's still alive. Someone always has to be with him, just in case. And at the same time, neither one of us should just disappear from our normal lives in case it arouses suspicion.' He sipped his tea loudly. 'Well, nobody's going to miss me for a week or so, but you've got Roger.'

'What about May?'

He rubbed his eye with his index finger and said, 'She's angry with me so I've probably got a few days before she cools down. But I'll probably have to pop by the other warehouse, just to make sure the place hasn't collapsed, and to keep everything away from here.'

When he tilted his head back to scratch his beard, she saw the bluish-red bruises from where Morley had throttled him. She yawned and blinked, black orbs floating in her vision.

'Fine, I'll head home then, if you think it's a good idea.'

'Of course it is,' he said. 'Get some sleep. Can you come back here tonight?'

Tonight? she thought sluggishly, and then remembered they had started a whole new day.

'Yeah,' she nodded. 'What're you going to do?'

'I'll get some rest. I brought a sleeping bag and some cushions so I'll be perfectly comfortable.'

She nodded. She was so tired she could have fallen asleep on a washing line. 'What if he wakes up?'

'I'll talk to him,' he said, smiling.

She got up to leave, reeling dizzily. He walked her to the door. Just before she left, she said, 'I don't want to torture him.'

A shadow passed over Jack's face. 'What do you mean?'

'I mean, I want to know why he killed Kate. And I think he'll tell us, in time, or maybe right away, who knows. But I don't want to torture him.'

'What difference does it make?' Jack asked defensively. 'He deserves a slow death.'

'I don't want to be involved in anything *sadistic*. I said I would help you… kill him. I didn't say I was going to torture him like an animal.'

'That's what he is. An animal.'

'Whatever he is, I don't want to do it like that. OK?'

'Sure,' Jack said without emotion.

She opened the door and stepped out into the frigid morning air, her hair whipping into her face. 'What time shall I come back?'

'Let's say nine.'

She nodded and left without another word.

Jack closed the door and then walked to the oiling room. He did not feel excitement or any sense of contentment, not yet anyway. He felt nothing at all; not so much as a flicker of satisfaction in the void. Maybe when he looked into those green eyes for the last time, he would feel peace.

He opened the door. Jack could hear the man's ragged breathing now, more like snoring. He walked over to the box by the fire exit, and then retrieved his sleeping bag cushions. He rolled the sleeping bag out on the floor, untied his boots and kicked them off, and then got inside, securing a cushion beneath his back.

He turned on his side and watched Morley. Less than ten minutes later, he was asleep.

He did not dream.

Chapter Twenty

Dillon had been fast asleep when Leila rushed into the room, yelling his name. Usually he was a very light sleeper, his ears attuned to the slightest disturbance. On some primal level he supposed it was because he always wanted to be alert and in control of his environment, even when he was unconscious. This subliminal instinct had kept him in good stead all through his adolescence in St Joseph's and beyond: he had caught two potential burglars trying to break into his hostel a few years back, and on another occasion had managed to hotfoot his way to safety when the police came to raid the flat he was renting.

He snapped awake so violently at the sound of Leila's voice that his fists were already in a fighting stance, ready to swing. There was no grogginess. He was immediately and acutely aware of everything in the room, but she was talking to him as though they were already involved in some deep-rooted conversation. He only heard 'Craig' and 'Frazier Avenue' and stood up, his erection jaunting against the fabric of his boxers. When she finished with '…on the TV,' and paused for breath, Dillon said, 'Stop,' and raised his hands. 'What the fuck are you going on about?'

Leila rolled her eyes in that impatient bitchy way that always made him want to launch her across the room. She inhaled and said, 'They've just raided Craig's flat on Frazier Avenue. It's all over the TV.'

He looked at her for a second, trying to gauge whether it was a wind-up or not, and said, 'You're not having me on, are you?'

'No,' she said, mouthing the word exaggeratedly. 'I've just paused it on the TV. Come, I'll show you.'

He followed her into the front room. Cora was sitting in the high chair with clumps of porridge hardening around her mouth, slapping her tray with her chubby hands. Dillon saw the TV paused on the reporter's face while he was in mid-sentence, the wind sweeping his hair.

'Rewind it,' he said to Leila, who went straight for the remote and did as she was bid.

When she pressed play, the TV showed the Frazier Avenue car park cordoned off with blue-and-white police tape.

'Thanks, Ian,' the reporter began, looking over his shoulder at the armada of police vehicles. 'Well, the scene you see behind me is the aftermath of a suspected kidnapping that has led to a truly bizarre turn of events. Late last night, an eyewitness reported the assault and kidnapping of her boyfriend, Craig Morley. However, her description of the incident prompted a raid on Mr Morley's residence by the Metropolitan Police. After a thorough interview with the witness, who has to remain anonymous for legal reasons, it is believed that Mr Morley had live firearms in his flat. Now the police have confirmed that they did not find any guns or ammunition, but they *did* locate over eight kilograms of pure heroin...'

Dillon's knees gave out and he fell back onto the sofa. His body ran cold. He covered his eyes with his hands and groaned. Leila was talking over the TV, asking him what was wrong. Cora was slapping her tray and singing merrily, and the reporter was still talking about an 'extensive search' to find Craig.

Dillon's intestines tied themselves in a knot. He shot up from the sofa and went back to his bedroom to get dressed.

They don't know who I am, and even if they did, what would they want from me? He wondered this as he pulled on his jeans. *Someone has to pay for that heroin,* his mind answered. *And if Craig isn't available, then it's going to fall back on you, sonny boy.*

'Where are you going?' Leila was in the doorway bouncing Cora on her hip.

'I need to go out.'

'Where?'

'Shut up, will you, and just listen.' He spun around, tugging his T-shirt on. 'I don't have time to explain everything to you. It's probably better if you don't know anything anyway.' He whirled around the room searching for socks, and settled on a dirty pair from the laundry basket. 'I don't know what's happening right now, but I need to find out where Craig is.'

'Why?' Leila asked over the sound of Cora's babbling. 'You're not wrapped up in any of this, are you?'

'Of course not,' he snapped, slipping his feet into his trainers and barging past her.

'So what is this? Will you just slow down and talk to me?'

'You know what Craig's like. He's always getting himself into some shit. So I need to find him.'

'What's that got to do with you?'

'Stop asking me so many fucking questions, will you?'

'I'm the mother of your child!' she said authoritatively. 'Your business is here in this flat with us, not out there getting mixed up in this fucking nonsense.'

'Listen to me carefully,' he said, his hands clenching into fists. 'I'm going to leave now, and I don't know when I'll be back.' As he said this, Leila made a dismissive grunting sound and walked off, leaving him talking to thin air. Dillon punched the hallway wall and then went into the living room after her. Her eyes were wide and attentive, betraying her defiant demeanour. 'When I walk out that door, you bolt it behind me and you don't answer it for anyone, do you understand me? I don't care if it's your mum, your sister, or if Jesus Christ himself comes down from heaven. You do not answer that fucking door, do you understand?'

'You're frightening me,' she whispered.

'Good. Then hopefully you'll do as I say. Don't leave this flat under any circumstances. You're under house arrest until I come back, got it?'

'Yeah.' She shrugged. 'Fine.' Then, as he was walking off, she added, 'You are coming back, aren't you?'

I hope so, he thought, and left.

He had to speak with Tara, find out what happened. Had she set him up somehow? Dillon didn't think so, but he didn't rule it out either. For a man who, by the very nature of his work, had to remain discreet about all aspects of his social life, Craig certainly did his best to make his business public. He had these schoolgirls fighting over him in the street, with their friends recording it and putting the footage online. Craig's discretion only went as far as offering them an alias upon meeting them, but it didn't matter if he called himself Daffy Duck or Batman, they all knew who he really was. They knew because they'd heard all the urban myths about him, swapping rumours and putting their own spin on the stories until he was crazier and scarier with each retelling.

At least he didn't cut the girl, Dillon thought without much relief. Craig and his morbid obsession with knives – Dillon could never understand it. He liked to *cut*. He didn't have a clue as to what had happened back at Craig's flat, but if there was any solace to be had in the situation it was that Craig didn't go berserk and start cutting her. If he had, surely they would have reported that?

Dillon jogged to the lift and thumbed the call button. The up arrow glowed, showing that the lift was ascending from two floors below.

Perhaps the news would show CCTV footage of the incident. He got his phone out of his pocket and typed 'Craig Morley' into the search engine. The reception was awful in the foyer and his results were stuck on the load screen. He kept his eyes on the phone as he walked out into the sunshine, thumbing the blue 'GO' icon to refresh the search. A couple of seconds later the page loaded showing news items. He was almost at his car door when he felt a hand on his shoulder. The phone dropped from his grasp and bounced on the concrete.

'Mr Dekkers would like to speak with you, please.' It was the golem that guarded the door at Dekkers' town house. His massive frame eclipsed the sun, bathing Dillon in shade.

One second Dillon was thinking about his phone, the screen's contents distorted by a snarl of cracks, and in the next his mind was a total blank. The fear ambushed him and robbed his ability to speak. He opened his mouth and uttered a nonsensical sentence that his daughter Cora would have probably articulated better.

'This way,' the man said, guiding Dillon to a Bentley that was as out of place among the surrounding cars as a flying saucer would have been.

Dillon's muscles became rigid. He saw Dekkers in the back seat reading a newspaper, and a word flashed in his mind like a beacon: RUN. He knew he if he shrugged the golem away and made a dash for it they wouldn't catch him on foot. He'd run back through the estate and lose them in the warren of hallways. That thought was glorious for the second that it lasted, before his rational mind returned and reminded him of Leila and Cora, and what this bastard might do to them in his absence.

The golem opened the back door and Dillon got in.

'It seems your friend found himself in some bother,' Dekkers said, without looking up from the newspaper. 'He didn't make the morning edition but I suspect he will have a couple of column inches this evening.'

Dillon opened his mouth to feign ignorance, but he decided against it. Dekkers was already many steps ahead of him. The best he could do now was co-operate and try to negotiate some breathing room.

'I just saw it on the news. I'm still trying to figure out what's going on.'

'Hmm…' Dekkers licked his thumb, turned the page, his white hair flowing over his shoulders like spun silk.

Dillon saw the golem's eyes watching him in the rear-view mirror. 'Right now, I don't… I don't have any leads, but then again, I haven't made any calls.'

Dekkers laughed softly. 'Leads. You sound like a detective.'

Dillon gulped audibly. 'There's a girl he was fucking around with, she'll know something. He'll turn up. And then...' He ran out of steam. He hadn't thought further than locating Craig and he didn't want to mention the heroin.

'Then we have a tea party?' Dekkers suggested.

Dillon tittered. To his ears it sounded like a very feminine laugh. He cleared his throat and said, 'I'll find him for you because I know you were involved in some business.'

'Were we? What business was that?' Dekkers asked, his white eyebrows arching.

Oh god, how had he wriggled his way into this position? He squirmed in his seat. 'He was going to export something for you.'

'Are you referring to the eight kilos of heroin now in police custody?'

Dillon nodded and bit down on the side of his tongue until he tasted blood.

'I think I might have a better plan. Would you mind if I told you?' Dekkers asked, perfectly polite. 'I'm going to put some men on the street, and we are going to comb the city. London is not so big, so we will soon see who knows what. I'll start with the big lady that *you* brought to his home, the one that was going to smuggle some of the eight kilos up her vagina.' He smiled at this, and in the rear-view mirror, Dillon saw the golem's eyes glitter. 'Then, when we find Craig, we will expect the nine hundred thousand he owes us for the heroin. But of course, we now have to factor in my other expenses.' He held out his hand and began counting off his fingers.

'My men don't work for free and they must be compensated. Then you have petrol and any other miscellaneous costs. So for now, let's estimate the bill in total at an even million. Does that sound fair?'

Dillon's stomach growled loudly. He felt a burp building up in his chest that eventually lodged in his windpipe.

'So Craig will owe me one million. And, because I am not completely unsympathetic to the situation he has found himself in, I will give him seven days to pay it. Are you with me so far?' When Dillon remained silent, Dekkers said, 'Excuse me? Are you with me so far?'

'Yes.' Dillon nodded and swallowed the acidic burp down, his throat burning with the taste.

'Good. I knew you were a clever man. However, we haven't factored in the other scenario. What happens if we can't find Craig or, god forbid, he's dead? Well, that's nothing to do with us of course. These things happen. But I am still one million out of pocket.' He tapped Dillon's knee with his index finger. 'Which is where you come in.'

'Mr Dekkers, I swear, let me talk to this girl, she'll know something and then—'

'Please, allow me to finish. Craig's debt will transfer to you. And likewise, you'll have a week to find the money. After that, things get a little bit more serious, I'm afraid. Not only will you incur interest, but you will also find your health severely compromised. But don't worry.' He rested a gentle hand on Dillon's arm. To Dillon it was like an anchor dragging him to the bed of the ocean. 'You will not suffer until your loved ones have suffered in front of you. How old is your daughter, by the way?'

Dillon's lips glued together. Dekkers' hand slapped him in the face, his rings cracking against Dillon's cheekbones.

'Now you speak. How old is your lovely daughter?'

'Eight... eighteen months,' Dillon said, rubbing his face, tears pricking his eyes.

'Such a wonderful time, isn't it? When they start developing their own little personality, and you can see glimpses of the person they're going to become. Or maybe not.' He sighed. 'To cut my sermon short, it's in your best interests to ensure we find Craig. You know Craig, you know his patterns, his associates. So if you get a lead, give us a call.' He handed Dillon an old mobile phone and added, 'There is only one number in the address book. Phone it, and you will reach Mikkel.' He pointed to the golem. 'He will call you back straight away. Let's stay in touch, yes?'

'Y-yes,' Dillon stammered.

'Good man. You can go now.'

Dillon opened the car door and rushed out. He walked toward his car, numb. As he touched the car door handle, Dekker called from his window, 'It would be unwise of you to think about leaving. Please do bear that in mind.'

Then the tinted window went up and the Bentley drove away.

Chapter Twenty-One

It was a short, lonely walk back to the station from the warehouse. Emily hadn't realised it until she was sitting down on the train, but her left hand was freckled with Morley's blood. She had sweated buckets throughout the course of the night's activities and now felt cruddy all over, but knowing that she had Morley's blood on her skin made her itchy and nauseous. Now she wanted a shower more than she wanted to sleep; she had to scrub herself clean, wipe away the residue of her nocturnal sins and wash them down the plughole.

And then do it all over again tonight, she thought bleakly. She remembered the sound the hammer had made on Morley's head. It was dull, not the dramatic *thwack* you got in movie violence. She felt her gorge rise, sure that she was going to be sick, and then closed her eyes and concentrated, waiting for it to pass. She didn't have the stomach for this. How was she expected to help murder Morley? Did she even still want to do it? After all, what was stopping her from just backing out now? She'd done her part, and if Jack tried to say any different, then she would remind him that it was her that had knocked Morley unconscious. She had saved Jack's life. Her finger-prints weren't on the hammer and nobody had seen them. She could just call it quits.

But it didn't matter if she stopped now or if she shovelled the last bit of dirt on Morley's grave. She had helped seal his fate. She had helped kill Craig Morley.

It was a long journey back on the train and paranoia began to scuttle around in her mind. How long had they spent scuffling with Morley before they finally got him in the back of the van? It had felt like an eternity but it couldn't have been longer than a couple of minutes. How much noise had they made? Morley had been shouting – screaming at one point – and then there was the sound of Jack choking. Had they woken anyone up? Could someone have seen them clearly in the car park? Surely not. Anyway, as rough as that area was, the residents were probably used to all manner of madness. It probably wasn't enough to arouse their interest, she told herself, and then repeated it in her head, trying to make the idea gain weight so she could believe it.

Then it hit her like a bucket of water – so sudden and forceful that she sat upright in the seat and gasped, making the woman sitting next to her jump in fright. Jack had been wearing a balaclava and she had not. Christ almighty. What if someone recognised her from when she was lurking around outside Morley's flat a few days before? That's all they needed to tell the police, wasn't it? *A weird woman had been roaming the hallway and then we saw her again hitting Morley with a hammer.* She was on the cusp of hyperventilating.

She looked out the window, saw that they were slowing to a halt and realised it was her stop. She squeezed through the herd of commuters, making it off the train just before the doors shut.

She slid the key quietly into the lock and opened the front door slowly in an attempt at making a quiet entrance. She felt like a teenager sneaking back home from a house party hours past her curfew. She was halfway up the stairs when Roger caught her. He pushed his glasses up the bridge of his nose and threw his arms out in a gesture of exaggerated exasperation.

'Well?'

'Roger, don't start, OK?'

'Don't start? You've been out all night. I've been worried sick.' Behind him in the living room, she could see his bacon sandwich and tea on the table. The worry hadn't robbed him of his appetite apparently. 'I've sent you about twenty messages, tried calling you. What is this?'

Her nails dug into the banister. 'I was in the hospital.'

'What?' His eyes bulged behind their lenses. 'What do you mean?'

She shook her head. 'Not for me. You remember Jack? He came to the door the other day?'

'Your sister's husband?' He nodded. 'What about him?'

'His mum's not well,' she lied. 'She's on borrowed time and they reckon she could go at any minute. Jack's all broken up about it, like you would imagine.'

'Well, that's sad and all, but you'll excuse me for being blunt here, what does that have to do with you staying out all night and not telling me where you were?'

'She's at death's door, Roger. I don't know when you were last in hospital, but they don't want you to have your mobile phone on in the ward. The signals mess with the X-ray machinery.' She could see that he knew that was a load of nonsense and he still wasn't budging. 'We thought she was going to go last night, so I waited with him.'

'Right, OK.' Again his hands flew up theatrically. 'Perhaps I'm not enunciating my words properly or something. I'm a bit scatty this morning because I didn't get much sleep last night. But what does his mum dying have to do with you? I thought you were in trouble, like maybe you'd been raped and murdered or something.'

Raped and murdered, she thought. *And you seem so relieved that I'm home.*

'Let me stop you there, Roger, before you say something even more stupid. Jack is family. He was married to my sister. I was very good friends with his mother, all right? I know it may seem difficult for you to believe, but I did have a life before you, you know.'

She stomped up the stairs. Everyone in the house should already be at work, but if by any freak occurrence someone was using the bathroom, she planned to kick the door to pieces and drag them out. Thankfully, the bathroom was unoccupied. She went in and began stripping out of her clothes. In the mirror, she saw that her wrist was striped with Morley's blood. She was in her underwear when Roger banged on the door.

'Go away,' she said, clutching the sink for support. Her eyes were sunken and had a wild, witch-like quality to them.

'No, I'm not going away. Look, perhaps it was insensitive of me to question you like that, but you can see where I'm coming from, can't you?'

She couldn't have this conversation with him now. She needed to get clean and go to bed. She turned on the shower, removed her underwear, and stepped in.

'Emily?' He knocked on the door again. 'Em, don't bloody blank me and treat me like an idiot when I'm trying to talk to you. All I'm asking for is a little common courtesy here.'

Common courtesy. She would've laughed if she'd had the strength to. Roger was perhaps the most inconsiderate man she'd ever met. He was a freelance digital illustrator who worked from home, picking and choosing his own hours. He stayed up all night watching Netflix and keeping her awake with the glow of the screen and the volume cranked up, which she could hear even when he put earphones in. He only ever did his own washing up and cooking, and never thought to prepare her something to eat when she came home after a traumatic commute during rush hour. And here he was talking about common courtesy?

The water was scalding hot, almost unbearable, but that's how she wanted it. The crash of the shower blocked out Roger's voice as he began to say something about Jack not technically being her family any more, and that Roger himself was actually more family than Jack was now. She grabbed the bar of soap and scrubbed herself pink.

When she was clean and satisfied that she had no traces of Morley on her skin, she stepped out of the shower and wrapped a towel around her body. A bank of steam followed her out of the bathroom. Roger wasn't there. She could hear his fingers clicking and clacking aggressively on the laptop keys downstairs. He probably wasn't even writing an email to anyone, just hammering the keys to make noise. Creep.

She entered the bedroom. The quilt was curled in a heap on the bed and the pillows were askew. He couldn't even make the fucking bed in the mornings. She removed her towel, grabbed her pyjamas off the chair and slipped into them without drying herself. Then she got into the bed, pulled the quilt over her and closed her eyes.

She knew almost immediately that she wouldn't be able to sleep. The house was too quiet now that Roger had settled back into the rhythm of his work and this left too much invitation for her mind to roam. She thought about the hammer, the gun, the windows of the tower block. She thought about Jack, how he had turned to stone the moment they pulled up to Frazier Avenue. And she thought about Morley, how she had struck him in the head, the way he had folded on the concrete, the puddle of blood, so much blood. Without treatment, he would surely die from that head wound. Or maybe Jack had already killed him now that she wasn't there to keep him at bay.

That's what you wanted, her mind whispered. *For Kate, remember?*

She's my sister. I love her. And she didn't deserve what she got. She did not deserve it.

She reminded herself that Kate was the innocent one in all this, that it was her life that had been snatched away by Morley. It didn't matter how much of a coward Emily was, Jack was right: Morley deserved to die.

It was no good. She sat up and turned the TV on, hoping a bit of background noise would help lull her to sleep. She flicked to another channel and was about to lie back down when something caught her eye. It was the news. The reporter was speaking into a microphone, live at the scene of a crime.

He was standing outside the Frazier Avenue estate.

Chapter Twenty-Two

It was risky as hell, and Dillon didn't think the girl would fall for it, but he had to keep reminding himself that he was dealing with a teenager and not the adult she pretended to be. When she answered his message, it occurred to him that she might be trying to set him up, to lure him straight into the hands of the law for questioning. But given his choices, he wasn't in much of a position to do anything else, and he couldn't give her time to settle. He had to pounce.

He watched Tara get off the bus, her long hair bouncing on her shoulders, her face oddly unsettling beneath badly applied makeup. She wore knee-high boots and a red bra was visible through a flimsy, see-through blouse; a schoolgirl dressed up as a streetwalker, shivering because she probably didn't own a coat that went with the ensemble.

Dillon flashed his headlights at her. She didn't wave or give any indication that she had seen him, concentrating instead on remaining upright in those ridiculous heels. While he waited for her to wobble her way to the car, he poured a clumsy line of coke onto a CD case and hoovered it up. His synapses exploded like fireworks, and he could almost hear his nerves crackling beneath his skin. An aftertaste of washing powder lingered at the back of his throat. He coughed, sneezed, and scratched his nostrils furiously.

He leaned across and opened the door for her, wondering whether she would need help getting in. If the circumstances were different, he would have found her baby giraffe strut hilarious, but as things stood, he had very little to laugh about. When she was settled in the passenger seat, he released the handbrake and broke away from the kerb with his tyres screeching and the exhaust belching black smoke.

'How'd you manage to get out?' Dillon asked. It wasn't on his original list of questions but curiosity got the better of him. There's no way she would have been able to sneak out in those boots, so her parents must've let her go willingly.

'What do you mean?' she asked flatly, examining her face in the wing mirror.

'I mean, you would've had police all over you, and now you're out here like nothing happened. Your parents just let you go?'

'My mum can't tell me what to do,' she said. The sentence was edged with annoyance, as though she were indirectly hinting that *he* couldn't tell her what to do either.

Keep it up, he thought, putting more weight on the accelerator and flying through an amber light that was a millisecond away from turning red. He thought he had a pretty good idea of what her mum was like, and if his intuition was right, she was either strung-out high or black-out drunk.

'Where are we going?' she asked.

'Thought we might go to the drive-through. You hungry?'

'I've lost my appetite.'

'Because you're worried about Craig?'

'Yeah. I still can't get used to thinking of him as *Craig*, and not Jerome.'

'He was using that name to try and protect you,' he said, turning off into a retail park that boasted a selection of fast-food restaurants. He wasn't surprised to see that the Clucky's car park was virtually empty; he hadn't eaten there since getting food poisoning as a kid from one of their greasy chicken burgers, and all he ever heard were horror stories of workers performing malicious acts on the food. He slotted the car in the space furthest to the back, and could smell the sweaty odour of the menu through his closed windows.

'You sure you don't want nothing to eat?' he asked, turning the engine off.

'From Clucky's?' she lifted a tweezed eyebrow and shook her head. 'No thanks.'

'All right, then let's get down to it.'

A smile tugged at her lips. She leaned back into her seat, the leather squeaking beneath her skirt. 'Get down to what?'

'What happened last night?'

The smile dissipated. She rolled her eyes and expelled a short, exasperated breath. 'You've been watching the news, haven't you?'

'Yeah.'

'There you go. Everything you need to know.'

'I want to hear it from you.'

She huffed and shook her head, as though this was all a terrible inconvenience to her. 'I thought you said you knew where he was. I thought you said he wanted to see me.'

Dillon pressed the button to lock the doors. 'You saw who took him. I don't care about what they're saying on the news. I want to hear it directly from your lips.'

'Did you just lock me in? Open the doors. Open these fucking doors or I'm going to scream.'

Dillon grabbed her by the throat, his fingers tightening around her windpipe. 'You fucking listen to me. You'd better drop this bad girl routine and tell me exactly what you saw, and if I even *think* you're lying I'm going to break your fucking neck.'

Tara watched the colour drain out of the world. Tiny black ants scurried across her vision and she felt something pop inside her skull. She reached up to his hands and tried to pry his fingers loose, but his grip was like a vice. Just as she teetered on the brink of oblivion, he released her. She coughed violently, desperately trying to suck in air, the muscles in her neck throbbing painfully. Her lungs constricted, stomach muscles tightening.

It was a few minutes before she could form words. By now, the windows were misty with condensation from their breath, and she could no longer see outside to appeal for help. She watched him snort cocaine off a CD case and could just about make out the devilish appearance of his bloodshot eyes in the gloom.

Without further delay, she told him what she knew. She told him that Craig heard his car alarm go off, went outside, and was ambushed by a man and woman. The man wore a mask, the woman didn't, but it was too dark to make her out clearly. She thought maybe the woman had brown hair, but it could have just as easily been black. After that, a woman from the estate tried to help her, but left before the police arrived, not wanting to get too involved.

Dillon listened to every word, his face an unmoving, stone mask. When she was finished, he said, 'You really haven't told me anything, have you?'

'I did,' she said hoarsely, massaging her tender throat. 'That's all I know.'

'The woman, the one that hit him with the hammer. You think you would recognise her again if you saw her?'

'I d... don't,' she hacked and winced from the pain. 'I don't know.'

'Well, we're going to find out, you and me.' He turned the key in the ignition, starting the car.

'Where are we going?'

'I have some ideas of who might have him. So you're coming on an identity parade with me. And you're not going anywhere until we've found the people that have him. So that foggy fucking memory of yours better get a whole lot clearer, fast.'

He blazed out of the car park, wiping his nose on the heel of his hand.

In a weak, childish voice he heard Tara say, 'But I've got school tomorrow.'

Chapter Twenty-Three

Jack was sitting on a chair in the doorway of the oiling room when Morley regained consciousness. It began with a gurgle, then a few feverish, incoherent words, like a man talking in his sleep during a particularly nasty nightmare. Then, slowly, Morley's eyelids opened. He blinked rapidly and then squinted at Jack, trying to focus his jittery vision.

'Where am I?' he tried to ask, but it left his mouth in a long, fractured croak. He tried to move against his restraints and Jack watched the confusion animate his face. Jack smiled, vaguely amused at the man's expression. Morley's pupils swelled to pennies, and as he strained to move, his waxy white skin became an angry shade of plum. Jack had washed the blood off Morley's face and replaced his bandage, after applying a line of superglue to the cut on his scalp. He'd thought about trying to stitch the wound closed with a needle and thread, but he knew he would butcher it.

'You're tied up,' Jack said. 'You should try and relax or you might pass out again.' Jack stood up and grabbed a packet of pills and a bottle of water from the workbench. 'These are called co-codamol. They're painkillers. They should help with your headache.'

'Where am I?'

'Tablets first. I need you thinking clearly.' Jack broke two co-codamol out of the blister packet and approached Morley. 'Open up.' Morley's mouth remained resolutely closed. 'Your head hurts, doesn't it? These won't get rid of the pain completely but they're very strong. I take them for my sciatica. Open up.'

Morley's eyes burned with hatred. 'You're trying to poison me.'

'You're still a little bit muddled up from the blows to your head. But I can assure you that I didn't go through the trouble of getting you here just so I could poison you. Now do you want the pills or not?'

The pulsing pain in Morley's head sent shock waves through his spine. The floor tilted like the deck of a sailing ship in rough seas. His mouth was scorched dry, and he wanted the water more than the drugs, really. Reluctantly, he opened his mouth and received the tablets and the blessed, cool water.

'They'll kick in after about twenty minutes or so. Don't worry if your chest starts to feel funny. They give you heartburn.' Jack sat back down in the chair and took a gulp of water for himself.

'Where am I?' Morley asked huskily for the third time.

Jack could see the cunning gleam in those green eyes, could almost hear the cogs in his damaged head clicking away.

'You're in a warehouse.'

'Why am I here?' Morley asked, barely moving his lips.

'We'll get to that.'

'Who are you?'

'Do you think you're interrogating me?' Jack said, unable to conceal the smile on his lips. 'You may be used to throwing your weight around, Craig, but you don't call any shots here. You're tied up and I'm not. You'd better make peace with it now.'

A thick cord bulged in Morley's neck. His mouth was turned down in a sneer. 'Who are you?' he growled through gritted teeth.

'WHO ARE *YOU*?' Jack bellowed back, his voice exploding in the silence of the warehouse. Morley's eyebrows rose in surprise, but beyond that, no fear registered on his face. He did not look around the room for anything that might help him. Instead, he kept his attention firmly fixed on Jack. With the rope pressed against his inflated neck, his breathing sounded phlegmy, and he opened his mouth to inhale deeper. 'Who are *you*? That is the real question.'

'I'm an innocent man tied up in a fucking warehouse,' Morley said.

'That's not who you are,' Jack said, his calmness contrasting eerily with the volatile outburst. 'Let me explain how this is going to work. I'm going to ask you questions, and when you lie to me, or I think you're lying to me, I'll hurt you. Simple enough, yes?' He went into his pocket, withdrew his folding knife and pulled out the blade. He ran the serrated blade of the knife over the scored surface of the workbench, curling off a thin rind of wood.

'I don't know what you want,' Morley said. He was sweating now, beads of perspiration rolling down the ridges of his ruddy face.

'I want to know who *you* are,' Jack said.

'I'm nobody.'

Jack used the tip of the knife to dig out a chip of wood from the bench. 'I'm only going to be able to hold my patience for so long. You can keep trying to mess me around, or you can start talking your way out of this awful situation you find yourself in. So I'll ask again. Who are you?'

'My name?'

'I know your name. Your name isn't who you are.'

He tried to shake his head on instinct, and grimaced as the rope chaffed the skin on his throat. 'I don't understand the question then,' he said.

'Who is Craig Morley?' Jack asked, blowing splinters from the knife. 'Imagine this is a job interview, not that a bag of shit like you has any idea what that would be like, but let's pretend. Tell me some trivia about yourself, some defining characteristics that make you who you are.'

Morley's lips moved wordlessly, and now his eyes drifted around the room like a fly, never settling on anything for longer than a heartbeat. Jack knew he was trying to formulate an answer, do anything he could to gain some ground. Jack clapped his hands together loudly, disrupting Morley's concentration.

'Who is Craig Morley?' he said again.

'I'm…' He sucked in air. 'I'm just a normal guy.' Jack's face was as cold and hard as the ground Morley sat on. Dull pain chipped away at the base of his skull, making him jerk involuntarily. 'I'm a dad. And I have a girlfriend.'

Jack nodded, but his face remained grim and unreadable. 'So you're a father. How many children do you have?'

'Two.'

'Boy, girl, what?'

'Two girls.'

Jack nodded once and put the blade of the knife away. Morley exhaled. 'You have both your kids with the same woman?'

Morley tried to nod. The rope strangled him. He winced and said, 'Mmm.'

'Didn't fancy marrying her?' Jack asked. 'Don't worry. I'm not marking you on this.'

Morley's tongue slithered out of his mouth and licked the sweat away from his stubbly upper lip. 'We plan to. Some day.' It was a lie. Monica hated his guts and he hadn't seen the girls in over three (or was it four?) years.

Jack seemed satisfied with the answer. 'So that's Craig Morley, is it? Father, devoted partner, generally all-round decent human being. Would you say so?'

Morley could see that Jack had set a trap for him but he wasn't brain-damaged enough to go bumbling into it. He knew that all he had to do was keep his answers simple and direct.

'We've all got our flaws,' Morley said.

'That's certainly true, Craig. What would you say is your main flaw?'

Their eyes met in a moment of silent understanding. Morley could sense the oncoming violence the way animals could sense an earthquake before the tremors started.

'Listen,' Morley began, craning his neck so that the rope wasn't pressing down on his Adam's apple. 'You're obviously upset with me about something, and I think you're gonna hurt me no matter what I say. So why don't you just tell me what I'm supposed to have done wrong?' He stared at Jack, and perhaps in some insane way he was trying to psych him out. 'I don't even know who you are. You don't work for Dekkers, I can see that for myself. But…'

'Here is what I'd say your main flaws are.' Jack stood up and rolled his shoulders. 'Firstly, you're a scumbag, aren't you? If I had to guess, I'd say you were a drug dealer, which makes you a piece of shit, but maybe that's all you're really qualified to do. After all, with an arrest record like yours, employers aren't exactly going to be climbing over each other to get at you, now, are they?' Jack saw a spark of recognition fly behind the man's eyes. It was as good as an admission. 'You've probably done a whole list of horrible things. But if I had to sum up who Craig Morley is, I could do it with one word.'

'Killer?' Morley said. 'That's what you keyed on my car, wasn't it?'

'Bingo. You're a killer. A cold-blooded, soulless murderer.'

Morley closed his eyes.

And then he smiled.

'Who am I supposed to have killed, Columbo?'

Jack cracked his neck to the side and rolled his shoulders again. A nerve in his back went numb from the tip of his spine down to his buttocks; sleeping on the floor had been an awful idea, but the pain, which would usually stop him in his tracks, was barely even noticeable. He left the oiling room and returned with a framed picture of Kate that showed her smiling and toasting the camera with a glass of wine. It was a photo he had snapped when she had accepted his wedding proposal.

'This is who you killed. Katherine Belinda Bracket. My wife.' He held the frame in front of Morley's face and watched his expression carefully. Morley analysed the woman in the photo.

'I have never seen her before in my life.'

'You're a liar,' Jack said coldly.

'I am a liar. And you may be right about a lot of things, but this isn't one of them.' He looked up at Jack fearlessly and said, 'How did she die?'

'You fucking know how she died,' Jack shouted, and the effort left him breathless. His chest rose and fell, his fists shaking at his sides.

'What's your name?' Morley asked, so casually that they might have been a couple of old friends having a discussion over a pint.

'My name is Jack Bracket. Kate Bracket was my wife. And you' – he thrust out an index finger as though it were a dagger – '*you* murdered her.'

Morley expelled a weary sigh. 'Jack, I've never killed anyone in my life.'

'You're a liar.'

'I've never seen you or your wife before. I'm sure of it.'

Jack punched his fist through one of the boxes lining the wall, which spewed polystyrene. Something sharp bit into his knuckles but he kept punching.

'Twelve years ago, you knocked on our door and you stabbed her!'

'Stabbed her, did I?' Morley chuckled weakly. 'Twelve years ago I stabbed her? No.'

'All you're doing is making this worse for yourself.'

'Really? I don't think so,' Morley said. 'I think you plan to kill me no matter what I tell you.' He didn't seem afraid at the prospect of dying. In fact, Jack thought he seemed relieved. Morley licked his lips, which were starting to harden and peel, and said, 'You might as well kill me now then. But you'd be killing an innocent man, which would make *you* the murderer now, wouldn't it?'

Jack was awed by Morley. All the years of thinking about this encounter, plotting what he might say to him, what he might *do* to him, and now he was completely disarmed. Morley had nerves of steel and he wasn't going to admit fault in a million years. But how could he look in Jack's face and lie so boldly?

'So what are you gonna do, Jack? You gonna torture me? You gonna murder me? You gonna leave me tied up here like your little slave?'

Jack ran his hands through his hair and then smoothed down his beard. He exhaled slowly, waiting for his heartbeat to settle, and then sat down on the chair.

'I might do all those things, Craig. But first, I'm going to tell you a story.'

Chapter Twenty-Four

2007

'You stink!' Kate said, giggling as she pulled away from his embrace. 'Oh my god, you smell like a caveman.'

She shooed him away with her hands but he grabbed her wrists and pulled her closer, burying his face in her neck and growling. She was ticklish by her collarbone so he blew his lips on that spot until she cringed away, breaking into hysterical laughter.

'Stop it!' she managed, 'I can't breathe.'

Jack continued, pinning her arms at her side. 'Say I'm the king.'

'All right,' she said, feigning defeat. 'I'm the king!'

'I gave you a chance.' He went back to her neck and blew down on her collarbone. She convulsed with laughter. He let her twist away and back up down the hallway.

'You're an idiot,' she said, pouting. 'And you stink.'

'Well, what way is that to treat your husband? You should have my dinner on the table and a bath already run for me. So, where is it?'

'You're too rough with me, as well,' she pointed to her stomach.

'You don't know rough,' he said, bending down to untie his boots. He kissed her stomach gently and then

153

followed her into the living room. *Judge Judy* was on the TV and a glass of lemonade sat on the coffee table.

'Seriously, though, did you make any dinner?'

'I literally got in and fell straight asleep,' she said, fanning her face with a copy of the local paper. 'I can make a salad or something if you want?'

'No, I don't want that, I'm starving,' he said, peeling off his T-shirt. It felt soggy in his hand and the white cotton was stained grey with sweat. The hair on his chest was slick; his forearms and neck burnt red.

'Get a takeaway then,' she said and glanced over at him briefly. 'My god, look how sunburnt you are.'

'We took some chairs and sat in the sun through lunch. I fell right asleep.'

'I'm pregnant, I have an excuse to fall asleep all the time. But you're not supposed to be falling asleep on the job.' She knelt on the sofa to inspect the redness of his arms. 'If you're going out in the sun, you have to put sun cream on, Jack.'

'Oh, stop being silly. What do you fancy for dinner then? I think I could do with something from Golden Dragon, what do you reckon? We could eat it in the garden.'

'You've got too many freckles on your arms,' she said, ignoring his segue and settling back into her chair. 'You're going to end up getting skin cancer if you keep sitting in the blazing heat without any sun cream on. You're too fair. You can't sit out in the sun like that, Jack, honestly.'

Jack stripped down to his boxer shorts and collapsed onto the sofa. Through the open window, they could hear the chime of the ice cream van jingling down the street, like the Pied Piper luring children away from their homes.

'I could really do with a witch's hat right now,' Kate said, abandoning *Judge Judy* in favour of a DVD of *The OC*.

'Witch's hat? What's that? Something your mum used to wear?' She leaned over and slapped his sunburnt forearm. 'Ouch!'

'You know what I'm on about,' she said as the disclaimer screen came on. She had a thing for these damn soppy dramas, and Jack couldn't stand them. If it wasn't *The OC* box set, then it would be *Dawson's Creek* or *Party of Five* or some other show full of attractive twenty-something-year-olds with perfect teeth. Didn't matter much to him what she watched now, though. The heat was already knocking him out and he estimated that he'd be asleep before the end of the opening credits.

He yawned, leaned back into the sofa and stretched his legs out onto the footstool. 'I don't know what a witch's hat is, honest.'

'Maybe you called them something different as a kid. It's an ice cream with an ice lolly stuck in it. We used to love them.'

'That sounds like an abomination.'

'It wasn't. It was the best thing ever.'

'You were feral children,' he said sleepily. 'And our child will not be eating any of that junk.'

'Oh yes, he will.'

'He?'

'Or she?' she amended, rolling her eyes. 'But it's a *he*. I know it.' She knitted her fingers lovingly across the small paunch of her stomach.

'Jack Junior,' he said, smiling, before leaning down to kiss her hands.

'I could kill for one of them now,' she said, nudging him with her bare foot.

'Kill for what?'

'A witch's hat.'

'So what do you want me to do about it?'

'Go and get me one.'

'What? No way. I've just sat down.'

'Exactly. You've just sat down, you're not settled yet.' She nudged him again. 'Please. I'm so hot.'

'I'll get the fan down later.'

'The ice cream isn't for me. Jack Junior wants it,' she said, giving him the puppy eyes and rubbing her stomach. 'You're going to deny your child?'

'I'm denying the child on the basis that I don't want to encourage any occult-themed refreshments in this house.'

'Come on,' she whined, digging her heel into his thigh. 'The ice cream man is going to drive away.'

'He's probably a mile down the road anyway.'

'He isn't. I heard him.'

'You heard the echo. It's probably leapfrogged to us from about five streets away.'

'So you're really not going to get me an ice cream? I'm going to go through hours of intense agony to push your baby out and you can't even go to the ice cream van?'

He looked over at her to gauge how desperate she was. Her face was stern and unwavering. She pointed at her stomach and then tapped her wrist to indicate he was wasting time.

'OK, I'll look down the road for him, but if I can't see him I'm coming back and you can't sulk.'

'You'll find him. I have faith in you. Now go quickly.'

He pulled himself off the sofa and jogged upstairs, slipped into a pair of shorts and a vest, then put a pair of flip-flops on. As he left he said, 'Don't fall back asleep before you order my food.'

'You got it.'

He stepped out of the house and shielded his eyes from the sun, looking up and down the street. He walked to the corner and found a swarm of kids clustered around a pink-and-white ice cream van about two hundred yards away. He thought about jogging to the van but didn't have the energy. Judging by the number of kids waiting, Jack supposed he could afford to stroll. He reached the van and waited for the kids to finish harassing the ice cream man. The little buggers took their time, asking a dozen questions about each lolly or modifying their ice creams with all kinds of crazy coloured sauces.

In a few years I'll be buying ice cream for the kid, he thought, imagining himself standing in the queue with an arm around little Jack or little Kate. Ever since their first scan, he had spent a lot of time daydreaming about what their child would eventually look like. It filled him with the loveliest kind of anxiety he'd ever known. The pleasant giddiness was offset by the dread that dwelled in the crevices of his mind. Every night before bed, he had to wait until Kate was asleep before he would allow himself to drift. He wanted to be alert in case she suddenly felt any twinges or sharp pains. And when he did finally sink into the pillow, he would mentally mutter the word *healthy* over and over until unconsciousness took him.

Please god, I don't care if it's a boy or a girl, I just want it to be healthy.

When it was finally his turn to order, Jack said, 'Do you do something called a witch's hat?'

The bald ice cream man scratched his hairy forearm and nodded.

'Really? I didn't think you'd know what that is.'

'Popeye, witch's hat, same thing. Two pound, boss.'

Jack paid and watched the man plonk a strawberry rocket into his ice cream, and then took it home, licking his knuckles when it dribbled down.

'You got it?' Kate was kneeling on the sofa when he entered the living room. Upon seeing the witch's hat, she smiled and clasped her hands together over her heart. 'Oh, my hero.'

'Here.' He handed it to her, sucking ice cream from his thumb. He plonked himself back down on the sofa, his eyelids drooping heavily. Kate removed the rocket from the ice cream, licked it in a way that was vaguely erotic to him, and then sighed contentedly. She leaned over and kissed his sunburnt nose; her soft lips were cold and soothing. He smiled and fell asleep.

When the doorbell rang, he stirred awake and saw the red-stained lolly stick on the coffee table. He could've been out for ten minutes or an hour, he wasn't sure.

'That'll be your food,' she said, patting him on the calf as she rose from the sofa and padded into the hallway to answer the door.

Jack could feel sleep trying to seduce him, but he was hungrier than he was tired and knew if he dozed off again then he would lie awake all night. He sat up, rubbing his eyes with the heels of his hands, and released a yawn that almost dislocated his jaw.

Then he heard the disturbance in the hallway. It sounded like a slap, then a thud, then a short, sharp shriek.

Jack stood up and through the curtains saw a hooded boy running down his garden path. His mind erupted with questions – what was that sound? Why was the delivery man dressed in a hoody when it was so hot out, and why was he running away?

It wasn't the delivery man.

Jack raced out into the hallway and found Kate on the floor. There was a split second of confusion before he saw the blood, and then the strength melted away from his legs. He knelt by his wife and looked up through the open doorway in time to see the car pull away, and the boy peering out the window at what he had done, admiring his work. The fading sunlight shone into the boy's pale face, illuminating a set of sparkling green eyes. In that instant, the world slowed down long enough for Jack to see the boy wink at him. He was *laughing* at Jack.

Jack felt a hand touch his face and looked down at Kate.

'Ja…' A bubble of blood burst out of her mouth as she tried to speak. She was clasping her neck. Blood pumped between her fingers and was splashing the skirting board and staining the wallpaper. In that moment of insanity, his thoughts a riot of noise in his head, Jack wondered if he would need to paint the skirting board again or whether he could just sop it up with a sponge. Then all thoughts vanished along with the feeling in his body, and he was alone with his dying wife as gouts of blood poured out of her neck in rhythmic spurts.

'Katie!' He pulled off his vest and pressed it over her hand, which was covering the neck wound. The white vest turned red in a matter of seconds. He could feel her hot blood soaking through the vest, dyeing his hands. 'Someone help me!' he screamed, and then pressed the vest harder against her. He looked into her eyes. They were wide with confusion and fear. Her lips continued to move silently as though searching for the right words that would convey her utter astonishment.

Jack had no idea what to do. The pressure he was placing on her neck didn't seem to be helping. He didn't want to move her in case it worsened her condition. Her condition? He didn't even know what was wrong with her, except that blood was gushing out of her neck and it was scaring him witless.

'Honey, can you hear me?' he yelled, one hand over her neck and the other cupping her cheek. 'You're going to be OK.' But as he said this his voice warbled, changing octave. He screamed out through the doorway again: 'SOMEONE FUCKING HELP ME! PLEASE, SOMEONE HELP ME!'

Her eyes didn't seem to be focusing on anything; they were just two glassy balls, staring past him.

'Look at me, love,' he said, desperately trying to get her to focus on him. Her lips had stopped moving and now her mouth hung open slackly, and obscenely, he could smell the sweet strawberry flavouring of the witch's hat amidst the metallic stink of her blood. 'Listen to me now, Kate,' he said, trying to keep his voice level so as not to panic her. 'I need you to try and focus for me, honey. Can you do that? Don't go to sleep. Don't…' The dam broke and a single, wracking sob shuddered out of him.

'What's going on?' One of his neighbours, a tall, thin man who lived across the road, was standing in the front garden.

'Call an ambulance,' Jack shouted.

'What's happened?'

'I don't know!' he snapped. He looked down at Kate, and in the second that he'd taken his attention off her to speak to the neighbour, she had slipped away. He couldn't quite work out why, or how this had happened, and the confusion separated his mind from his body.

Maybe she isn't dead, he thought, knowing that it was a lie, knowing that this was some kind of defence mechanism to stop his sanity from shattering. He bent down and placed an ear to her lips, but could not feel any breath. She had lost so much blood that it had drained the colour from her face and lips, and now her complexion was so ashen she looked almost a pale shade of green. He pressed his fingers on the opposite side of her neck, feeling for a pulse, but couldn't find one. The blood was no longer pumping from her neck, but merely spilling out, spreading in a pool that stretched to the base of the staircase.

She couldn't be dead. There was no way she could really be dead, because just moments ago she was getting ready to watch *The OC* and he had just bought her an ice cream, and this sort of thing couldn't happen on such an ordinary day. There was no reason for this to happen, and it was that thought that caused a tidal wave of unreality to crash over him. The house began to quiver and spin. His body was on fire, the heat seeming to emanate from his brain, and the only thought that survived the flames was that none of this was fair.

This couldn't happen to people like them.

When the delivery man pulled up on the moped outside his gate, Jack screamed, and the furnace erupted.

Chapter Twenty-Five

Morley listened to the whole thing without interruption. When Jack was finished, his hands were shaking. Jack inhaled deeply and then released the breath slowly and steadily, pulling himself back from the brink of hyperventilating. He hadn't told that story in such detail in a very long time, not since he was featured in the re-enactment for the TV appeal.

'You only have one chance to live,' Jack said, wiping the corners of his lips with his fingertips. The effort it had taken to relay the story made the moisture evaporate from his mouth. 'All I want to know is why you did it. Just tell me.'

'And then what?' Morley replied quietly. 'You'll just untie me and let me go about my business?'

'Yes,' Jack said.

'Now who's lying to who?' He gasped and grimaced, his face shiny with perspiration. 'I might be a lot of things, Jack. But I'm not a fucking idiot.'

'I can cause you serious pain. I'm not sure that I want to. But I will if you don't tell me what made you do it.'

A tired, almost sad look passed over Morley's face. He closed his eyes and was quiet for several seconds, as though lost in thought. Then he said, 'You're going to kill me no matter what I tell you. There's no way that you can let me live. Not after going through all this to get me here.'

Jack smiled. 'All right. You're right. You're not a fucking idiot.' Then the smile died and Jack's expression was like a cliff face weathered by years of grief. 'How you die is up to you, Craig. If you tell me what I want to know, then I'll do it quickly. I'll give you something you didn't give Kate. I'll kill you with some dignity. And I'll bury you properly.' He leaned back in the chair, his palms pressed flat on his thighs; the shaking had stopped and he felt he was in control of himself once again. 'If you want to lie to me, I'll make sure the pain drags on and on. That's the only deal I'm going to offer you.'

Morley spat on the floor. 'I'm dying of thirst,' he said, and laughed mirthlessly to himself. 'I don't suppose I could get another sip of that water, could I?'

Jack stood up, took the bottle of water to Morley and let him have two large gulps.

'Thanks. That's better.' Morley cleared his throat, and then winced against the pain it caused in his head. 'Am I allowed to ask you a question, Jack?'

'You're not going to talk your way out of this.'

'I know. You said that already. It's just, something confuses me about the story you just told me.'

'Yeah?'

'Yeah. You still haven't told me why you think it was me that stabbed your wife.'

'It's you because I saw you.'

Morley looked at the floor, his face stoic with concentration. 'When did you say this happened again?'

'You know when.'

'And you saw me running into the back of a car? What did I look like?'

'Don't fucking play mind games with me,' Jack growled, flexing his fingers. 'You think you can outsmart me? You think you're going to confuse me?'

'Jack, why don't we assume I've done a lot of drugs over the years and my memory might not be so great.'

'This isn't a court of law. You're not going to get off on a technicality.'

'I know. I know. But if you want the truth out of me, why don't we just assume that my memory is all fucked up?'

Jack left the oiling room. He came back a moment later with a laptop in one hand and a nail gun in the other. He set the laptop down on a box and clicked play on the video.

Morley's dragon eyes squinted for a second, his mouth hanging open stupidly. Then he frowned, before a wry smile tugged at his dry lips. 'I haven't seen this in a long time.'

'*Money Up Front,*' Jack said, and then, to Morley's surprise, Jack began lip-syncing the words to the opening verse.

Morley tried to clear his throat but there was no saliva, so instead he swallowed painfully, and said, 'I don't know what—'

'This is my favourite part,' Jack said, cutting him short. '*Money up front or I'll be at your door with the blade out. Pay what you owe or I'll carve your face out.* You must have realised that you rhymed "out" with "out" when you wrote this, didn't you? You're not exactly Eminem, are you?'

'I was only a kid. I was just… I was just talking, you know.'

'Just talking? That's not what it sounds like to me, Mister Flashy. In fact it sounds very specific, doesn't it?'

A single bead of perspiration ran down the bridge of Morley's nose. 'No. Come on, you can't be serious.'

'You came to my door and you stabbed my wife. *I'll be at your door with the blade out.* That's what you say in the video. You meaning to tell me that it's just a coincidence, is that it?' Jack was spitting as he spoke.

'No, I mean… yeah, it is. That music shit was just a phase, everyone was doing it. My friend, he had a studio and… we'd say all kinds of stupid shit and—'

Jack snatched the nail gun off the workbench. 'Do you know what this is?'

'No,' Morley said.

'It's a nail gun.'

'Look, you said you saw me through your curtains and then you went into the hallway and I was in the back of a car. You said I looked at you and smiled.' He heard the low squeak as Jack's hand tightened around the nail gun. 'When I was running away, what did I look like?'

Jack's lips pressed together tightly, his nostrils flaring to accommodate the force of his exhalations. 'You had your trousers hanging off your arse.'

'What else?'

Jack raised the nail gun and fired. There was a loud thud behind Morley's head as a nail flew out and thumped into a box.

Morley's face remained impassive. 'You saw someone from behind, running into a car. You can't describe them better than that?'

Jack walked over to Morley and crouched in front of him. Face-to-face, Jack could smell the stink of the man; his sour breath, his salty sweat.

'You laughed at me,' Jack said, so quietly that even in the silence of the warehouse Morley had to strain to hear him. 'You laughed because you thought I'd never catch up to you. But you didn't think past tomorrow, did you? You thought you were invincible. Now here you are. You don't have a smile for me now, do you, Craig?'

'No,' Morley replied, without meeting Jack's eyes.

'Oh? Why not?'

'There isn't much to smile about.'

'That's exactly right. You knocked on my door, and when my wife answered, you stabbed her in the neck and ran off like a little coward.' He pressed the nail gun against Morley's bandaged forehead. 'You will tell me why you did it.'

'When am I supposed to have killed your wife? Will you tell me that at least?'

'You're a snake and you think lying will save your skin. But it won't.'

'Are you saying this all happened back then, before I made that video? I was a kid! Look at the size of me in that video. I couldn't have run down your driveway if you had paid me a million pounds.'

'You want me to kill you, don't you?'

'No. But you're going to anyway. Even though you know I'm innocent.'

'Innocent? How dare you?' Jack shook his head and laughed darkly. 'Innocent? That offends me. It offends me that you would apply a word like that to yourself. You have never been innocent of anything in your entire disgusting life.'

'Fine. I'm a bastard. I'm a worthless piece of shit. But I didn't kill your wife.' Morley's lips curled at the corners and his face seemed to brighten and come alive. 'And I think you're starting to realise that, aren't you?'

Jack pulled the trigger on the nail gun. Morley made a sound that was something between a scream and a grunt, and then laughed airily. Jack looked at the nail gun, perplexed. It was jammed. Colin had probably been dicking around with it, shooting cans on his lunch break or something. *Thank god it had jammed*, Jack thought. That momentary loss of control almost blew everything.

Jack set the nail gun down. He went into his pocket, opened the blade of his knife and brought the tip to the dark flesh beneath Morley's eyes.

'I could live to be a thousand years old, Craig, and I'd never forget these pretty green peepers of yours. I bet these eyes have got you into trouble a lot in the past, haven't they? Wouldn't take much to pick you out of a fucking line-up. Isn't that right, Flashy Boy?' Gently, Jack prodded the tip of the knife toward the rim of Morley's eye. 'I wouldn't make any sudden movements if I were you.'

The knife pricked the thin membrane of skin just beneath the lashes. Craig turned his head away from the knife and felt the blade slice across his cheek. He screamed. It was more from a release of tension than from the sting of the cut. 'I didn't do it! I can prove it! Just give me the chance to prove it!'

'It's too late for words now, Flashy.' He grabbed hold of Morley's throat and squeezed. 'I'll start by taking your eyes.' He pinned Morley's head in place and brought the blade nearer. Morley writhed and tried to twist his face away, kicking his legs. Jack had the blade a millimetre from Morley's eyeball when there was a banging on the warehouse door. Immediately Jack's hand clamped over Morley's mouth. 'Not a sound,' he whispered, listening.

There was another banging at the door, and then the bell rang.

'Jack! It's me.'

He heard Emily's voice and glanced down at his wrist-watch. It was only five in the afternoon. She was early. He placed the knife atop a nearby box, stood up, grabbed the masking tape gun and taped over Morley's mouth before going to the door.

When he opened it, she quickly sidled past him, removing the hood of her jacket. Her face was wild and flushed.

'What's wrong?' he asked. A sound travelled out of the oiling room; Morley was screaming through the masking tape.

'How long has he been awake?' Emily asked, her face a painting of panic.

Jack closed the door behind her, locked it. 'A couple of hours. I've just been talking to him.'

'And?'

'He's saying just about everything he can to get out of it. He's going to take some softening up.' He looked her up and down, saw the tiredness in her bloodshot eyes. Her hair was frizzy and uncombed, and for the first time he saw silver threads at the crown of her head. How had he not noticed she was going grey? 'What's the matter?'

'We have a huge problem.' She was about to say more when Morley's muted screaming became fiercer, more animalistic. 'He's making so much noise. Someone's going to hear.'

'Do you wanna speak to him?' Jack asked.

'No.' She shook her head. 'I just want him to shut up.'

Jack nodded, signalled for her to follow him. They walked to the oiling room. Through the open doorway, Emily saw Morley writhing and straining against his restraints. Beads of sweat rolled down his angry red face and dripped off the edge of his jaw. He twisted and bucked, but could not find any wiggle room that might help his cause. Morley's eyes fixed on Emily and he was nodding as though trying to convey his need for help. Yet when he saw that she was in no rush to assist him, the screaming and thrashing began to ebb. Finally, realisation dawned on him and he began to tally together what he was seeing. She wasn't an ally. She had been there last night when they snatched him out of the car park. His face slackened, his shoulders slumped, and he became still.

'Flashy Menace, meet Emily,' Jack said. 'Look familiar? She should do. She's Kate's twin sister.'

Morley shook his head, his eyes pleading with Emily. She looked away, and Morley started babbling behind the tape. The noise drifted out of the room and created a jagged acoustic in the warehouse. Jack shut the door and locked it. On a stack of boxes that lined the outside wall of the oiling room sat an old, battered radio with a broken cassette deck. Jack tuned it until he picked up 'When Doves Cry', and turned the volume up, drowning out Morley's protests.

Chapter Twenty-Six

They walked away from the oiling room and Jack said, 'He's so slippery. He knows every trick in the book. Maybe I underestimated him. He's a lot smarter than I thought he would be.'

'Jack, we need to talk.'

He nodded. 'Shall we go up to the office?'

They went upstairs to a small, cluttered office that housed one desk, two office chairs and a laptop. 'Shall I make some tea?' Jack asked as Emily sat down.

'No, forget the tea,' she snapped. 'Just sit down.'

He recoiled from her reaction ever so slightly, and then eased himself into the chair.

'You didn't get any sleep, did you?' he said.

'I didn't get a chance. I was a little bit occupied by the fact he's all over the news.'

Jack's casual, almost bored expression hardened into steely concentration. '*What?*'

'I got home and turned the TV on. There was someone else with Morley yesterday. They saw everything.'

'No,' he shook his head. 'Of course there wasn't.'

'Jack, he was with a girlfriend and she saw us take him. She phoned the police—'

'There wasn't anyone else there,' he butted in.

'You need to be quiet and let me finish,' she said, closing her eyes and raising her hands to touch her temples. The stress was congregating in the centre of her forehead and had been trying to burrow out all day. 'His girlfriend phoned the police and gave a description of us. So far, I think all they have is that it was a man and a woman that took him. But she must've told them that he had a gun on him, so they raided his flat. You know what they found? Eight kilos of heroin so pure that they've linked him to all kinds of criminal organisations across Europe.' She paused for breath. 'Now they're out there combing the city for him.'

Jack thought about it. Emily could not read his expression. Eventually he shrugged and said, 'It makes no difference to us. In fact, it only makes things easier, doesn't it?'

'What are you talking about?'

'That fucking piece of shit downstairs is not just a murderer, he's a drug pusher too. So it isn't just our lives he's ruined. Who knows how many others he's brought misery to with these drugs?'

She closed her eyes against the tension in her skull. Her frustration only fed the migraine. 'No, you don't get it,' she began as calmly as she could. 'This changes everything.'

'It changes nothing,' he replied immediately.

'Jack, he's got half the Metropolitan Police trying to find him so that he can give up the source of the heroin. And it gets better,' she said, her voice rising to a manic pitch. 'Imagine who else is looking for him – the people that want to make sure he doesn't get questioned. You see what I'm getting at?'

Jack was quiet for a very long time. He seemed to be contemplating what she had said, but there was no worry or alarm in his face. He stood up and said, 'Well, I'm going to make tea. I haven't had one all day and I'm gasping.'

He walked out of the office, crossed the long, bare stock room, and went into the kitchen. Emily had to grit her teeth together to contain the scream of annoyance that was lurking in her throat. She went to the kitchen and saw him eating a digestive biscuit placidly.

'Why aren't you taking this seriously?' she demanded, slapping the counter so hard that a teaspoon jumped. 'Do you know what could happen to us? We could get thrown in prison for years or we could get horribly murdered. Doesn't that mean anything to you?'

He waited until he'd swallowed the mouthful of digestive before saying, 'It leaves us in about the same position we were in anyway.'

'No, it doesn't. What planet are you on, Jack?'

'Look, don't start getting all spooked on me now, Em. You can handle this. I never would have chosen you if I'd thought you couldn't.'

She flinched. 'Chosen me? What's that supposed to mean?'

He shook his head irritably and then pinched the bridge of his nose. 'I mean... fuck's sake, I haven't slept properly, my mind's turning to mush. What I'm trying to say is I wouldn't have got you *involved* if I didn't think you were strong enough. There, is that better? Kate's your sister. I just thought you'd want to be *involved*.'

'Yes, I know she was my sister, Jack. You don't have to keep beating me over the head with it.'

Jack closed his eyes and took a deep breath. Calmly he said, 'They've made a big fuss about him on the news this morning. And yet here we are.'

'I don't believe you.' She shook her head. Then quietly, to herself: 'What have I got myself into?'

'If they had any real leads on Morley, then they would have got him by now.' He walked up to Emily, placed his hands on her shoulders and softly said, 'I've changed the plates back on the van. Nobody knows he's down there except us.'

The kettle clicked, distracting Jack. He poured hot water into the cups he'd prepared. 'We just need to stick to our original plan. We find out why he killed Kate, and then we make him disappear. And think of it this way, Emily. By taking him out of this world, we could be helping put away these disgusting drug dealers that prey on innocent people like Kate.'

She wasn't convinced, but Jack's calmness was almost contagious. Maybe if she did manage to get some sleep she would be able to think straight, and perhaps this whole thing would make sense to her again.

'Did he admit it?' she asked wearily. 'Did he say anything at all that made him sound like he was the one that did it?'

'Morley? No, course not. But I could see it in his eyes when I described what happened. I saw the panic, the fear. He's been involved with people that are far scarier than me, Emily. And he's probably talked his way out of far scarier situations.' He grabbed the teaspoon, drained the teabag and tossed it into the bin. 'This man is a different animal to us. We have to bear that in mind.'

'You're not at all worried about him being on the news this morning, are you?' she said, and almost laughed at how absurd a notion it was.

'Right now, all I care about is getting what I need from Morley and then getting rid of him.' He smiled, but it was a caricature; like a robot giving their interpretation of what a smile was supposed to look like. 'You know something? This news could help us.'

'How?'

'He's not afraid of me, but I'll bet he's afraid of whoever that heroin belongs to. Might give him the kick up the arse he needs to start talking.'

'There's one other thing,' she said. It was something she had been thinking about all the way over to the warehouse, a piece of the jigsaw that didn't adhere to the rest of the puzzle. 'They didn't find his gun. Or the hammer.'

Jack paused mid-sip. 'So?'

'Well, I mean, they didn't say they found them. Normally they would, wouldn't they? They'd say the police recovered a gun and a hammer at the scene of the crime. But they didn't.'

'So what are you getting at?'

'You have your fingerprints and Morley's blood on that hammer. That's enough evidence to implement you in the kidnapping. And that leaves the question, doesn't it?'

'You're gonna have to spell it out for me, Emily, I'm not sure what you're getting at.'

'If they don't have the hammer and the gun, then who does?'

Chapter Twenty-Seven

May had almost eaten her way through a whole tin of chocolates but she didn't feel the least bit guilty. In school, she'd struggled with her weight and had shuffled her way through a plethora of diets, never quite having the willpower to stick to one long enough to see any change. She had always been pretty and the rest of her body developed early, which gave her an advantage over the flat-chested girls in her school year. Adolescent boys were drawn to her large breasts, which had ballooned by the time she was fourteen. She discovered makeup and after getting past the fear of allowing a boy to fumble around with her, she began to rather enjoy it. Of course, her new-found reputation didn't ingratiate her much with the other girls in her year, but by then she didn't care.

The weight was no longer an issue – until she was married. The second she said 'I do', she opened up the floodgates for a torrent of abuse. If there was fluff on the carpet then she was a lazy fat pig who didn't do housework. If she went shopping and had forgotten to buy something as simple as bacon or the specific kind of bread he liked, then it was because she was too busy buying snacks to eat on the way home like the greedy fat bitch she was.

Eventually that sort of negative reinforcement corroded her sweet tooth and killed her cravings. She began weighing her food, preparing child-sized portions for herself, or skipping meals completely. That regime, combined with the stress of living with her then-husband Carl, helped the weight to melt off her. In six months, she lost four stone. She could see her ribs, her cheekbones, started noticing new things about herself.

She lost all the excess fat and after a couple of years she found that she had lost the desire for the sweets and snacks that she had coveted as a girl. Yet every now and then she would reward herself with a little something as a reminder of how well she had done, and how far she had come.

Today was a special occasion. The willpower she had demonstrated in losing the weight paled in comparison to the nerve it had taken to retrieve the hammer and the gun. She had saved Jack and proved her worth.

Having those items in the boot of her car as she gave her statement to the police was the most nerve-wracking and electrifying thing she had ever done. For the first time in her entire life, she felt powerful. Now, as she sat there watching BBC News, she felt a pride that far surpassed what she felt when she had pulled herself up from the dungeon of depression.

There were still things that bothered her about the incident, but they would be easy enough to figure out once she spoke to Jack. Again, it had taken every modicum of self-restraint she had not to go running after him like a dog with her tail between her legs. He would like that, wouldn't he? For her to trot after him with her tail wagging, so eager for a pat on the head. Well, the dynamic of their relationship had shifted somewhat, hadn't it? She had his freedom tied up in a bin liner and stuffed into the cupboard beneath the stairs. And that's where it would remain until he showed her the respect she deserved.

The mystery woman didn't grate on her so much, not after the news had reported who it was they'd kidnapped. May was quite sure that their relationship wasn't sexual, and therefore the woman wasn't a threat to her. Still, she wasn't exactly thrilled that he had a double life and dealings with this woman, but that could be ironed out. That would be one of the parameters of their new relationship: no secrets, no living in separate houses, no more treating her like a toy he could pick up and discard whenever he grew bored. She would be in full control, and that was best for everyone really.

She dragged herself away from the TV and freshened up. It was time to phone Jack and talk things through. She didn't care how busy he was with whatever trouble he had cooked up. She was going to click her fingers and he was going to jump through her hoop. He owed her that much at least.

She phoned his house phone. The line wouldn't connect. She felt the anger rising in her. She wanted to throw her mobile phone through the window and scream the house down. How could he continue to exist like an ape? Why couldn't he just get a mobile phone so that she could talk to him wherever he was? His stubbornness enraged her, but then she thought about the bag beneath the stairs and a cool balm of reassurance caressed her. It was good to feel reassured and in control.

Fine. If she had to make a concession in order to kick-start her plan, then she would. She swept her hands through the empty wrappers in the chocolate tin and settled on a toffee, unwrapped it and popped it in her mouth. Then she headed out to her car.

If he wasn't at his house, then he would be at the woman's. And if he wasn't at either of those places, then the little boy he worked with at the warehouse might have a good idea where he was.

She drove to Jack's place and rang the bell. The windows were dark, and when she peered through the letterbox she could neither see nor hear anything stirring within the house. Sometimes when she made an impromptu visit, she'd hear the clang of weights from behind the garage door. She walked across to the garage and placed an ear up to the door. She couldn't hear anything. She reached down and tried the handle but it wouldn't budge, nor had she really expected it to.

As she walked back to her car, she wondered whether this mystery changed the way she felt about Jack. In the last twenty-four hours, she had learned that he was an incredibly dangerous man. And until then she had thought of him as her sweet, quiet Jackie, a man that wouldn't hurt a fly. How wrong she was.

No, it didn't change how she felt. If anything, it amplified her love for him, made her want to rip his clothes off and make love to him over and over again.

She wasn't annoyed when she got back behind the wheel and began driving to the mystery woman's house. She hadn't expected him to be home anyway, the same way she didn't expect him to be at this woman's house, but she wasn't going to leave any stone unturned.

Finding the house was easy. When she had followed his van there yesterday afternoon, she'd made a mental note of the street name and house number. Google Maps did the rest.

She pulled up at the house. The street was silent as she stepped out of the car, walked up to the front door and rang the bell.

A man answered and gave her a quizzical look before saying, 'Can I help you?'

'Yes,' May said with a smile. 'I was wondering if Jack was here, please?'

'Jack?' The man cocked his head. 'No, sorry. Nobody called Jack lives here.'

'Oh, I know he doesn't live here. But he was visiting a friend here yesterday and I thought he might be here again. Sorry, I forgot the woman's name.' She smiled sweetly again to reassure the man that she didn't intend to bring any drama to his doorstep. 'Blond, about five seven?'

The man seemed to remember something because he nodded and said, 'Can you give me a minute? I think my housemate will know.'

'Sure.'

She stuffed her hands in her pockets and waited.

Another man came to the door. He was chewing something, and didn't stop to swallow before asking, 'You're looking for Jack?'

'Yes. I'm his fiancée,' she said proudly. 'I don't suppose he's here?'

'No,' the man said, and shook his head to remove the hair from his eyes. 'I think he's at the hospital.'

'Hospital?'

'Yes. My girlfriend's with him.' When he saw no sign of understanding on May's face he added, 'Emily?'

'Emily?'

'Yes. She's his sister-in-law. Well, I don't know if they're technically still in-laws now that his wife is dead, but, you know.'

May had never been good at masking her emotions, especially when something caught her by surprise. She felt the hinges of her jaw loosen, her mouth dropping open. She had known Jack had been married, but always assumed it had ended in divorce. She hadn't exactly had a desperate urge for the messy details; in fact she felt sick at the idea that another woman had once shared his bed. But she had no idea that her Jack was a widower.

'Yeah,' the man replied, and the first trace of doubt lined his face. 'His mum. Didn't he tell you?'

'Tell me what?' she said, barely able to follow the conversation now.

'Well, I think his mum's really sick. Emily says she hasn't got long. She's been at the hospital with him, you know, saying their last goodbyes and just waiting really.'

'Really?' May said exaggeratedly. 'That's strange.'

'Why's that strange?' he asked, his voice lowering to accommodate the suspicion.

'It's strange because his mum died when he was a teenager.' She let it linger a moment before adding, 'Maybe you heard your girlfriend wrong.'

'No.' He stepped out and said, 'They're definitely visiting his mother.'

'Then they'd be at a graveyard and not a hospital.' She smiled and then added, 'I'm sure this is just a mix-up. Anyway, I'm sorry to have disturbed you.'

May walked away with a smile on her face.

Chapter Twenty-Eight

Bernard finished his twelve-hour shift and shambled out of the police station with the sound of the cell buzzers still ringing through his head. It had been a full house since two in the morning and now the exhaustion had settled into his marrow. He squinted at the fading daylight, his eyes achy and raw, sparks of pain jumping up through the arches of his feet.

He got into his car with a huff and allowed himself half a minute or so before slotting the key into the ignition. It was the first time he had sat down in half a day, and had he not hated the sight of the station so much, he could have quite happily fallen asleep right then and there. He was also very hungry. One of the benefits of being a detention officer was that he could help himself to all the ready-made meals his heart desired from the selection kept in the freezer, provided because it wasn't the sort of job you could leave the building mid-shift to get a snack. But when you spent most of your shift watching detainees smear shit on the walls or drink out of the toilet, it robbed you of your appetite somewhat. Apart from that, the ready-made meals stank as bad as some of the filth they scooped off the streets. And the coffee was even worse.

It usually took him about twenty minutes to get home if the traffic was light, but that wasn't the case this evening.

The roads were clogged, and the shrill sounds of sirens sang in the distance. Maybe there was a pile-up somewhere.

When he turned the corner onto his road just over an hour later, he saw the gaggle of boys playing football outside his house and felt a stab of pain in his stomach. That fucking African family had been nothing but trouble since they were gifted a council house opposite his. The kids ran wild, booting the ball off the parked cars or running up and down the street screaming their heads off into the early hours, and the parents were just as bad. Well, *parent*, he thought; he had only ever seen their mother, and all she did was sit on the porch talking on her fucking phone so loud he could hear the conversation from his bedroom.

A big heap of a woman with her clan of noisy kids, all looking at *him* like he was the one who had something to be ashamed of. Him – a hard-working white man who paid his taxes so she could live rent-free. What a joke this country was.

The boys saw him approach and made no effort to stop their game or at least postpone it so he could park in his space. He honked his horn. The boys imitated the sound before cackling like a pack of hyenas. He wound down the window.

'Get out of the road,' he shouted.

'Get out of the road,' one of the spindly boys repeated, altering their accent to match his. He wasn't sure why, but that childish needling set his blood on fire. Perhaps it was the fact that these foreigners had the nerve to mock his English accent in his own country. He gripped the handbrake, yanked it up and then flung the door open.

The boys scattered, shrieking gleefully as they ran away from him. He looked over at the mother who was on her phone. She stared back at him defiantly, unwilling to pause her conversation or so much as yell her usual ooga booga at the boys.

'Next time I'll run them over,' Bernard said, pointing at the boys who were now taunting him at the next speed bump further down the road.

'Wha?' the mother said, her expression turning mean.

'Oh, you heard me?' Bernard said and got back into his car before he could say any more. He was so agitated that it took him three attempts to reverse park into the spot that was wide enough to slot in a limo. He got out of the car and trudged up to his house, wishing that he could just turn round and call her exactly what he wanted to call her. He slammed the front door behind him and heard the noise echo down the street.

The tension gnawed at his muscles. The pain in his head, which had been a manageable dull throb for most of the day, now felt like screws tightening into his skull. Even his gums seemed to hurt from clenching his teeth.

Thank Christ there was beer in the fridge. He slapped together a three-tiered cheese, mayonnaise and ham extravaganza, grabbed two bottles and slumped down in his threadbare armchair.

Before he turned on the TV, he could hear the boys outside his house again, circled in a game of kick-ups. The sandwich turned to glue in his throat and he cringed every time he heard the thud of the ball. Quite sincerely, he thought he would go out and beat the living shit out of one of those black boys if that ball came through his window. The pain pinched in his stomach again.

Angrily, he snatched the remote up off the floor and turned on the TV. There was no way he was going to be able to sleep now, no fucking way at all. He thumbed through the channels, hoping to catch a film that would distract him from the bag of shit his day had been. Outside, the African woman guffawed, bellowing laughter that climaxed in a high-pitched squeal. The sound cut straight through him.

He put on the news. Maybe there'd be a segment about benefit cuts or a crackdown on illegal immigrants that would brighten his mood. He twisted the cap off his first beer and killed half the bottle in one mouthful. The alcohol burned as it swished through his belly. He'd have to get that checked out at some stage; he was sure it was an ulcer.

The screen showed a grim tower block the colour of cigarette smoke, cordoned off with police tape. Bernard turned the volume up. The reporter, a pretty *white* woman with blushing cheeks and blond hair, addressed the camera:

'...and we're told an unusually high number of calls have come flooding in with information about the possible whereabouts of drug boss Craig Morley, who was abducted from this car park late last night.'

An acidic burp worked its way up Bernard's throat and he grimaced at the taste of it. Craig Morley? He knew that name, didn't he? Had he booked him in the cells before? Bernard couldn't recall. He set the beer bottle down and leaned forward, watching the TV intently.

The screen cut to a middle-aged woman with thinning hair scraped back into a ponytail. 'I don't know what he's involved in, but I will tell you this for free,' the woman began, her steely glare fixed on the interviewer behind the camera. 'I'm sick to death of all the drugs around here. We've got babies, little kids that want to play in the park, but they can't 'cos it's too dangerous. So, if he's keeping guns and god knows what else up there, then, well, you know what I say? What goes around comes around. Good. Get him off the estate so the rest of us can go about our lives in peace.'

Her impassioned monologue earned mutters of agreement from a group of Frazier Avenue residents that had gathered nearby.

Craig Morley. Why was that name so bloody familiar? Bernard picked up his phone and ran the name through Google. An ugly brute of a man appeared on the screen above numerous breaking news reports. Bernard didn't recognise him, but he definitely knew the name. Craig Morley... Craig Mo–

'*I have a friend and she's dating someone, but I have my suspicions about him. I get a weird vibe off him and I just know he's dodgy...*'

He leapt up from the chair, knocking the half-empty bottle of beer over. An electric charge pulsed through him, and in less than a heartbeat, he was flooded with sweat. He became short of breath, a bolt of panic pinning him to the spot. The room tilted ever so gently.

'Emily,' he whispered, and grimaced as claws ripped at the walls of his stomach.

Outside, a football bounced off the bonnet of his car.

Chapter Twenty-Nine

Emily had been watching the news on the laptop in the warehouse office for hours. Staring at the screen in the darkness didn't go a long way toward helping her migraine, but the fear exceeded her discomfort. It enslaved her.

The reporter had just begun touching on a conspiracy theory that was spreading through social media, detailing the possibility that Morley had staged the kidnapping to get out of his obligation to a criminal organisation, when Jack entered and interrupted.

'I think I'm going to have to do something about how he's tied up.'

'Shh,' she hissed, flapping her hand.

'What is it?' He stood next to her and watched the laptop.

'He's trending on Twitter,' Emily said. It felt like something was lodged in her throat, and her neck muscles had to work around it in order to speak. She exhaled slowly and touched the back of her hand to her forehead, which was hot and moist despite the chill in the warehouse.

'What does that mean?' Jack asked, his brow furrowing with confusion.

'It means he's all over the internet. Everybody's talking about it.'

Jack shrugged and put a hand on his lower back, wincing. 'Who cares? Tomorrow something else will happen. Someone will get stabbed or some poor kid will get his head blown off and everyone will be typing about something else.'

'Oh Jesus.' Emily cupped her hands over her forehead and peered at the screen. 'It's like it's turning into a game. There's a hashtag and everything.'

'Let me see.' He squinted at the laptop, saw the wall of messages ending in #FindMorley and shook his head. 'This doesn't mean anything. Why are you getting so stressed out about this? I can't believe people have the time to type all this shit.'

'It's picking up speed. This is how it starts. You know how many crimes get solved by these internet detectives?'

'Internet detectives? Don't make me laugh. What does that even mean?'

She thought about trying to explain it to him, detailing the lengths that some true crime fanatics would go to. Social media was just the tip of the iceberg; there were forums, clubs, gatherings. There was even a Facebook group that discussed the mystery surrounding Kate's death, although, after a year or so, the messages had fizzled out.

'I'm going home,' she said weakly.

'You can't.'

'I can't?' She turned and gave him a look full of poison. 'I can't? What do you mean, I can't?' Her voice was shrill and frayed.

He shook his head irritably. 'I didn't mean you can't leave, I just meant not right now. I need your help with something.'

'Well, that's too bad. Because I don't want anything to do with this any more.'

'Excuse me?' Jack's bushy eyebrows rose.

'You fucking heard me. I don't want anything to do with this any more. I've done my part, and that's it.'

'No.' Jack shook his head, laughing humourlessly. 'No, that's not it. There's more to do.'

'Then do it yourself. You seem to have everything else figured out anyway.'

She went to walk past him. He stepped in front of her, preventing her progress.

'Your chance to back out has been and gone. You don't get to pick and choose how much participation you have in this, not now. You're in it until the end.'

'I've done my fair share,' she said, trying to remain firm, but couldn't quite project the confidence she needed. She could feel hot blood rushing in her ears. 'You seem to forget that it was me who got him off your back in the car park. He was going to kill you and I hit him with the hammer. If it wasn't for me they'd be reporting your murder on the news instead of Morley's disappearance.'

'So?' Jack shrugged. 'This is a partnership. That's what you were supposed to do.'

'Can you move out of the way?'

'No.'

'So now I'm your prisoner too?'

He made a disgusted spitting sound and scowled. 'You're not the victim here, Emily. This isn't about you. It's about Kate, or have you forgotten that?'

She opened her mouth to say something but no words came to her. Jack rubbed his forehead and said, 'Look, he's tied up wrong down there. I need to untie him and make it so that he has some movement.'

'What on earth for?'

'Because if I don't he's going to end up soiling himself. I need him to be able to use a bucket. And besides, if he stays all cramped up like that for too much longer then he might get blood clots, you know, like how you get on aeroplanes.'

'So what? I thought you wanted him dead anyway?'

'I don't want him dead before he tells me the truth. And I don't want him sitting in his own shit and piss for days on end, because it'll make an already difficult task that much harder.'

'I don't think I have the stomach for this,' she said. 'At first, when we were just talking about it, I thought I did. I thought I was tough. But I'm not.'

'I know that now.' He sighed deeply. 'I thought you were like me. I thought you wanted to put an end to the torment.' He stepped away from the door. 'It doesn't mean you love Kate any less. I don't want you to feel guilty about that too.'

She stepped toward the door in preparation to leave, and then stopped abruptly. She thought about their twenty-first birthday, when she and Kate and a bunch of their girlfriends went out to a nightclub to celebrate. Emily had just bought a vodka and Coke, and as she was leaving the bar, some drunk girl banged into her, spilling the drink all over Emily's new blouse – a birthday present from Kate. Emily protested and found herself surrounded by a gang of girls, all screaming and shouting at her. And then suddenly Kate appeared, like a wild cat, forcing her way into the circle to Emily's side. Emily had never seen

Kate so fierce. In that instant she looked like she could have ripped the whole club apart with her bare hands. The girls sensed it too and backed down, fleeing to the dancefloor.

Then a thought occurred to her, with such certainty that it heaped a whole new helping of shame and guilt onto Emily's plate. *If it was me that had been murdered, Kate would not think twice. She would kill him.*

She would do it for me.

'What do you need me to do?' Emily asked.

'I have a nail gun downstairs. It jammed up on me earlier but I've got it working again. I just need you to keep it trained on him while I undo his ropes and then tie him up again. I'm gonna make him a leash so that he can crawl to a bucket.' He looked down at his boots and said, 'Just help me do this and then that's it. You can go home and I'll take care of everything else.'

She nodded. 'Fine.'

They began downstairs. Emily noticed that Jack was limping as he walked. Madonna was singing 'Lucky Star' when they reached the oiling room. Jack turned the volume down a touch and then fished the keys out of his pocket. He unlocked the door and opened it wide.

Morley wasn't there.

Chapter Thirty

Snatches of masking tape and a tangle of frayed ropes lay in a bundle by the pipe. To Jack it seemed like an optical illusion he couldn't quite wrap his mind around.

Jack felt in his pockets for the folding knife. It wasn't there. When had he had it last? He had cut Morley's cheek with it and then what? The doorbell rang and it was Emily, but what had he done with the knife?

He had just remembered leaving the knife on top of the boxes when Morley burst out from behind the door. He charged over the threshold and tackled Jack back into a metal shelving unit, dislodging a stack of shower radios. Pain arced through Jack's lower back. Morley brought his hand up and drove the knife toward Jack's chest. Jack caught Morley's wrist but still felt the knife tip bite into his skin. It didn't sink deep enough to cause any major damage, but it hurt enough for him to scream out. Morley swung his other fist and connected with Jack's temple. Jack's teeth clicked together and a blast of pain boomed through his skull.

Emily stood stunned, watching as Morley hurled Jack to the floor like a rag doll. Jack's body bounced and slid across the floor, the knife still sticking out of his chest. He tried to sit but Morley was already there, sweeping a foot across his face. The trance broke and Emily's head whipped around, looking for something to use as a weapon. She knew that once Morley had beaten Jack into oblivion – or killed him outright – then he would turn his attention to her. A whisper of déjà vu sang in her mind as she thought back to the car park, of how she had struck Morley with a hammer. She thought she had killed him and now look. He was like a bull raging through the stands of a bullfight. He was literally fighting for his life, and all at once she felt a hollow sickness inside of her, knowing that she would not be so lucky with him in the rematch. In the car park, they had the element of surprise; now, it was the complete opposite.

'Stop it!' she screamed. It was such a pathetic thing to say, something a child might say to her arguing parents. Jack curled up into a tight ball while Morley stomped down upon him with all his weight.

The closest thing to a weapon that she could see was the old radio. She yanked the cord out of it, cutting short the static-crackly sound of Whitney Houston's voice, and carried the radio over to Morley. She gripped the handle and swung feebly. The radio thumped into Morley's back, but did no damage. Morley did not seem surprised by her interference. He swatted her with the back of his hand, his knobbly knuckles knocking against her forehead, but the adrenaline kept her on her feet.

She had provided just enough distraction for Jack to get himself to a standing position, reeling from the culmination of blows. He yanked the knife free from his chest and lunged for Morley, but he was too battered to launch any kind of attack. Instead he lumbered into Morley, and they became entwined in a drunken dance.

Emily saw tendrils of Morley's greasy hair flapping from beneath the bandages and grabbed two fistfuls. He arched back, momentarily at her mercy. He started to regain his composure, bending his head toward the direction in which she was pulling his hair, when Jack slugged him. Morley fell back on top of Emily, pinning her to the ground. The immense weight of him was like a hydraulic press, flattening her against the concrete.

Jack pulled his arm back, ready to drive the knife straight into Morley's windpipe, or maybe puncture one of those gremlin green eyes. But at the last second, he folded the knife away, removed his belt and wrapped it around Morley's neck, rolling him off Emily. Jack crossed his arms over behind Morley's head, strangling him with the leather. Morley's arms flailed and fought for purchase, searching for something of Jack's that he could clutch, squeeze or claw, but his face quickly bloomed with colour and he passed out. Jack let go of the belt and Morley crumpled to the ground.

Jack collapsed, his back finally betraying him. He could feel the nagging ache of the knife wound, but the enormous pain in his back completely eclipsed it.

The three of them lay on the ground in a triangle.

'We'd better tie him up quickly... he won't stay quiet for long,' Jack eventually gasped.

A second later, he fainted.

When Jack regained consciousness, he heard Morley snoring. Jack's entire back and neck were numb.

'Em...' he said, wiggling his fingers, thankful that he was still able to feel them.

'I'm here,' she replied quickly.

'Can you give me a hand, please?'

She leaned over him, her face waxy and pale. 'What's wrong? Can't you stand up?'

'I think I can, but I just need you to help me.' He reached out a hand to her. She took it and heaved back, playing tug of war with his dead weight. He groaned as the numbness gave way to flaring pain. He paused for breath and then used the metal shelving unit to assist him the rest of the way. He touched the tuft of bloody stuffing poking through the hole in his body warmer and hissed.

'You're bleeding,' Emily said, blinking through her astonishment. 'He stabbed you.'

'Just a scratch,' he grunted. 'If it had been a couple of inches higher…' He didn't finish the sentence. He palmed sweat from his forehead, biting his bottom lip as his sciatic nerve screamed. He waited a few minutes until he felt confident enough to walk unassisted, and then fetched the trolley. He had the distinct feeling that the moment he bent down to load Morley onto it, his back would finally quit on him. Having no choice, he delicately crouched by Morley's head and grabbed hold of him by the armpits.

'His legs,' Jack said through fresh sheets of sweat.

Seeing him struggle, Emily used every ounce of strength she had to hoist Morley's lower half onto the trolley. Jack's face brightened to a feverish red as they picked him up, a thick vein bulging on his forehead.

Once Morley was on, Emily pulled the trolley back to the oiling room with Jack limping behind her.

'How did he get out?' she asked as Jack uncoiled more rope and went about tying Morley's wrists together again. Jack had to stop every few seconds to hiss from the pain, and as he hobbled or held his back to support it, Emily thought he looked very old.

'I made a couple of mistakes. I tied his hands in front of him with… I probably shouldn't have used masking tape. Normally it wouldn't have mattered but I left my knife on top of those boxes.' He flicked his head toward the incriminating tower of toasters. 'He must've kicked the boxes, the knife dropped and…'

'He could have got away,' Emily said, raking her fingers through her sweat-greased hair. She didn't have the strength to yell, nor could she summon the energy needed to give him the lecture he deserved. She flopped against the wall, her blood turning to treacle in her legs, weighing her down.

'I know,' Jack said in a low voice. 'It was an error on my part. It won't happen again.'

'I just can't…' She shook her head in frustration. 'Why're we even using fucking masking tape and rope? I mean…' A dull ache stretched through her ribs as she exhaled. They were probably bruised from the impact of Morley's weight. 'How badly did he stab you?'

'I'm fine,' Jack said, working at the knots.

'Maybe I should look at it.'

'He barely nicked me. I'm telling you it's nothing.'

'Jack?' He winced and looked up at her. '*Can* you do this?'

'You don't need to worry,' Jack said, looping the rope around Morley's wrists. 'He's out like a light.'

'Maybe I do need to worry,' she groaned as she breathed in. 'He nearly got away.'

'Yes,' Jack said through clenched teeth. 'I know.'

Chapter Thirty-One

It was dark and raining lightly when Emily left the warehouse. She walked through the desolate industrial estate and found her way to the train station. She stood swaying on the empty platform, struggling for a deep breath.

Her hands were shaking badly by the time she reached her doorstep and her key scratched around the lock until it slid home. She trudged upstairs, a new layer of dread enveloping her as she neared her and Roger's bedroom. She couldn't hear the sound of his laptop, which was strange, and the thought of him being asleep gave her a small pinch of relief.

When she entered the room, he was awake and sitting on the edge of the bed. She could smell the alcohol as soon as she walked in. The stink of belched Budweiser hung in the air like smog.

'You're back,' he said sloppily, without turning to face her.

'Yeah.' She kicked out of her shoes and began to undress, letting her clothes fall to the ground where she stood.

'How's Jack's mother?'

Wearily, she said, 'She died.'

'When?'

'Earlier tonight.' She got into the bed, and when she lay down on the mattress, she thought she might be all right; she felt herself sinking, deeper and deeper, and it was lovely.

'She died tonight?' he asked, looking over his shoulder at her.

'Mmm. It was sad.'

'Was it?'

'Yeah. It's been a sad night. I just want to go to sleep if that's OK, Roger?'

He remained quiet enough for her mind to drift away, and just as she neared the precipice of sleep, he said, 'You're a fucking liar.'

She hadn't heard all of what he'd said, not in the low, throaty way he was speaking. But she caught the tone and that snatched her back to reality.

'What?'

'I said, you're a fucking liar. You weren't at the hospital.'

Her eyes snapped open and she was wide awake. 'What are you talking about?'

'You're fucking him, aren't you? Just admit it. I know the truth anyway.'

'Don't be an idiot, Roger, I'm not in the mood for this.'

'How convenient.'

'I've had a dreadful evening, all right? His mum's just died and you accuse me of sleeping with him? He was my sister's husband, for god's sake.'

'Yeah, twin sister, so I bet there's a natural attraction.'

'You're drunk and you're talking shit. Go to sleep.'

The bed springs whined as he stood up. 'His mum's already dead. She died when he was a teenager. Jack's fiancée came by tonight and told me, so don't bother denying it.'

Emily pulled the quilt back and got out of the bed. Now she had no idea what was going on.

'Are you gonna deny it?' he asked, with a sour smile on his lips. 'Go on, deny it like the liar you clearly are.'

'What is all this?' she asked, not quite ready to dig herself any deeper into the hole she'd found herself in.

'I want you to stand there and look me in the eyes and tell me that you were at the hospital with Jack tonight. If you can look me in the eyes and say that, then I'll have no choice but to accept it and believe that his fiancée got her facts wrong.'

It was strange, considering she'd already woven a web of lies to protect herself, but she found that she couldn't do it. Lying to him about her whereabouts had been self-defence, a necessary evil. But he deserved better than that. Then she felt that unmistakeable tremor in the air, that same one she'd encountered so many times before in her life in varying degrees of intensity. They were going to break up.

'Fine. I lied,' she said, and the air sailed out of her lungs. She felt herself wilting beneath his wounded gaze. 'We weren't at the hospital.'

He straightened up, pinned his shoulders back. 'So, you're sleeping with him then?' he asked casually, as though her answer made no difference to him.

What alternative did she have? There was no other logical reason that she could offer Roger to explain why she was spending so much time with Jack. She was about to say that she was working for him at the warehouse, but closed her mouth again.

'Roger,' she began, his name little more than a brittle whisper. 'I have to go.'

'Go where?'

'I just… away. I'm sorry.'

'I see. Just like that? No explanation at all? Well, why would I get an explanation? You seem to keep everything so close to your chest these days.' His mouth pulled into a pout and in that instant he looked like a scared little boy. 'What have I done to deserve this?'

'Nothing,' she answered, her voice thick with grief and exhaustion. 'I just need to get away.' Her hands trembled at her sides, the anxiety riddling her body, tenderising her muscles. A helpless scream was locked behind her lips, ready to leap out at any moment.

'Without me? And there's me thinking we were going to get our own place,' he said with a derisive snort. He swallowed down a burp and shook his head disapprovingly at her, his distended belly pressing against the fabric of his stained T-shirt.

'Did you really think that? Or was it just something we told ourselves?'

Suddenly, he slapped his chest and yelled, 'I thought it! Why do you think I've been saving like a dog for all this time? Look at me! I haven't bought any clothes, I haven't gone anywhere. I've been here' – he spread his arms and stumbled, off-balance – 'I've been right here with you because I thought you loved me!'

She looked at the carpet, saw a pair of his socks that he'd peeled off and left on her side of the bed a few days ago.

'I thought so too,' she said. 'I thought we could've had our own life together, I really did, but…' *But I threw it all away*, she wanted to say. How much easier would this be if she could just explain everything to him properly? She was sick of always feeling like a horrible person, but this was the best way – the only way – to ensure he didn't get caught up in it all. Their relationship simply wasn't strong enough to endure the strain of what she was now involved in.

'I want you to get the fuck out of here,' he said, ripping open the doors of her wardrobe. He reached inside, grabbed a handful of clothes that she'd spent a large chunk of her previous weekend ironing and folding, and tossed them at her.

'Please stop that,' she said. 'I'll pack, OK? Just don't.'

'No, I can't stop. You'll need your clothes,' he said, stumbling on the words. He yanked hangers from the wardrobe and flung her dresses and blouses on the floor.

He sat with his back to the wall, his forearms resting on his knees, watching her pull the suitcase from beneath the bed. She could feel his smouldering stare and knew his bottom lip would be sticking out sulkily. It made her pack faster. She opened her drawer and removed underwear indiscriminately, stuffed it in the case and then zipped it.

'Wow, that was quick,' he mumbled. 'Did you rehearse this beforehand? Did you do a speed run?'

She pulled the suitcase off the bed. It felt as though it was still empty, but everything she'd packed would keep her covered for at least a couple of days.

Her nakedness now made her feel very uncomfortable. She picked up the clothes she had taken off less than half an hour before, and put them back on. She could smell the warehouse on the fabric, could pick up Morley's scent woven into the folds. 'I'll be back in a few days for the rest of my stuff,' she croaked, opening the bedroom door. 'I'll text you before to find a time that's convenient for you.'

She wheeled the case out onto the landing and heard him lurching across the bedroom after her. She was on the stairs when he crashed out of the bedroom.

'Wait, Emily!'

She dragged the case and it bumped down the stairs after her; she bit the inside of her cheek to keep from blubbering.

'Don't go like this,' he said, grabbing hold of the case to prevent her descending further. 'I don't get it. This morning we were in love, and now… now everything has fallen apart.'

'Just let me go, Roger.'

'No. You can't just breeze out of my…' He was trying to make some elaborate sweeping gesture but leaned forward in the process. For the second time that evening a man fell on her, but on this occasion, she had anticipated it and managed to put her hands up, letting go of the suitcase in the process. She pressed against his chest to stop him from clattering down the stairs and breaking his neck.

'I just don't know why this is happening.'

Charles came out of his room in his dressing gown and poked his head around the stairs. 'Everything all right, guys?'

'Yes,' Emily said.

'No,' Roger said.

Emily picked up her suitcase from where it had dropped and continued down the stairs. She opened the front door, the cold night air blowing in her face. Roger's hand closed the door before she stepped out.

'Just wait a second,' Roger said quietly, his breath bitter and warm. His hand remained pressed against the door, preventing her from opening it. 'Just tell me. Tell me what this is all about. If something's wrong, I can help you fix it.'

'No,' she sighed wearily, the weight of all the evening's emotion pushing down on her shoulders. 'I don't think you can. It's better this way. Just trust me.'

His head tipped to the side, bumping the door. 'Just… I don't know. We had so much planned.' The sulky expression morphed, became vengeful. 'You fucking time-waster. You've wasted…' He closed his eyes, tried to calculate the duration of their relationship. 'You've wasted everything.'

She shouldered past him, the suitcase now weighing heavy as a boulder as she clanked it onto the porch.

'I fucking hate you,' he said, and slammed the door behind her.

–

The Uber arrived and the driver took her to the hotel without any small talk, which was just as well. She spent the entire journey crying into her hands.

She spoke to the hotel clerk, booked the cheapest thing available, and headed straight to her room.

When she was in bed, she reached down into her jeans pocket and removed her phone to make sure her alarm was off. She didn't want anything waking her up in the morning. She wanted to sleep forever. She squinted at the glow of the screen in the darkness and saw four missed calls. Three of them were from Roger. One of them was from a number she didn't recognise.

She scrolled through her call log and saw that she had called the number before. She thought for a moment and then realised it was when she was trying to get in touch with Bernard, to take him out for coffee and probe him for information about Morley.

Bernard had also sent her a text message. It read:

'I think you and I need to have a little chat about your friend… call me.'

Chapter Thirty-Two

When he had finished tying up Morley, making a noose for his neck that would keep him tethered to the pipe but allow him two feet of slack, Jack crumpled in a heap just outside the oiling room. Jagged teeth gnawed at his tailbone and the surrounding muscles felt like coils of razor wire. He lay there for a very long time, fresh sweat breaking out of his pores and soaking through his clothes. His right thigh was cold and numb all the way down to his kneecap.

Whenever he tried to shift his weight in an effort to stand up, new and vibrant messages of pain blossomed through his body, and the warehouse lights dimmed before his eyes. He could not believe that his brain was still allowing him to process this much pain without shutting down. There were several times when he thought he was going to black out and he actually looked forward to it.

It felt like hours later when he finally rolled onto his side, panting, with perspiration dripping from his hair. A helicopter propeller of pain whirred angrily in his head as he pressed his clammy palms against the floor and tried to push himself up. Like a grotesque parody of the evolution of man, he struggled to a kneeling position and then, much later and with the help of the oiling room door handle, got to his feet. This triumph was not without its indignity; the effort pinched his bladder and he urinated in his jeans. He didn't care. Pissing himself was a small price to pay considering he was back on his feet.

He made it to the stairs and clutched the metal banister as though it were a piece of driftwood that had just saved him from drowning. He pillowed his head on his forearm and spat on the floor.

'FUCKING BASTARD, LET ME OUT!' The groggy voice travelled out of the oiling room. Jack could hardly believe it. They'd hammered Morley's skull, punched him and choked him unconscious with a belt, and he still had the energy to yell like that. Tough bastard. Jack didn't even have the strength to tell him to shut his trap.

Jack looked up the stairs. There was a bottle of Bells whisky in the kitchen and he wanted it badly, especially now that the pills were wearing off. But the stairs scared him. He visualised the ascent, thinking about the shift in weight as he pressed his foot down and raised another, an act he had taken for granted all his life. Now the action was a calculated risk. He could imagine the muscles in his back stretching and snapping, and his legs giving way beneath him.

He leaned all his weight on the banister and negotiated the stairs slowly and steadily. A swarm of black dots floated in his vision, and he felt the gentle tug of unconsciousness pulling at him.

He wanted to stop and take a break but knew there was no chance he'd be able to sit down on these stairs. The only choice he had was to forge ahead. He thought about Morley and the smug, condescending way the man had spoken to him. He had no fear, no remorse, no *soul*. Jack didn't know if there was anything he could do to get the truth out of him. He didn't think Morley would confess even if Jack tortured him. Jack could pull the man's teeth and fingernails out and Morley would probably laugh at him, the same way he had laughed when he got in the back of that car.

The first note of defeat began to resonate within him. He wasn't built for this kind of thing any more; his back just wasn't up to it. Morley had had the better of him twice now. Were it not for Emily's help, Jack would be dead, no doubt about it. How could he have been so stupid as to leave his knife in the room? It was those kinds of mistakes that reaffirmed what he already knew: he couldn't keep this ship sailing for much longer. It might be better to just kill Morley right now.

But first, he would have a drink. He got to the top of the stairs and walked, hunchbacked, to the kitchen. He uncapped the whisky and drank deeply, ignoring the burn.

Two large squares of damp foam leaned against the wall, presumably the insides of sofa cushions in their former life. He dropped them on the floor and went about trying to lie down.

–

Colin saw the woman on the security camera and released an exasperated sigh. 'Christ, not again.'

'What is it?' Amanda asked, looking up from her laptop.

The buzzer droned through the warehouse again.

'You ever met Jack's missus?'

Amanda pushed her glasses up the bridge of her nose and shook her head. The buzzer went off again in three short angry bursts. 'Well, are you going to answer it?'

'She's a nightmare,' Colin said. 'Can you talk to her?'

'Me? I've got nothing to do with deliveries.'

'She's not here for—' He paused as the buzzer went off again. 'She's here for Jack.'

'Well, Jack's not here and I've got invoices to chase. I'm snowed under.'

'Please. I'd do it for you. Come on, please. I'm busy too.' He gestured to the pallet of boxes. 'I'm a day late with some of this. I'll get you a sticky bun tomorrow?'

The buzzer went off again. 'What's the matter with her?' Amanda said irritably, rising from the desk, peering across the room at the security screen.

Colin began jogging to the back of the warehouse. 'Answer it. If she asks, I'm not here.'

'You owe me more than a bloody sticky bun,' she said, making her way to the door. When she opened it, the woman flinched back, surprised.

'Who are you?' May asked.

'I'm Amanda. I work in accounts. How can I help you?'

'I need to see Jack. I'm his fiancée.'

Amanda feigned surprise. 'Oh, sorry. Jack's not here.'

'Yes, I know. Where's that other boy, the blond one?'

'Colin?' Amanda shrugged. 'I think he's with a client at the minute.'

May's eyes narrowed, her tongue probing the inside of her cheek. 'Really? Well, I was wondering if you could let me know when Jack is due in.'

'I don't know, he didn't say.'

'So he just dropped everything and took off without any word about when he might be back?'

'Well, he's the boss,' Amanda said, as politely as she could. 'He doesn't really need to tell us anything.'

'What about the boy? He would know, wouldn't he?'

'I don't think so.'

'Yes, he would,' May said matter-of-factly. She didn't like this girl. She was pretty, probably had her pick of the boys. An accountant? So she was smart and pretty and a bitch. Funny, May couldn't recall Jack ever mentioning her. But she forced a smile, knowing you caught more flies with honey than you did with vinegar, and said, 'Do you have an idea of any big orders he would have to oversee? He had something going on with that German wholesaler, didn't he?'

'I really don't know,' Amanda said.

'Does he have a diary here?'

'Not that I know of.'

'All right.' May shrugged. 'I'll just come in and wait for him. I'm sure he'll be coming by at some point, won't he?'

She went to step inside when Amanda said, 'He could be in Cheshunt. Have you tried there?'

'Cheshunt? What's in Cheshunt?'

Amanda frowned. 'Um, the new warehouse. He's been taking the stock over there, ready for the merger.'

'Merger? What are you talking about?'

'Strident was bought out by Greco Kitchens. We'll be operating out of the new warehouse in April, so he's been trying to get that ready.'

A smile slid across May's face. 'I couldn't trouble you for the address and number, could I?'

Jack could hear Morley scratching around in the oiling room before he opened the door. It reminded Jack of a time when Kate thought they had rats in the walls, and she would wake him up at three every morning, saying, 'There it is, listen. You hear it?' Turned out that it wasn't rats at all, but a single mouse, which he caught a few days later with a glue trap. He had wanted to stomp on the trap to make sure the mouse wouldn't come back, but Kate forbade it. 'Can't you just take it to the park and release it?'

'Maybe I can buy a leash and take it for a walk while I'm at it,' he'd said, before taking it into the back garden and crushing it underfoot.

Morley was bent over on his knees with his hands tied behind his back. It looked like he was praying to Jack as he entered.

'You'd better fucking kill me,' Morley said, the veins in his forehead like fat worms feeding. 'If I get out of here again, I'm going to...'

'You're going to what?'

'I'm going to skin you alive. You think I'm lying, don't you? Oh, you'd better believe me. I'm going to skin you alive and then I'm going to piss on your body.'

'Really? That another one of your little raps?' Jack said disinterestedly and threw a bucket at him. It hit Morley's head and bounced off a nearby box. 'That's for you to go to the toilet.'

'Toilet? You fucking stupid cunt. How am I supposed to get my trousers down with my hands tied behind my back?'

'That's your problem. I would have kept them tied up the way they were if you hadn't tried to escape.'

'You'd better kill me...'

'I'm not going to do anything until you tell me why you murdered my wife.'

Morley's eyes shone in the shade like two emeralds reflecting the sun at the bottom of a well. 'Look, that song was just some dumb shit. I made a hundred tracks like that, just dicking around in my friend's room. Your wife – that has nothing to do with me. Why won't you believe that I didn't kill her?'

'Because I saw you on that day. July eighth, 2007, you came knocking,' Jack said, leaning one hand on the workbench for support. A few hours' sleep had helped mend some of the niggles, but the main points of pain still throbbed and held his every movement hostage. 'I can keep going in circles until you get bored, or hungry, or thirsty, and then you can tell me. Or we can just speed this whole thing up.'

Morley scooted awkwardly back against the pipe. 'You want me to be honest with you, don't you?'

'I'll be able to tell either way. But of course, it'd be better for everyone if you just gave it to me straight.'

'All right.' Morley nodded in a resigned way that suggested defeat. 'Here's the truth. You know that you've never seen me before in your life, and you know I didn't kill your wife. You also know that you've taken this too far, and the only way you can make sense of your mistake is by forcing a confession out of me.'

'So, we're back to this, are we?'

'Fine. I killed your wife. There's your confession.'

'I already know you did it,' Jack said monotonically. 'I want to know *why*.'

Morley pressed his cheek to the floor and giggled. The giggle graduated into gales of laughter. 'Can I…?' He choked out more laughter, and then continued. 'Can I tell you something?'

'By all means,' Jack replied stoically. 'But if it's more bullshit, you're better off saving your breath. Because I'm not giving you a crumb of food or a drop of water until you tell me why.'

Morley smiled through a bloody lip. The threat didn't mean a thing to him.

'Earlier you asked me who I am,' Morley said. 'You're so interested in me? Well, how about some trivia?' He cleared his throat. 'My older brother was a deeply paranoid schizophrenic. I was always frightened of him. He had a bad temper, would just explode at something and you wouldn't even know what was happening. But that wasn't really what scared me about him. It was the other stuff he did. Like he wouldn't sleep in a bed, he would sleep under it, or in the wardrobe. And then one day I came back from school and he had blacked out all our windows with shoe polish because he thought there was a witch that lived in the building across from us.

'I remember this night when he ran into the living room completely naked, screaming that he had bugs under his skin. My mum had to tell him, "No, Maurice, you haven't got any bugs under your skin, calm down." But he couldn't be told. So he'd start clawing at his skin, biting it. I watched him bite right through the back of his hand like a dog or something… blood everywhere. But that only made him go even crazier because now he'd let all the bugs out and they were crawling over everything.'

'I don't want to know about your brother, Craig. So stop with the sob story.'

Craig's eyes rolled toward him. 'Let me finish!'

Jack shifted his weight and leaned against the far wall. He was sure that he could feel a bulge in his lower back and wondered if a disc had ruptured.

'I couldn't understand how he could go about like that, worrying about everything, thinking up all these mad conspiracies. He just wouldn't stop. The doctors put him on medication, and that sort of helped, but he still did weird things.

'When I was about thirteen, I pulled back the covers to get into bed one night, and he'd put all the knives from the kitchen on my mattress and under my pillow. He said, "Craig, you need to hide these because otherwise someone might break in and try to kill me." About a week after that he slit his wrists and bled to death.

'The reason I'm telling you all this is because I know madness. Whatever you want to think of me, you know – I'm a bastard, a piece of shit, all the rest of it – understand this also: I know the darkness. I'm not talking about crime or things that go on in the streets. I'm talking about real darkness that closes in on you every second of every day. And you' – he inclined his chin toward Jack – 'you have that same look about you that my brother had. There's nothing behind your eyes. So I could sit here and tell you that I didn't kill your wife. Or I could tell you that I did kill your wife, and I did it just for fun. But none of it is going to satisfy you, is it? Because once you break through that wound, the bugs will come out.'

Jack eased himself down and sat on one of the boxes. 'Are you finished?'

Morley yawned and split his lower lip wider. 'If I told you I killed your wife because she embarrassed me in front of my friends, would that work for you?'

Jack stiffened. A small, sharp breath escaped him. 'What did you just say?'

'What if your wife was walking down the road and I was acting up, showing off in front of some girls, maybe trying to get a bit frisky with one, and your wife tried to tell me off. And maybe I didn't like being embarrassed, so the next day I knocked on your door and stabbed her.'

'Is that what happened?' Jack roared and got to his feet, ignoring the distress flares shooting up his spine. 'Is that why you did it?'

'Or,' Morley began, his voice smooth and calm, unruffled by Jack's temper, 'let's say I knocked on your door and killed your wife as an initiation.'

'Wh-what?' The panic and confusion pulled Jack's face into a dumb, slack mask. 'What do you mean, "an initiation"?'

'Like a gang initiation. You've seen that on TV, haven't you? These gangs, they get kids to join by maiming someone, or killing them.'

'What gang?' Jack asked desperately, raking his fingers through his hair. He straightened up, took a deep breath and swallowed painfully. 'Craig, tell me the name of the gang. I want the leader's name.'

Morley looked to the ceiling and clicked his tongue, mulling over his thoughts. 'Or, maybe the twin sister, the woman that was with you before, maybe she was in love with you. And maybe she was jealous of your wife and she wanted her dead. So she paid some little piece of shit with no morals to knock on your door and stab your wife. There it is, job done.'

'No.' Jack shook his head. 'No, she wouldn't.'

'Maybe it was one of those things and maybe it was none of those things. But I can't tell you because I had nothing to do with it.' He spoke firmly, making direct eye contact with Jack. 'I want you to listen to me, Jack, and I want you to really think about this.' He watched as Jack started panting like a dog. 'Jack, by now you have some idea of who I am. But what you probably don't know is what I can do. The police didn't catch your wife's murderer, and do you wanna know why?'

Jack opened his mouth to say yes, but then clamped it shut stubbornly. He did not want Morley to be the one granting *him* favours.

'Some boy stabs your wife all these years ago and there are probably a dozen people that know he did it. But they're not talking, especially not to the police. Nobody gives a fuck about your wife, so why should they go to the police and get themselves in trouble for something that doesn't have anything to do with them?' Jack stood there, chest heaving, his eyes like loose ball bearings rolling around in their sockets. 'That same handful of people that know the boy that killed your wife are still out there. One or two of them might've moved on, but the rest will still be in the same streets, doing the same shit, going to the same nightclubs and bars.

'Jack, I need you to really concentrate on what I'm about to say to you.' He scooted forward as much as the rope would permit. 'You might not believe it, but I have a lot of influence out there. I'm not just some little wannabe

214

hustler. If you let me go now, I'll round up the people who know the boy that killed your wife. I'll have his name within a week, and I'll have him caught three days after that. I'll catch him for you, Jack.'

Jack frowned, his eyes skittering back and forth rapidly.

'If I… if I let you go, you'll kill me,' Jack said absently. He was standing not six inches from Morley and yet seemed very far away. 'You won't let me live after all this.'

'You've done me wrong, and you do deserve some payback. I'm not going to try and butter you up. I'm very fucking angry with you, but, given your situation and the fact that apart from splitting my fucking head open, you haven't treated me too badly, I'm willing to be reasonable. Now, I'm not going to let you off the hook entirely. If you let me go and I catch the bastard that murdered… what was her name again?'

'*Kate*,' Jack said softly, and then exhaled, making a thin, whining sound.

'Kate. If I do you this favour and catch him for you, then you'll need to do me a favour in return. That way, I don't have to think about coming back to hurt you, I can just chalk this up to a big misunderstanding.' When Jack didn't respond, Morley continued. 'She didn't deserve what happened to her. Nobody deserves to be murdered without any good reason. Trust me, Jack, getting this fucker would be like a good deed for me. But we have to sweep all this shit under the carpet.'

Jack nodded. 'She was beautiful,' he said thickly, as though the words had fought their way up from the base of his stomach. 'We loved each other so much. It wasn't fair. None of this is fair.'

'Of course it isn't,' Morley said, getting to his knees. He looked like a dog begging for a treat. 'I don't know how you managed to keep yourself together for all these years. If someone killed the mother of my kids, I'd…'

'She was pregnant,' Jack said, pressing his fists against his forehead. A cry escaped his lips and he struggled to get his breathing back on course. 'It wasn't supposed to be like this.'

'Oh Christ, that's awful,' Morley said, shaking his head. 'Oh Jesus Christ, that's just… what a monster. What a fucking evil monster. Jack, look at me, mate.' It took a long time for Jack to look through his fingers at Morley. 'Let me help you. Let me catch him.'

They stared at each other in silence for a long time.

'I need a cup of tea,' Jack said. He walked to the oiling room door then turned and said, 'Do you want a cup of tea?'

'Tea?' Morley faltered for a second. 'Yeah. Sure. Why not?'

'How do you take it?'

'Milk, three sugars.'

'Three sugars,' Jack laughed lightly. 'It's a wonder you have any teeth left.'

'I know,' Morley smiled. 'I've got a mouthful of fillings.'

Jack nodded and walked off.

–

Morley angled his ear toward the door and listened to Jack's progress through the warehouse. He heard the slow, thudding footfall up the stairs. It seemed to take him forever to climb them. Then Morley's eyes rolled to the ceiling as he heard Jack directly above him. He exhaled and it felt like every breath he'd ever taken came out at once. The relief was almost orgasmic, and far greater than that he had felt when he finally managed to saw through the ropes. He'd done it; he'd cracked the bastard, had him making cups of tea for him. With the relief came an almost delicious sense of pride. He had been worried that this mad man would actually kill him, but Morley had outsmarted him at his own game. He'd won.

Not quite. He still had to get him to untie this rope, and once he did, Morley would snap his neck. He'd seen it done in plenty of films and thought himself more than capable of the task. He'd let Jack cut the rope off his wrists and then, as he was undoing the rope around his feet, he'd reach forward, clasp Jack's head between his hands, and twist as hard as he could.

He was sure that he would be free soon, and that knowledge went a long way toward soothing the dread that had slowly been building inside him. He could feel the anxiety fading, his muscles uncoiling. His heartbeat went back to a steady, healthy drumming as opposed to the constant sledgehammering he'd felt since the car park.

The conundrum he had found himself in had kept his mind occupied. Now that he had solved this particular riddle, he found that he had freed up the mental bandwidth to focus on the pain. His skull sang in a dull, endless choir that blurred his vision. He wondered if that hammer had broken up the plates in his head, and whether there were any bone chips stabbing into his brain. Wouldn't that be just his luck? He'd escape from this warehouse, take two steps outside and then die of a brain haemorrhage.

He had sweated so feverishly that he was dehydrated, his tongue rough and dry, his throat coated in sandpaper.

Maybe he wouldn't twist Jack's head off straight away. Maybe he'd have that cup of tea first.

The clanging on the stairs distracted him. It wouldn't be long now. His toes curled in anticipation and he felt a tingle of excitement in his groin that made him shudder. Was he getting an erection at the thought of freedom? Yes, he thought he was.

Jack opened the oiling room door holding the steaming kettle. He did not have any cups.

'You thought you could confuse me, didn't you?'

'What's going on?' Morley watched ribbons of steam coiling out from the spout of the kettle.

Without another word, Jack walked over to Morley and poured the hot water over his head.

The screams that left Morley's mouth as his skin blistered did not sound human. It reminded Jack of the awful, hideous shrieking of the foxes that fought in his garden in the middle of the night. Morley's guttural screams made his voice change octaves until his throat seized up and would no longer permit sound. He writhed and rolled on the floor, strangling himself with the rope, his face a painting of abject terror. He made one last piping noise, a whistle almost, and then trembled.

When he passed out, Jack smiled.

Chapter Thirty-Three

Emily had never been to a restaurant so fancy in her entire life. Perhaps it was because she had never had a partner that thought her worth the expense. As she sat down at the table, enveloped in the dreamy piano music, she couldn't help but laugh to herself at the irony. She had always wanted to go somewhere like this, but now that she was here she had absolutely no appetite. She didn't think that she would be able to keep a starter down, even the pretentiously small morsels she'd seen the woman at the neighbouring table eat.

She felt woefully underdressed in her jeans and scoop neck top, but consoled herself with the idea that people might think she was too hip to make such an effort. In her current state, she could pass for a stressed-out journalist, or maybe some kind of fringe celebrity that wanted to let their hair down. But when Bernard arrived in an expensive-looking suit, she felt less like a celebrity and more like some kind of cheap escort he'd picked up at a gritty bus station.

A waiter made a beeline for the table and asked in a French accent too thick to be natural if Bernard wanted a drink. Bernard picked up the wine menu, scanned it briefly, and ordered a bottle of Châteauneuf-du-Pape.

'You look lovely,' he said to Emily, unfolding his napkin and placing it in his lap.

She couldn't tell if he was needling her or not. 'So do you. That's a nice suit.'

'Armani,' he said with a shrug to indicate that it was no big deal. 'Have I kept you waiting long?'

It was close to two in the afternoon. He'd told her to meet him at one.

'No, it's fine.'

'Have you ordered any food?'

'No, I don't think I'm going to eat.'

'Yes you are,' he said, looking over the food menu. 'We're going to have lunch and enjoy ourselves. That's the reason we're here.'

She said nothing. The waiter returned with the wine and poured a drop for Bernard to taste. He savoured it, and nodded for the waiter to continue pouring.

'Madam?' The waiter angled the bottle over her glass.

'Thanks,' she said, and the waiter filled her up.

When they were alone again, Bernard said, 'How about a toast?'

'Sure,' she said wearily and held up her glass.

'How about we toast to new beginnings?'

She nodded and clinked his glass, then gulped the wine. She couldn't tell if it cost ten pounds or two grand.

'So what did you want to talk about?' she asked.

'Let's eat first, enjoy ourselves.'

'What's the big mystery?'

His eyebrows rose. 'I was hoping you could tell me.'

'Bernard, I don't know what you're getting at, but this isn't cute, what you're doing.'

'I see.' He put his glass down. 'You just want to dive right in, do you? Well, I can see why. You've already sort of admitted guilt by meeting me, haven't you?'

'What on earth are you talking about?'

'Let's face it. You wouldn't have agreed to meet me if I didn't have a carrot dangling over your nose now, would you?'

'I invited you for coffee the other day, didn't I?'

'Oh yes, coffee. And let's not forget the bored and disinterested way you sat there, staring at your phone, gulping down the coffee quickly to hurry the process up. All you wanted was information about' – he paused and gave her a grin dominated by his front two teeth – 'you-know-who. Which brings us on to the next point of business, doesn't it?'

The waiter returned with a smile. 'Would we like to order food now?'

'Yes, please,' Bernard said, happy as a pig in shit. 'I'd like to have the steak, rare, and my friend here will have the cassoulet.'

'Ah, very nice,' the waiter replied, without jotting the order down. 'Any appetiser for you?'

'No.' He looked over at Emily. 'We'd like to get right down to it, please.'

'Absolutely.'

The waiter left with the menus.

Emily said, 'So you saw Craig Morley all over the news. I told you he was a nasty piece of work, didn't I?'

'Yes, you did. What was it you said again? Your friend was seeing him. I'm assuming this is the same friend that filed the police report?'

'No.' Emily shook her head. 'He was cheating on her, obviously.' She looked down at her lap, wringing the napkin in her hands. 'I'm just happy this came out now, before my friend got too involved with him.'

Bernard nodded, unable to shake the grin. 'I just found it all very strange; didn't you?'

'Well, yeah, of course...'

'You come to me wanting details about you-know-who,' he said, blurting over her, 'and a couple of days later he's the biggest story in the country. Have the police questioned your friend?' He had an arrogant, knowing look about him that made her want to throw her wine in his stupid face.

'I don't know.'

'Well, surely you spoke to her? After all, you were so concerned about her well-being before. I took that to mean you were really good friends.'

'Frankly, Bernard, I don't think it's any of your business.'

'I'm afraid I'd have to disagree. You've made it my business.'

'How?'

He lifted his glass, swirled the wine, and sipped. 'Did you see the news last night?'

'No.' She had actively been avoiding it. It was childish but she didn't want to face up to her involvement. The less she knew about the escalation, the quicker she could forget the whole thing.

'I don't know. I just find it all a little bit... convenient. You come to me asking about Craig Morley, and then someone gives a description of a man and a woman' – he made the slightest gesture toward her with his hand

– 'kidnapping him. Then everybody wants to find Mr Morley. That puts me in a strange predicament, doesn't it?'

'I don't see how.'

'Because, indirectly I suppose, I have something to offer this case. The ethical thing to do would be to talk to my sergeant and tell him that you came to me asking about Mr Morley.'

'You could do that,' she said, pouring more wine into her glass, 'but then you'd have to admit that you breached data protection. Then you'd lose your job, wouldn't you?'

'I'd say that it came out in passing conversation, a momentary slip of the tongue. I'd get a slap on the wrists. But of course, if I said that you might be a person of interest in this case...'

'A person of interest?' She laughed. 'Why? I asked you to check his record out because I was scared for my friend's life. That's it.'

'That may be true. But the police would probably want to question you anyway. And you never know' – he shrugged, feigning innocence – 'you might have information that could really help the investigation. Sometimes it's the smallest things that make a difference. If you're worried about any possible ramifications of you snitching, I can assure you whatever you say would be purely confidential.'

She looked away from him and saw a handsome man and an elegant woman enjoying what appeared to be their first date.

'Yeah, right. I'm sure that there'd be no way of people finding out I gave a statement, same way there should be no way of finding out Craig Morley's arrest history.'

Bernard's mouth turned down at the corners, his buck teeth resting on his lower lip. His eyes gleamed slyly.

'You could help put a very dangerous man behind bars with your information.'

'I'm not talking to any police, Bernard.'

'I thought you'd say that.' He leaned forward. Emily flinched back. 'But you know what? I am going to talk to the police, because now I know you're hiding something.'

The uneasiness stirred inside her as though he had woken some dormant sickness. She did her best to appear indifferent with a shrug and a shake of the head. 'Bernard, what is it you think I've done?'

'I have a theory,' he said nonchalantly. 'Would you like to hear it?'

'I'm sure it's fascinating.'

He gulped the last mouthful of wine from his glass and then dabbed his lips with his napkin. 'I think that you were the one that was seeing Craig Morley, not this imaginary friend of yours.' He paused, pleased with himself, and added, 'Would you like another bit of insider info? They haven't made this public yet, but the girl who made the call about the kidnapping was only fifteen years old. That's why they can't identify her.' He covered his mouth and chuckled as though he'd just delivered the punchline to a joke. 'That must sting a little bit. He was fucking a schoolgirl, not even of legal age.'

'Like you said, I had my doubts about him.' She pushed her chair back. 'Go to the police if you want. I don't really care. Tell them that you think I was sleeping with Craig Morley and I'll deny it. I've never even met him.' She stood up and watched his face sour. 'Enjoy your lunch.'

'I wasn't planning on telling them that you were sleeping with him,' he said. 'I was going to tell them that you know who kidnapped him.'

'Good luck with that.'

'You think I'm bluffing, don't you?' He stared at her and then pointed to her seat. 'Sit down.'

Her eyes fixed on the exit, desperate to be away from him, to be outside in the cool air.

'Sit down, Emily.'

Reluctantly she obeyed his command, but continued to regard the exit like a missed opportunity.

'Here's what I'm going to do,' he began. 'I'll go to my sergeant on my night shift tonight and ask if I can have a word with him. Then I'll say that a friend of mine – namely you – had been seeing Craig Morley as recently as a week ago. I'll also add that in our little date today, you gave me reason to believe you know who took him.'

'But I don't,' she hissed.

'Maybe you don't, but it'll still be enough for them to interview you. And believe me, with the heat that Morley's got on him at the moment, they will put every aspect of your life under the microscope. They'll grill you so intensely that if you *do* have something to hide, they'll get it out of you, trust me on that.'

'They can do what they want because I don't have anything to hide.' She tried to make the statement sound concrete, but the words sounded shaky when she delivered them.

'That may be true, and if the police don't find anything, then maybe the newspapers will.'

There it was. Checkmate. He leaned back in the chair, satisfied with his work.

'It's the hottest story of the year so far,' he said. 'I'd bet people are phoning in their stories right now, everybody from Craig Morley's primary school teachers to his barber to the newsagent he gets his milk from. Now imagine a nice juicy story about the "other" woman in his life, someone who could offer some intimate insight into what it's like to fuck a high-profile heroin dealer.'

A waitress came to the table and presented their food. 'Oh, this looks delicious,' Bernard said, and immediately cut into his steak. Bloody juice ran out of the meat and filled his plate, turning Emily's stomach.

Her eyes drifted down to her cassoulet. It might as well have been a bowl of vomit. She felt an oncoming avalanche of self-pity threatening to descend. How had her life become such a mess in such a short amount of time? Perhaps it was better to let him go to the police, she thought. Maybe it would be better to just own up to what she had done and face the consequences.

You'd go to jail for a very long time. They'd make an example out of you.

Would that be such a bad thing? She didn't have anywhere to live, she no longer had a job or a boyfriend, or a future. What *did* she have? The memory of her dead sister that visited her in gruesome nightmares?

'Why would you want to do that to me, Bernard?' she asked as he emphatically chewed his steak. 'You're talking about ruining my life. Why would you want to do it?'

'I don't *want* to do it,' he said, in an obvious attempt at sincerity, a shred of beef between his two front teeth. 'But let's face it. If I can help end these awful events, then surely it's my duty. I mean, I can't have something like this on my conscience, can I? Unless…' He trailed off and resumed work on the steak.

'Unless?'

'We work something out. You and I.'

'Work something out,' she repeated slowly, as though he had spoken in some foreign tongue. 'What did you have in mind?'

'I think you know the answer to that already.' He continued to eat as he spoke, dipping the steak in the peppercorn sauce. 'You and me, one night. If you treated me nicely I'm sure I'd forget this whole thing.'

She had never felt such revulsion in her entire life. Even Morley didn't disgust her as much as Bernard did right now.

'You want me to sleep with you?' She almost gagged on the sentence.

'No, I want to *fuck* you.' His features hardened, and his eyes blazed darkly. His lips curled back over his plaque-lined teeth. 'You walk around thinking that you're something special, that you can just play with people, lead them on, *manipulate* them. I know your type, Emily, you're nothing but a user. But maybe if I fucked you like an animal, treated you like a filthy whore, you'd know what it is to really feel used by someone.' He looked away from her, his mouth tightening into a line, his knuckles whitening as his hands clenched the cutlery.

She could not quite believe that she was still sitting there, listening to such a lurid proposition. But it was too late now, she'd played this whole thing wrong. She should never have even agreed to come to lunch, let alone listen to his disgusting fantasy, and yet she had blundered right into his hands.

'And you expect me to go along with this, do you?'

'If you want to avoid going to prison until you're old enough to ride the bus for free, then yes, I do.'

'How do I know you'd keep your word?'

'Don't you trust me?' he asked, suddenly amiable, pouring more wine, topping her up. 'I could put it in writing, a contract signed by both of us. That way, if I went to the papers or spoke to the police, you could show that I... well, blackmailed is quite a strong word, but for lack of a better one, you could say that I blackmailed you. That'd be my career over and I'd be open to just as much media scrutiny as you. Then again, if you tried to go to the police after the act, you'd be implicating yourself in the crime by showing them the contract.'

Frustration and resentment stole her voice. She opened her lips to speak but could not find any words that would adequately portray how she felt. Bernard saw her struggling and decided to help her out.

'Don't give me an answer now,' he said, wiping his mouth with the napkin and rising from the table. 'You can let me know by tomorrow evening. Oh, and by the way' – he signalled to the waiter and pointed down at their table, before looking back to Emily – 'thanks for lunch.'

Chapter Thirty-Four

Dillon couldn't remember the last time he'd slept. He had endured the marathon by knuckling cocaine into his nose. He had two twisted knots of tissue wedged into his nostrils to stem the bleeding, and his face was so numb it felt like his skin had turned to cotton wool. He didn't care. He just had to keep moving in the hope that inspiration would strike again, because right now he was all out of ideas.

The night wrapped around the car in a blur of lights. He was so wired that he was losing basic motor functions, cranking the gears and burning the clutch. He'd thrashed the arse off the car and now it was almost toast. It had been running on fumes for the last hour or so. (Was it an hour? It felt longer and shorter at the same time, not that he had any concept of time any more. All he knew were the lights.) The engine was starting to complain. He burned through a red light, narrowly escaped a collision with an oncoming car, and took a right turn so violently that he thought his car might tip over. Tara screamed, both hands pressed against the dashboard, begging him to slow down. The tyres screeched and the car began to swerve. He wrestled the wheel in an effort to stop the car from fishtailing, and floored the accelerator.

In his rear-view mirror, he thought he saw an ocean of flashing blue lights. He weaved down the carriageway, zipping dangerously close to the other cars as he changed lanes. When he checked the rear-view mirror again, there were no blue lights at all. *Paranoid, you're being paranoid.* He knew this, and yet couldn't shake the feeling that there were plain-clothes police officers in all the cars along the motorway. He remembered Craig's words of wisdom just then like a fleeting déjà vu – *Just because you're paranoid it doesn't mean they're not out to get you, dummy.*

'I know, I know,' he said aloud before cranking the gears and threading through a narrow gap between the middle and far right lane.

'Wh–what?' Tara asked, her face the colour of curdled milk. He had smacked her a few times earlier, and now her upper lip looked like a leech, bloated on blood.

'We're going to find them,' he rasped, the inside of his nose itching like crazy. 'We're going to find who took him and you're going to point them out.'

He saw the sign for the exit about a mile up the stretch and a spark jumped inside him; it was not quite relief, nor was it a reprieve from the madness he had endured since all this began. His hands were slippery on the wheel and his feet danced across the pedals with a leaden heaviness.

He had been all over the city in search of Craig, dragging Tara into just about every drug den he knew. Reality melted and dissolved, leaving only a warped mirage of places and things he barely recognised.

Tara had complained that she was hungry, but when he bought her a Snickers bar, she moaned that she couldn't eat it, mumbling something about a broken tooth. She whined about needing the toilet, and when he refused to pull over anywhere, she eventually wet herself, crying into her hands. *Let her sit in it*, he thought. *If I have to wade through all this shit, she can sit in a bit of piss.*

Dillon knew of only one woman that moved in the same circles as he and Craig. In East London was Bertha, a heavyset Jamaican with an accent so thick he only ever managed to decipher about one in every ten words she said. She moved 'hard food' – crack cocaine mostly, but occasionally heroin. Dillon relayed this to Tara, more to get things straight in his own head than for her benefit.

'The woman I saw take Jerome... *Craig*, wasn't black,' Tara said, as Dillon dragged her up to Bertha's front door. The stink of urine was very obvious; it had settled into her clothes throughout the course of the journey.

Bertha came to the door wearing a bright red velour tracksuit. She was scowling at the unannounced house visit, her hard features accentuated by a deep scar that ran from the corner of her eye down to her chin.

Dillon began by apologising, before asking whether she knew anything about the pair that took Craig. Was she aware of any white woman with dark hair that might have been looking to go into business for herself?

In an angry burst of patois, Bertha explained that she didn't know anything about it, and said something about Dillon moving away from her front yard before she lost her temper, or at least that's what he took from the exchange. She slammed the door in their faces, and he had better sense than to knock again, especially without any backup. She wasn't as dumb as Craig to keep any guns or drugs where she lived, but that didn't mean she wouldn't grab a machete and try and take his head off.

He was running out of options as he marched Tara back to the car, shoving her inside before climbing into the driver's side and roaring off. Where else could he go?

'Please, I just want to go home,' Tara croaked miserably. Her mouth had pulled down into an inverted horseshoe, and her voice had taken on a childish timbre. 'Please, I won't say anything to anyone, I j-j-just—' She broke off, choking on her sobs.

'Just shut up!' he yelled. 'Real tough bitch, weren't you? You wanna fuck around with drug dealers? Now look at you, crying like a baby. Well, this is what happens! This is what happens!'

'I'm sorry, I'm sorry!'

'*I'm sorry,*' he mimicked, punching the steering wheel, causing the car to drift. 'You're the only one that saw them. So where am I supposed to go now? Shall I just start putting up flyers? What the fuck do I do now?'

He was screaming. Spit flew from his mouth in foamy gobs. His heart kicked in his chest.

'I don't know,' she yipped.

'That's right, you don't know anything. You're going to get me killed, you stupid little bitch. You're going to get my family killed! Do you understand that? Do you?'

'Please slow down… please, you're going too—'

He took the exit and roared past a Mitsubishi as he emerged onto a large roundabout. He was going too quickly to follow the bend and felt the car pulling away from him. He drifted close to a lorry, narrowly missing it. His hands struggled with the steering wheel in an effort to regain control. He pulled too hard and the wheels locked.

Tara's terrified scream filled the car, piercing Dillon's eardrums. A hand clenched around his madly beating heart as the roundabout became a whirlpool around them.

Their car slammed into a metal barrier, crunching the bonnet into an accordion. His head smacked into the steering wheel, and he thought suddenly how weird it was that the airbag hadn't deployed. Then he thought that he really needed something to drink because not only was he extremely thirsty, he was sweating like a bastard. It was only when he touched his face and saw that his palm came away red that he realised it was blood.

'Craig, you nearly killed me,' he mumbled through a numb jaw, wondering why Craig wasn't laughing or calling him names. 'You… talk about my driving? You nearly… killed me.'

He turned his head, his neck stiff as a rusted lock, and looked at the passenger seat.

Tara's skull had smashed through the side window. Blood painted her skin and dripped down her neck, which was bent at an awkward angle. Her blouse, which she had worn because it was see-through and would reveal her bra beneath, was drenched. Her chest was not moving.

It took a few seconds for the image of her limp, crumpled body to calibrate in his mind, for he had temporarily taken leave of his senses.

Dillon, surprised that he had actually been wearing a seatbelt, unclipped it, opened the door and fell out of the car. He stared up at the sky and allowed himself a few breaths, listening to a chorus of confusion as other cars began to stop. He began the painful climb to his feet. The stink of burnt rubber and petrol filled his nose. His legs and side hurt, but he was walking now so he guessed they couldn't have been broken.

That was good, because now he could hear sirens.

Chapter Thirty-Five

In many ways, Morley was lucky. Had his head not been bandaged so thickly, the scalding would have been much worse. As it stood, he had only lost the skin on the bridge of his nose and some on his right cheek. His clothes had protected his body from any severe blistering, though the skin on his thick neck was bright red and blotchy. The scalding water had caused both his eyes to swell closed, and Jack was vaguely thankful that he didn't have to look into them any longer.

'Now maybe you'll understand how serious I am,' Jack said when he saw Morley stirring and mewling. 'Does it hurt?' Jack kicked Morley's foot. 'I thought you were a big tough guy. Doesn't look like it from where I'm standing. A little bit of hot water and you're crying like a fat little baby. Hey!' He kicked Morley's foot harder. 'Stop feeling sorry for yourself. You're the one making me do this. You have the power to stop it at any moment. All you have to do is—'

The buzzer rang shrilly through the warehouse. Jack stiffened. The buzzer rang again. He thought about going upstairs to check the security camera to see who it was, and then decided to ignore it completely. He stood completely still, his eyes fixed on Morley's bloody, blistered lips. The buzzer droned in a long, continuous burr.

He checked his watch. It was just after six in the evening. It could be someone from Greco calling. But they probably wouldn't just turn up without arranging something with Jack first. Had they been trying to reach him? How long had he been away from the Dagenham warehouse for? Was it two or three days? Couldn't have been longer than a week already, could it? He would have to sit and have a think about that. Couldn't afford to start losing track of the little details. He supposed that he should probably check in with the other warehouse soon, to make sure the place hadn't crumbled to the ground in his absence. Perhaps he'd make a quick visit there later this evening before closing, as soon as the person at the door stopped ringing that fucking buzzer.

There was a long stretch of silence. Jack exhaled and was about to go back to work on Morley when he heard a familiar sound: the hinges of the warehouse door's letterbox opening.

'Jackie?' May's voice infiltrated the silence. 'Jackie, I know you're in there. The van is a bit of a giveaway.' She paused and he could almost feel her eyes roaming around, looking for signs of life. 'All right then, have it your way. I'll wait out here.'

The letterbox snapped shut. Jack closed his eyes and stroked his forehead. The sound of her voice, or maybe it had been hearing her call him *Jackie*, had re-ignited a stress headache. He looked down at Morley, wondered if he was faking it. A reedy whimper whistled out of his mouth and his eyes remained tightly closed. Jack was about to tape over Morley's mouth but realised he would have to touch the field of bright red flesh on his cheek, which would probably snap him out of his stupor and send him into a fit of screaming. Then he remembered that the radio was broken, so he couldn't even use that to drown him out.

He inspected the knots around Morley's feet and hands, and then left the oiling room, locking the door behind him. Then he padded to the warehouse door and opened it.

May was sitting behind the wheel of her car with her head resting against the window when she spotted him. She sat up, smiled involuntarily, and then made a conscious effort to look stern. Jack offered her a sheepish wave, locked the warehouse door behind him, and walked over to her car. She made no signs of getting out.

The window rolled down as he neared.

'Hi May.' He saw her eyes wandering over his face, and the look of mild shock at his appearance. 'What are you doing here?'

'You're not very fond of phones, are you? I've been calling your house, been calling this place' – she pointed at the warehouse – 'but it seems you've unplugged the lines. You've left me no choice but to make a pest of myself, so thanks for that.'

He nodded, ignoring the bait. 'How've you been?'

She shrugged. 'I've been really well actually.'

'Good. I'm glad.' He looked back at the warehouse and said, 'I'd love to chat but I've got a lot of work on.'

'Have you? Working a bit late, aren't you? And that's funny because I thought you'd requested a couple of days' annual leave. Strange.'

'Yeah I did,' he said, placing a fist into the small of his back with a wince. His thigh felt cold again and he wanted very badly to lie down. 'I needed a bit of time to myself but I couldn't sit at home doing nothing, so I thought I'd get on with some stuff here. You know, keep my mind occupied.'

'Mmm.' She made a show of smiling. 'Is it working?' When he shrugged, she said, 'Back playing you up again?'

'Yeah. Sciatica.'

'Well you should be careful how you're lifting those boxes,' she said, her tone thick with condescension. 'Or maybe you've knocked it?'

'Yeah, well.' He cracked his neck to the side. 'How's everything with you?'

'You already asked me that and I already told you I'm peachy. In fact, I'm here to take you up on your offer.'

'What offer?'

'The offer of dinner at your place that you're going to make me.'

'May...'

'Time is already getting on, but I think nine is a good time to eat. Anything after that and you run the risk of feeling bloated for the whole night. So, I'll see you at seven.'

'May, I don't know what...'

'Can I just stop you there for a second,' she said, holding up her palm. 'I'm going to come to yours at nine and I expect a cooked meal, because I was thinking back and I couldn't remember the last time *you* cooked for *me*. It's always takeaways or dinner at some dingy little place. Well, tonight you're going to cook. I don't mind what it is, as long as you make the effort. And then we're going to talk about our wedding.'

Her words registered dimly inside of him, but they didn't mean anything. That tiny piece of emotional real estate reserved for dealing with May and her feelings was

238

now completely occupied. 'I told you I don't think that's a good idea.'

She looked at him as though he had just suggested flying to the moon in her Polo.

'I know what you did. I saw you that night on the estate. You and the woman took him.' She pointed through her windscreen and said, 'And he's in there, isn't he?'

May saw something change in Jack's face, and quickly pressed the button to close her window. He reached for the handle but the door was locked.

'May, open the door.'

'No,' she said, shaking her head.

'May, open it. Now.' She started the engine. He walked in front of her car and smiled, hoping it would look reassuring. The effort of the pantomime taxed him, pulling the last shroud away from his fatigue. He suddenly felt a lot older than forty-five. 'What do you think I'm going to do? You think I'm going to hurt you?'

'I don't know. I don't think I really know who you are any more.'

'Have I ever given you reason to think I would hurt you?'

'Not until the other night when I saw you hit the man with the hammer.'

'May, I can't do dinner at mine.'

'Why not? Your little girlfriend there?'

'No,' he said, shaking his head at her as though it was the most ridiculous suggestion in the world. 'And she isn't my girlfriend. My place is a dump. After our argument I got drunk, smashed the place up.'

'I don't care about the mess.'

'Well, maybe I do. If I'm going to cook you a nice meal I'd like to do it properly. You have a better kitchen than mine too, more pots and pans.'

She was suddenly struggling to fight back tears. The driver's side window came down an inch and she said, 'I tried to cook you a special dinner the other day. And then a single sob shivered out of her and she was crying. 'For god's sake, all I wanted to do was cook you a nice—' She broke off, her features scrunching together as she struggled to keep from brimming over.

'I know, and I screwed it up like I always do. But damn it, May, I'm a man and I make mistakes. Let me cook at yours, and then we can talk about whether we think marriage is the best thing to do.'

'You're trying to trick me, aren't you? The only reason you're saying all this is because I know what you did.'

'No, it's not.' He felt something bite into a nerve just above his buttocks and pinned his shoulders back. He pressed his palms on her bonnet. 'Last time at your house I reacted badly because I don't think marriage is a good thing. You know I was married once and—'

'She died. You didn't tell me that.'

A cold fist clenched around his heart. He didn't know why, but hearing her say it like that, with such casual detachment, hit him hard. Was that why he had kept the details of Kate's death from her, so that she wouldn't trivialise it?

'May, I'll come to your house at nine.' It took every bit of strength he had to smile, when what he really wanted to do was rip the bonnet off her car. 'You always were the voice of reason. Thank you.'

She nodded, grateful for his recognition of her effort. 'Do you promise you'll come, Jack?'

'I've never lied to you before, and I'm not about to start now. I'll be there at nine, traffic permitting.'

Her mouth twitched and finally broke into a smile.

He stepped away from her car, smiling, almost laughing at the lunacy of it all.

When she began to drive away, he blew her a kiss and waved her off into the sunset.

He went back inside, grabbed his address book, made the gruelling journey up the stairs and plugged in the warehouse phone. He gave himself a moment to catch his breath. His thoughts were crashing together and he couldn't quite lock onto any one thing to think it through. He dialled Emily's number and listened to the ringtone.

When she answered, he said, 'I know you didn't want me to contact you but I had no other choice, I'm sorry. But I need a favour.'

'It's all right,' she said quietly. 'I was going to call you anyway. What's wrong?'

'Are you all right? You sound funny. What's the matter?'

'Nothing's the matter.'

'Doesn't sound like nothing. You sick?'

'I'm fine!' she snapped.

He listened to her raspy breathing, worried. 'I need you to come and watch Morley for a few hours.'

'Jack,' she barked down the phone. 'Stop using his name.'

'What, you think our phones are tapped? Don't be ridiculous.' Her exhalation crackled through the receiver. 'Can you do it, Emily?'

After a pause, she said, 'Jesus Christ, yeah, sure. Why not? I haven't got anything else on.'

—

When she arrived at the warehouse, Jack had his jacket on and a key in his hand.

'This is for the oiling room,' he said. 'It's locked and he's all tied up. I don't think there'll be any reason to open the door, but if you do need to, don't get too close to him. Got it?'

'Yeah,' she said, pocketing the key. 'Where are you going?'

'I have a couple of things to take care of. I want to swing by the Dagenham warehouse and check up on a few bits.' He eyed her closely. 'He won't be able to get out, so you don't have to worry about that. Are you going to be all right here?'

She nodded and shrugged out of her jacket. 'I'm a big girl.'

'OK. I'm going to lock this door after me. If anyone rings the buzzer, which they shouldn't do, do not let them in.'

'I wasn't planning to,' she said.

'Good. I'll be back first thing in the morning.'

'Morning?'

'Yes. I've got to sort a lot of stuff out. That's not going to be a problem, is it?'

'I suppose not,' she said, and glanced toward the oiling room. 'Jack, when you get back I think we need to talk about a few things.'

'Fine,' he said irritably. He had a vague urge to inform her that he hadn't slept much in a very long time, but as he couldn't remember exactly how long it had been, he just shook the thought from his head. He opened the door to leave and then turned back to her. 'Emily? If you do have to talk to him, just remember that everything that comes out of his mouth is designed to trick you. He's as slippery as the devil. He'll try and talk circles around you, try to confuse you. He'll…' Jack got tied up in his own train of thought and flapped his hands in frustration.

'Got it,' she said with a firm nod of the head.

She was closing the door behind him when he said, 'Just out of interest, what did you want to talk to me about? Do I need to worry?'

'I don't know yet. We'll figure it out when you're back.'

When Jack left, she removed her phone and sent a text message.

Chapter Thirty-Six

Bernard stared at the message, his hand tightening around the phone. The mercury in his internal thermometer started to rise until he could feel the pulse in his neck and the kick of his heartbeat. He looked away from the screen, took a deep breath, and the anger cooled into a gelatinous sickly feeling in the pit of his stomach.

When that goblin of humiliation reared its head, as it had done so frequently in his life, Bernard thought about his teeth and his acne-scarred cheeks. Then all at once, cruel memories would rush through his mind, so fast and ferocious that he would have to cringe. He remembered getting his first job at McDonald's and how one of the girls that worked there – Cynthia, a big-boned black bitch – called him a goofy idiot after he had forgotten to pack fries into one of her customer's bags. He hadn't had the nerve to retaliate, but the words flashed in his mind like an angry beacon, and she had sensed it too.

'You want to call me something, Pocky?'

Yes, I do, he thought, but he settled for a meek 'Shut up.'

She had made some remark about him being better off working at Pizza Hut, because at least then his face would fit in with the food.

He remembered his first year working at the police station. He had been in charge of booking in two rather ragged prostitutes and escorting them to their accommodation for the night. The prostitutes were housed in neighbouring cells and had entertained themselves by shouting under the door to one another. They taunted him from down the hall, calling him a fat, dickless pig and asked him if his mum had been a horse. One of the prostitutes said, 'You look like you could eat an apple through a letterbox, you fat shit,' and his colleague working at the desk had chuckled, ever so slightly. She had tried to hide the laughter by saying, 'Don't listen to them, Bernard, they're drunk.'

But he had listened to them, the same way he had listened to all the others over the years. And then he had fantasised about what he would do to them, the pain he could cause if he really wanted to. He was six-foot-two and sixteen stone, not so heavy when you really thought about it, but the weight tended to collect on his chest and hips, giving him an awkward, almost feminine appearance.

The dating apps had been, for the most part, a disaster. Except for Emily. When she had agreed to a second date, and then offered to cook for him, he thought that was it. She had been different from the others, had seen past his flaws. They were getting on like a house on fire; she had even let him kiss her on the cheek, and then... nothing. She wouldn't answer text messages or calls. She did not even have the courtesy to accept his friend request on Facebook.

After weeks and then months of trying, his infatuation morphed and reshaped itself into resentment.

He re-read the message.

'I don't know what you're talking about. But I would rather kill myself than "be fucked" by you. You're pathetic. So do what you want and lose my number.'

His hand began to shake. Did she really think he was bluffing? Did she really think she could manipulate him like this, treat him like some fucking loser that would do her bidding at the snap of her fingers? Oh no, not at all. Pathetic? I'll show you how pathetic and petty I can be. Fucking bitch. He could lose his job, but he had been meaning to quit the station and do something else for far too long now. Maybe this was the kick up the arse he needed.

–

The station was relatively empty that night. Two teenagers were in for speeding on a stolen moped. A subsequent search had revealed an 8mm handgun and a knife as long as his arm. Those two fucking idiots were looking at a stretch in an adult prison, and were whiling away the time until their solicitor arrived by ringing the buzzer and asking for tea. Bernard was beyond surprised at how casual some of the criminals were.

Bernard had answered the buzzer of a man in cell five who was in on a drunk and disorderly charge. The man had quite casually informed Bernard that if he didn't get to see his solicitor in the next five minutes, he was going to kill every officer in the building. Bernard had closed the cell wicket and gone back to the desk to think. Thinking was always difficult with the constant shrill of the buzzers, but being in the job as long as he had, his mind had developed the ability to override the noise.

He had pondered on his dilemma all night and had almost talked himself out of it. Now, however, he had a point to prove – to himself, to Emily, and all the rest of them before her. He was not some cowardly tub of lard. He was *not*. He was—

Pathetic, pizza face, eat an apple through a letterbox...

Bitch. I'll show you, you fucking bitch.

He turned to his sergeant, who was sitting on a swivel chair and scrolling through his phone. Sergeant Richmond had transferred to the station a couple of years ago, and had shown little interest in the job beyond delegating tasks and drinking endless cups of the awful black station coffee.

'Sarge? Have you got a minute?'

Sergeant Richmond said 'Hmm?' but didn't look up from his screen. He was probably on a porn site if Bernard were to believe the rumours from his female co-workers.

'Sorry, sarge. I was just wondering if I could have a minute.'

Sergeant Richmond's brow crinkled. He locked his phone screen and set it on the desk. 'What is it?'

Bernard hesitated, nibbled his lower lip. He was losing his nerve and suddenly felt like a schoolchild standing before the head teacher. He opened his mouth to try and talk his way out of it, to say that he was just curious, when he heard Emily's voice in his head.

I would rather kill myself...

'Well,' Bernard began, 'you know this thing going on in the news about the man that was kidnapped? I think I might know something.'

Chapter Thirty-Seven

May opened the door and offered him a businesslike smile. She wore a respectable silk shirt and a black skirt.

Jack held up a shopping bag and said, 'You'll never guess what!'

'What?' she asked. Her eyes were as wide as saucers, ready to succumb to any one of her myriad emotions.

'I remembered the wine this time!' He stepped inside, slipped out of his shoes and then bent down to kiss her cheek. She smelled like a perfume shop counter. He knew that she had probably spritzed herself dozens of times, decided the fragrance was too weak, picked up a different perfume and repeated the process. He'd watched the infuriating ritual many times in the past whenever he sat waiting for her to get ready.

'Well, that truly is a first,' she said, following him into the kitchen. 'So Master Chef, what's on the menu tonight?'

'OK, well, I'm assuming you have rice?'

'Of course. Top shelf, the one by your head there.'

'Ah, great.' He clapped his hands and rubbed them together. 'I'm going to make chilli con carne. I haven't made it in a very long time, but it should be easy enough. And don't worry, I won't actually put any chillies in it.'

She couldn't handle any spice at all. They could never eat anything too exotic in case, god forbid, something tingled her delicate palate.

'Well, that sounds lovely,' she said. 'Can I be your sous chef?'

'My what?'

She giggled. 'Can I help you with anything?'

'No,' he said firmly. 'This is my dinner and I've got it all under control. Oh, wait, hang on. How do you turn on your cooker?'

She walked over, twisted the gas knob and pushed it in to ignite the hob. Then she stood by his side and rested her head on his shoulder. 'I'm glad you're here, Jack.'

He stroked her cheek and said, 'I'm glad to be here. I'm glad we're working this out like a pair of real adults. Look at us, huh?'

She tittered and sat down on a stool by the breakfast nook while Jack went about draining the blood from the mince. Now that he was engaged in the act of cooking, he remembered how much he had enjoyed it, once upon a time. His favourite thing had been to throw a few different bits of meat on the barbecue and experiment with his own marinades. It wasn't rocket science, but he enjoyed watching the meat darken, standing among the smells, squinting through the smoke with a beer in his hand.

'So,' he said above the hiss as he added the mince to the pan. 'Here's what I want to know. Do you really think getting married will be a good idea? Because, if I'm honest, I'm more than a bit superstitious. I come from the school of if it ain't broke, don't—'

'Jack?' She said his name so delicately that for a split second she sounded like a little girl. He looked over at her, expecting tears or some other dramatic display, but she was quite calm. 'Before we talk about weddings, maybe we should talk about the other thing.'

He peeled an onion, grabbed a knife from the block and began vigorously dicing it. The knife rapidly thudded into the chopping board.

'What's it all about, Jack?'

Jack picked up the chopping board and swept the onion into the pan, and then rifled through the drawers looking for the can opener.

'I saw you and that woman beat him up and then you threw him in the van.'

It was possibly the first time that he had ever heard her pick her words before speaking. He had never known her to be so articulate. He turned and leaned against the kitchen counter, crossing his arms.

'I've never lied to you,' Jack said. 'Not once. So don't ask me to lie to you now.'

'I'm not asking you to lie. I want you to tell me the truth. I want you to trust me.'

'I don't want you involved in this,' he said. 'The less you know, the better.'

'Well, I already know that you kidnapped him and that you're keeping him in that warehouse. What else do you think is going to get me into trouble?'

'Have you been watching the news?' he asked, turning away from her to concentrate on the sizzling pan.

Oh, you'd better believe I have, she thought. 'Bits and pieces.'

'Then you know he's a heroin dealer.'

'What's that got to do with you?'

'Nothing. But it should tell you that he's a nasty piece of work and he deserves everything that's coming to him. He's not some choirboy that I've just snatched off the street. He's the devil.'

And I'm his God, he thought absently. *I'm his Jesus Christ.*

'So you're a vigilante now?' When he ignored her, she said, 'That woman, she's your wife's sister. What's her involvement?'

He grabbed a wooden spoon and stabbed it into the mince. He was actually faintly surprised that the word 'vigilante' was part of her lexicon.

'Jack? What does she have to do with it?'

He was forgetting to do something but he couldn't remember what. Garlic, was that it? You put garlic in spaghetti Bolognese, didn't you? And mushrooms. But he wasn't making spaghetti, he was making... what was he making? He looked at the supermarket bag, saw the kidney beans and remembered. Chilli con carne, that was it.

'I know you're not having an affair, I'm not accusing you of that. I know that you wouldn't do that to me. But I just need to... Jack? Jack, will you look at me?'

'I'm cooking, honey,' he said. He wanted to ask her where the fuck she kept her can opener but waited for his temper to simmer down. Speaking of, the heat was too high for the pan. He was going to burn the mince. What was he cooking again? Chilli, for god's sake. 'Where do you keep your can opener?'

'The drawer on your left.'

He knew he had already checked that drawer, but he pulled it open again, perhaps a little too hard. The cutlery jumped in its compartments. He found the can opener, although it looked like more of a corkscrew or some sort of funky spoon and he started to wonder what had possessed her to buy such an awful contraption. He placed the can opener on the lip of the kidney bean can and turned the handle. It didn't bite through the metal. He tried again and still no luck.

'What is this?' he asked, holding it up. 'How am I supposed to use this thing?'

'You have to—'

'What? What do I need to do?'

'You just use it like a regular one, except—'

'Well, obviously I don't, because I can't get this fucking can open. What is this? Some new technology that's supposed to improve the experience of opening cans? In all my life, I've never seen something so stupid. Why change the fucking design?'

'Shall I do it?'

'Be my guest.' He tossed the can opener on the counter and turned back to the mince, which was starting to brown.

'Here,' she said, handing him the now open can of kidney beans. 'Easy peasy.'

He sighed. 'May, I'm… I'm sorry. My back is making me miserable and I've got so much on my mind, you wouldn't believe it.' He drained the water from the kidney beans and upended the contents of the can into the pan.

'What are you going to do with him?'

'Who?'

'Craig Morley. The man on the news that you kidnapped.'

'I just want to talk to him and then I'm going to let him go.' He'd lost interest in the food. He turned the heat all the way down and eased himself into a chair at the kitchen table. 'I don't want to talk any more about this now. I thought I came here to talk about marriage.'

'How can we talk about marriage if we still have secrets?'

'This isn't a secret. It's just something that had to be done, something that goes back to before I met you.'

'Is it something to do with your... wife?' She spoke with the caution of a woman talking to a crazy man who had broken into the house with a knife. She had never known Jack to lose his temper, but thought this particular subject might be the minefield to change that.

'All right,' he said with a heavy sigh, his elbows on the table, his hands clutched together as if in prayer. 'I'm going to say this once, and never again. I don't ever want to talk about my wife. I don't want you asking questions about her, and I don't want you trying to squeeze me for information about her. She's gone, and that's all you need to know.'

May stared down at her lap and pulled a piece of loose thread from her skirt. 'You still love her. Even after all these years, it's her that you think about, isn't it?'

'What did I just say, May?'

The way he looked at her just then made the hairs on the nape of her neck prickle. The pupils of his eyes were like two holes drilled through a piece of glass. Beneath the kitchen lights, he suddenly appeared very frightening. It occurred to her that she may have made a very big mistake. And still... she could not ignore the rapidity of her heartbeat, the flush of heat across her skin. So he was a bad guy? Wasn't that her type? Hadn't she always fallen for some kind of villain in her chequered list of lovers? And hadn't she always liked that aspect of danger about them? She felt as though she had always known there was an element of darkness to Jack, that he carried this long shadow with him everywhere he went, and this time she was right and – god, was she becoming aroused?

This was running away from her. How had she let him take the reins here? She was the one with the upper hand; she had to remember that.

'Jack, I want to marry you. And I want to do it soon. I think this is a fair request.'

Jack seemed to consider it. 'Fine. We'll get married then.'

'And I have conditions,' she added, and upon seeing that he had no reaction, she continued. 'You don't want me talking about your wife. That's more than fine by me. But if you want me to stick to that rule then you have to agree to never have any contact with that woman, your wife's sister.'

'That seems reasonable,' he said.

'Really?' she laughed, a mingling of surprise and nervousness.

'Yes. I told you, I just needed time to talk it through. I mean, I'm naturally a bit apprehensive, but I suppose we have to do the decent thing.' Pressing his weight down on the table, he rose from the chair and opened his arms. 'Come on. Bring it here.'

She skipped across the kitchen and buried her face in his wide, firm chest, wrapping her arms around his waist. Now she cried, but they were tears of joy and he was laughing and stroking her hair, telling her to stop being so silly. And then they kissed, long and passionately, her lips wet and eager, her tongue slippery and animated.

He broke the kiss off prematurely, leaving her gasping into his face. 'May, there's one more thing we do need to get straight, though,' he said. She tilted her head back and looked up at him wondrously, like an obedient dog ready to retrieve whatever object he let fly.

'What is it, love?'

He drew her tighter against his chest and was no longer stroking her hair but letting his hand linger on the back of her neck. She felt the muscles in his calloused palm, the strength of the wrist beyond it.

'Who have you spoken to about the other night?'

'Spoken to?'

'Yes. Did you mention me to anyone?'

'No, Jack.' She tried to pull back for eye contact but he wouldn't allow it. She tried to wiggle her shoulders but it was no use, so she spoke into his chest. 'I was in the car park. I followed you to see what you were doing with that woman and then, well, I saw.'

'Someone else was there too. Did you see them?'

'Someone else?'

'The one who made the police report.'

'I don't... I'm not sure...'

'You don't have to be afraid of me, May. I haven't given you a reason to be afraid of me before, have I?'

'I know.'

'So tell me the truth.'

'It was a girl. A young girl. She was with Craig Morley.' She kept referring to him by his full name as though he were a celebrity, and it was starting to irritate him. 'She watched you from the entrance of the block. She came out blubbering…'

'And what did you do?'

'Jack, please, I didn't say anything to the police. I was gone before they even showed up.'

'You sure? You seemed really angry with me the last time we saw each other.'

'So you think I would just chuck everything away because of a stupid argument?'

'I don't know. Would you?'

'No. She saw you kidnap her boyfriend and called the police. And that's it. I just wanted to know if she saw you, that's all. I was trying to look out for you.'

'You'd better not be lying to me, May.'

She could feel herself growing hot, the outrage lighting a fire deep inside of her. *You'd better not be lying to me, May*. That sounded like something her ex-husband would say before he cracked her across the face or chased her screaming through the house with a belt wrapped around his fist.

'You have the cheek to accuse me of lying?'

'Stop throwing a tantrum, and—'

She bit into his chest as hard as she could, her teeth sinking through the fabric of his shirt and pinching into where he'd bandaged the knife wound. He shrieked in pain and surprise and she broke free of his embrace. He looked down at his shirt, saw the wet ring of teeth impressions, and then turned his attention to her.

'Don't you dare,' she yelled with such authority that she actually stopped him in mid-step. 'Don't you fucking dare.'

'See,' he sneered, gingerly touching his chest. 'This is why we can't get married. You're an emotional wreck. You don't know how to control your—'

She grabbed a plate from the shelf – the special crockery that was reserved for special dinners like birthdays and Christmas – and launched it at him. It whistled past his head and shattered against the wall, showering him with shards.

'Make me break my nice china, you fucking...' She grabbed another plate and threw it. This time she was less discriminating with her aim. The plate flew wide and smashed against a cupboard. She had turned to retrieve more ammo when he caught hold of her wrists.

'This isn't a game, May! What did you tell the police?'

She was stuttering on her sobs, a thick line of saliva dribbling down her chin.

He let go of her. 'This is how you want it, is it? Maybe deep down you want me to put my hands on you like your piece of shit husband used to. But you know what?' He smoothed his hair back. 'I don't want to do this. I love you too much, May. Can't you see that? I love you, for Christ's sake. I always have!'

He sat down in the chair, the pain in his back pulsing like a heartbeat. He covered his face and now it was his turn to cry. He bawled loudly, his despair amplified against his hands. He cried until his sobs overwhelmed hers. He felt her touch his shoulder and flinched away.

'I don't want you to see me like this,' he said, without removing his hands from his eyes.

She had never seen him cry before. In fact, she had never seen him show any emotion other than tepid disinterest. His whole repertoire of feelings could be summed up in a single shrug. And here he was crying… crying for her!

'I'm sorry, Jack, I'm so sorry.' She tried to pull his hands away from his face, but he would not let her.

If he had, she would have seen that his eyes were completely dry.

'Jack, please. I have the hammer. And the gun.'

His sobs stopped so abruptly that he had to make a strangled groaning sound to make it seem natural.

'What did you say?'

'Yes. I have them here. Let me get them.' She scurried out of the kitchen and he heard her rummaging around by the stairs. When she returned with a black bin bag, he made a show of drying his eyes against his sleeve.

'I took them before the police got there,' she said hopefully. 'I did it to protect you, but I didn't want you to be mad with me.' She opened the bin bag to show him the contents. 'You'd think I was meddling and get angry with me, and all I was trying to do was make everything right again.'

'May, you… you don't understand what this means to me. Do you know what you've done?'

'What?' she asked tremulously.

'You've saved my life.' Using the chair for support, he knelt before her. 'I should have done this ages ago. I should have done this the day I met you.' He looked up at her. 'I don't have a ring, but I swear to god I'm going to buy you one first thing tomorrow and… May, can you forgive a stupid, sour old man like me and do me the honour of giving me your hand in marriage?'

As he offered the proposal, he watched her face brighten, the happiness breaking through the confusion.

She would love the way he worded it too, like something from one of those romantic comedies she tortured him with.

'Yes. Oh Jack, yes, you know I will.'

He hugged her stomach and then rose. He knew he would pay later for all the malarkey he'd put his back through today, but this had to be done. She had actually dug him out of a potentially detrimental hole, and yet he was not all that surprised. Even with all the stress, he knew there was a reason he'd kept her around, had sensed in some way that being with her was useful. At first, he'd thought that she was more of a convenience, and that a man his age living alone would seem strange, perhaps even sinister to those around him. Being alone brought unwanted attention that might have later led to suspicion, and he didn't need that one bit. May came with emotional baggage, and yes, she was high-maintenance, but she was also a brilliant counterbalance. She provided him with all the stage dressing he needed. Here was a woman that would do anything to stay with him, keep any secret, tell any lie. She was an invaluable asset, one he could shape, mould. She was coming along perfectly.

'Look, can we rewind and pretend that the last ten minutes never happened?'

'Yes,' she said, laughing and kissing his face enthusiastically.

He looked down at the debris and made a seething sound through his clenched teeth. 'Those were your good plates.' He slapped himself in the head. 'I'm such a fucking idiot.'

'No, they don't matter. I can buy new ones.'

His shoulders sagged. 'And I've ruined dinner.' He picked up the wooden spoon and stirred the mince. It was black and stuck to the bottom of the pan.

'It's all right,' she said, kissing his face. 'I wasn't hungry anyway.'

Chapter Thirty-Eight

Sergeant Richmond listened to what Bernard had to say without interruption. They were standing outside the station, away from the various sound-recording cameras that lined the halls. Richmond smoked his way through two cigarettes as Bernard spoke in stuttered whispers, using his fat pink hands to emphasise certain points of the story. When he was finished, Richmond patted him on his arm and said, 'I want to thank you for telling me that, Bernard. That took a lot of balls and I know it's been weighing heavily on your mind.'

'It has,' Bernard confirmed, and gave Richmond a smile that looked like he was ready to catch a fly with his tongue and swallow it whole. 'Really it has. She's a nasty piece of work, it just took me a while to see it. She tricked me, really. I mean, she's a bloody liar and...'

Richmond raised a hand, cutting Bernard's monologue short. 'Voice down, Bernard. Let's keep this between us, yeah?'

'Yes.' Bernard nodded and released a shaky sigh, rubbing his crinkled forehead. 'Thank you, sarge.'

Richmond dropped the butt of his cigarette and crushed the ember beneath his heel. He expelled twin streams of smoke through his nostrils and said, 'This Emily woman. You know where she lives?'

'I think so.'

'You think so? What does that mean?'

Bernard scratched under his chin, his fingernails grazing a rash of red razor bumps. 'Well, see, the thing is I know the house by sight, but I don't know if she lives there any more.'

For the first time since Bernard had relayed his information to Sergeant Richmond, he saw a flicker of annoyance in the older man's face. 'What does that mean, Bernard?'

'What I mean to say is, well, remember I said she cooked dinner for me once?' Bernard saw the sergeant's eyes glaze over, the bushy brows drawing together. 'Yeah, she cooked for me and what I'm saying is I would probably know the route there. In fact, yeah, I definitely know where that house is.' What he had neglected to tell the sergeant was that, when Emily went cold on him, he had spent numerous weeks driving past the house or parking directly opposite, hoping to catch a glimpse of her. On one of his nightly stakeouts, he thought he saw her silhouette drift past the upstairs window and managed to convince himself that she had just stepped out of the shower. He let this fantasy play out in his mind until he was rock hard in his pants, barely able to contain his excitement.

'Good work, mate,' Richmond smiled warmly. 'Why didn't you ever join the force? You'd have made a blinding copper.'

'It wasn't on the cards,' Bernard said with a grin, and then, sensing that the sergeant was looking at the plaque on his teeth, quickly closed his mouth.

'So here's what I need you to do,' Richmond began, removing another cigarette from the pack and placing it between his lips. Before lighting it, he said, 'I need you to knock off early, right now in fact. Go to the house and get me the exact address. Do you think you can do that?'

He was only two hours into his shift. Getting out of this godforsaken shithole to stitch up that bitch Emily was a welcome reprieve. 'Yeah, I can do that,' Bernard said. 'But what about me?'

Sparking the lighter, Richmond said, 'What about you?'

'I mean where does this leave me? Am I gonna get in trouble for this or what?' He wasn't thinking about his job at all, but there was a kernel of fear threatening to blossom into something greater at the idea of jail time.

'Trouble for what? As far as I'm concerned, we came about this intelligence via our internal investigation. It had nothing to do with you, did it?' He met his subordinate's eyes with a knowing stare. 'I look after my own, Bernard. Later, when we've got all this resolved, we'll throw you a bloody party, you silly bugger.'

Bernard snorted laughter. 'A party. Ha! All right. Well, should I go to the house now?'

'No time like the present, mate.'

Bernard nodded and headed back inside the station for his jacket.

When he was gone, Sergeant Richmond made a phone call.

Chapter Thirty-Nine

Emily had been listening to Morley wailing for an hour before she went to investigate. He had been making some vague attempt to cry for help, but his words were gibberish, lost in a soup of despair. He sounded like a toddler who had just learned to talk, stringing combinations of words together with incoherent nonsense.

This did not sound like the man that had shrugged off hammer strikes and rampaged through the warehouse. She tried ignoring it at first, but the warehouse was perfect for his acoustics. The boxes that Jack had assured her would dampen any sound he made, had not lived up to his claim. She had been sitting in the kitchen area, trying to think of some way to get out of this predicament.

'Just want… gluuurgh… pleaash…' Morley moaned. Emily wanted to slam her hands over her ears like a little girl and pretend she couldn't hear him. 'Eeeaghn DO IT!'

She ignored his mush-mouthed rambling until he fixated on two words, which he pronounced without any problem at all.

'He's wrong,' Morley said, and continued saying it over and over again until the mantra was practically bouncing off the walls. *He's wrong, he's wrong, he's wrong…*

Emily approached the oiling room, trembling with trepidation. She had found a Stanley knife upstairs and now she held it out in front of her, ready to swipe through the air if he came bursting through the door. She would not underestimate him again. She had seen his tenacity first-hand and understood exactly what she was dealing with: a very strong man who was in fear of losing his life. She did not rule out that his blubbering was all a ruse, designed to get her to the door.

'He's wrong,' Morley chanted, his voice gaining strength as she neared the door. 'He's...' He faltered, must've heard her approaching, and said, 'Don't burn me again! Please...'

Burn you? Was that why he was going out of his mind? She had assumed he'd be hungry or thirsty, or perhaps driven to screaming from discomfort. But Jack had burned him?

She tapped the door. 'Keep your voice down in there.'

'You,' he panted. 'It's you! Oh, thank god. You won't burn me, will you?'

'Nobody's going to burn you,' she said.

'He already did! He boiled up the kettle and... I'm in so much pain!'

'He poured hot...' She stopped, biting back the words. She didn't want to engage in conversation with him, not while Jack was away. 'Just keep your mouth shut and save your energy.'

'You've... got... the... wrong... person,' he said, labouring on the words as though each syllable physically taxed him. 'Please... please...'

Everything that comes out of his mouth is designed to trick you. He's as slippery as the devil...

Had she ever been completely satisfied that Morley was Kate's killer? She had managed to convince herself that he was, but that wasn't the same thing as truly believing it. And how could she truly believe it based on Jack's word alone? Even with the music video, which had struck her as nothing more than a young man showing off on camera, spewing vile and detestable lyrics in an attempt to amplify his ego, she still wasn't sure. But she made herself believe it, even with the doubts and inconsistencies, because she needed an end to the torment. Kate's murder had changed the course of all their lives, and none of them had ever been the same since. She needed to move past this horror; she needed a reason as to why this atrocity had happened so she could salvage whatever life she had left.

Jack had seemed so sure, and yet there was still that tiny, niggling doubt that ate away at her like a maggot through an apple core. No matter how much she had wanted justice, closure, or – call it what it was for god's sake, *vengeance* – it could not begin to equal Jack's own needs. He was completely obsessed, so blindly fixated on finding her killer that he had started to seem... *unstable*, was that the right word?

Still, for all her doubts, it still didn't mean that Jack was wrong and that Morley was innocent.

She pulled the key from her pocket and considered unlocking the door.

It is him. You know it is.

She put the key into the lock and was about to open the door when she stopped.

But what if it isn't?

'He's wrong...'

'Hey.' She banged the door with her fist. 'Listen to me. I'm opening this door. If you try anything I'm going to stab you, do you understand me?'

'He's wrong,' Morley groaned. His words had dulled and lost their potency. The fire in him was finally dwindling.

'Just shut up. I'm opening the door.' She turned the key and pushed the door open. She had been bracing herself for Morley to rush her the way he had done with Jack, but instead Morley cringed away from the light and whimpered.

There was a big puddle on the floor and she couldn't tell if it was from the boiling water, as Morley had said, or whether he had wet himself. Then she saw him peer into the rectangle of light from the open doorway. His face looked distorted and it took a couple of seconds for her brain to understand why. A roll of pale, boiled skin flapped off his cheek, revealing a large, oozing red sore. His eyes were nothing more than slits in golf-ball-sized welts. Blisters lined his lips and the skin on his neck was violent red.

She could not neatly compartmentalise the maelstrom of emotions she felt just then. She felt revolted at the sight of him, but whether that was because of his appearance or because of what he was – or what she *thought* he was – she couldn't tell. The fear felt like the worst case of heartburn she'd ever had. There was even pity, weakly trying to push through the crowd to make its presence known.

What she didn't feel was the one thing she was supposed to feel: hate.

She didn't hate Morley. She had thought she would eventually, when she became more convinced of his guilt. But that moment hadn't come. Not yet.

'He's wrong.'

'You killed my sister,' Emily eventually said.

'I didn't.' His tongue licked at the sores around his mouth. 'Look at me… he burned me! Please, it hurts so much.'

'That's the least of your worries.' She swallowed, still unable to keep her gaze on his face for longer than a second at a time.

His head whipped up and he dragged himself forward on his knees until the rope around his neck pulled taut. 'Do I look bad? I can't see properly… please, tell me…'

He looked like a horror show, like a melted Halloween mask.

'You'll live,' she said, and then bit her lip at her poor choice of words. Morley had picked up on it too. He rolled onto his side like a sick dog.

'He's wrong and he's still going to kill me,' he said, drooling.

'He isn't wrong. He saw you murder my sister. And there's no point in trying to build a case for yourself because I know exactly what you are.'

Tears, or maybe it was oozing pus, rolled down the sore of his cheek. 'I am whatever you say I am,' he said in a slow drawl, 'as long as you don't say I'm a murderer. Because I'm NOT.'

'You are,' she said, her voice rising and quavering. 'You killed my sister for no reason at all and he saw you.'

'He saw a teenage boy in the back of a car.'

'He recognised your eyes,' she countered, aware of how stupid it sounded now that it had left her mouth. 'You knocked on his door and you stabbed Kate in the neck and then you ran off. He saw you and he's not going to let it go.'

'He didn't see *me*.'

'Oh yeah? Think about this, then,' she began. 'Why would he be so insistent that it was you, after all these years? Why would a man like him – who has no criminal record, probably never even had so much as a parking ticket – want to go to all this trouble if he wasn't entirely sure that you' – she pointed the knife at Morley – 'killed his wife?'

'It's obvious,' Morley said, twisting around on the floor in a futile attempt at finding comfort. 'He's insane.'

'No, you're the one that's insane.'

'No,' he said, the word coming out in a short, flat note. 'I'm not.' He lay stretched out, resting his good cheek on the floor. 'You're not like him,' he said softly. 'I can tell.'

'Shut up. Just shut up.'

'You only hate me because he's told you that I've killed your sister. But he isn't right in his head. And you know that. I can see it in your face that you don't really think it was me.'

'And I'm supposed to take your word over his, am I?'

'Yes,' Morley said with a dry, chalky chuckle. 'Even if there is one tiny bit of doubt about me in your head, you should undo these ropes and let me go.'

'You disgust me,' she said with a sneer. 'Even now, lying there with half your face falling off, you think you can talk me round, don't you? Have you forgotten back in the flats, when you chased me down the stairs?'

'I didn't chase you…'

'You think I'm going to feel sorry for you because he poured a bit of hot water on you? Boo-fucking-hoo. Do you know the grief you've caused? The pain my family have suffered through, that Jack has suffered, because of what you did?'

'How could I know? I wasn't even aware of what you're accusing me of until the other day.'

'You would say that, though, wouldn't you? You think that if you deny it long enough he'll just let you go?'

'No,' he coughed weakly, his face scored in pain from the effort. 'I know he's going to kill me. I could admit to it, deny it, tell him that it was Santa Claus and it would make not a bit of difference to him because he's lost his fucking mind.'

She looked at the way he was flopped on the floor, the spill of his hairy stomach, the mess of his face. She wondered what it would feel like if she walked over and cut him with the Stanley knife. She wondered if hurting him would feel good. Because up to now, none of this had felt good at all. She thumbed the lever and brought the blade out another inch, but she knew she would never have the nerve to slice him. The knife was nothing but a useless prop in her hands, and by the dopey, awful smile on Morley's face, he seemed to know it too.

'If you let him kill me,' Morley began, still smiling grimly, 'then you'll be a murderer. You'll be no better than the boy that stabbed your sister to death.'

'*You* were the boy that stabbed her!' All her nervousness rocketed up through her and was expelled in one loud blast that left her reeling, light-headed. She steadied herself and said, 'Jack saw you and that's good enough for me, because I believe him. I believe you did it.'

Gently, he said, 'No, you don't.'

'It wouldn't make a difference if I did let you go. Everybody in the country is looking for you.'

No surprise registered on his damaged face.

'You had eight kilos of heroin in your flat, didn't you?'
As she said this, he began pushing himself up to a sitting
position. She finally had his attention. 'Well, the police
are looking for you because they want to link you to the
person you got the heroin from.'

She watched him untangle it all, his mind spinning like
a Catherine wheel.

'Where'd you...' he started to say and then shook his
head. In that one instant, he had shrugged away the pain
and swept any fear he harboured for Jack under the carpet.
'That's not...' His mouth struggled to find the right words.
Then he settled on a sentence so incredulous that it almost
made Emily laugh. 'This isn't fair.'

'Fair?' She shook her head, laughing drily. 'So you
understand the concept of fairness, do you? Or maybe
you understand it when it suits you.'

'Listen to me, you stupid fucking idiot, I didn't kill
your sister. I didn't kill anyone!' He jerked forward like an
angry pit bull leashed to a fence post. 'Do you know what
you've done? I didn't kill her! You have to let me go!'

'Really?' she said in a weak attempt at casualness.
'Maybe you see why your word is worth less than shit
to me. You're a fucking drug-dealing bastard.'

He didn't even flinch at the verbal jabs. She knew by
this new expression on his face – a stony, unwavering
seriousness surfacing through the welts – that she would
not be able to say anything more that would unsettle him.
Even battered and disfigured as he was, he now looked
fierce enough to spew fire and blow gouts of black smoke
from his nostrils. A renewed sense of strength seemed to
take him over and he began transforming right before her
eyes.

'OK, listen to me,' he rasped.

'No, you don't give the orders here, Morley.'

'Please, please just listen to me for a minute. Just give me that. *Please.*'

'What's the matter? You've grown a conscience all of a sudden?'

'I have kids. They're in trouble.'

'I doubt it,' Emily said. 'The police have probably interviewed them while they've been looking for you. Nothing is going to happen to them. You should be thinking about the innocent people that you've hurt throughout your miserable life.'

He tugged his head away from the pipe, trying to break the leash around his neck. A growl rumbled through him as he wrestled the rope, and then when he understood that it would not snap he turned and bit down on it. He snarled like an animal, his head vibrating with tension, the blood rushing to his face and turning his complexion purple.

'It's no use,' she said, hoping to dissuade him. His intensity had begun to frighten her, even though she could see there was no way he could physically chomp through the rope. Still, he yanked and bit down and screamed, drawing on some new reservoir of strength. 'You're not going anywhere.'

'Then kill me now,' he said, turning away from her, the muscles in his back flexing beneath the fabric of his shirt. He panted and rested his head on the pipe. 'You say I'm a coward?' he began breathlessly, wheezing as he spoke. 'But you're the one that doesn't have the courage to do the right thing. Just fucking kill me and get it over with.'

'Tell me why you killed Kate and I will.'

'Liar. Coward.'

'Fuck you,' she spat.

'Yeah, fuck me.' He sank to his knees. 'Fuck me,' he murmured again. 'I was obese as a teenager. I have asthma. He says I stabbed her and ran away; I say I couldn't have run two feet without collapsing. So fuck me.' He reared his head back and slammed it into the pipe. The sound of the impact resonated hollowly.

The shock startled Emily and she shed all pretence of toughness. She watched as he pulled his head back and slammed it into the pipe harder, screaming as his skull cracked against the metal.

'Stop it!' She rushed over to him as he was rearing back again. She was going to prevent him headbutting the pipe by grabbing hold of his shirt and pulling him back, but he whirled on her, quickly and fluidly, his rank, fetid breath smothering her. She felt the bulk of his stomach as it pillowed against her, and felt very small and very vulnerable. Up close, she saw the pus oozing from his scalded cheek, the blood blisters lining his lips like cold sores. Fresh blood seeped through the bandages around his head, adding a vibrant red to the cola-brown stains.

'Please,' he begged, beginning to cry, and his breath took on a character of its own. It was shitty smelling and sour, like a gust from an open grave. 'I've never killed anyone. Please, I don't want to die.'

'Sit back and behave yourself,' Emily said, trying to keep the panic out of her voice.

He reached up and touched the bandage. When he saw his fingers come away red, he said, 'Don't let him kill me.

Not for something I didn't do.' His head rolled, his chin falling down on his chest. 'My head. My head hurts so much. Please. He's crazy. He's—' he said, and then passed out.

Chapter Forty

Edward Dekkers had been working out of his central London office just off Tottenham Court Road since the unfortunate business began. He did not care for London and only ever came to the capital when it was necessary. Now, with everything going on, he wanted to be right there in the middle of things, to feel the city's heartbeat and be close to the action.

He had made a rare and uncharacteristic error of judgement in trusting a thug like Morley, but these hiccups occurred from time to time. They were, he supposed, a rather useful way of keeping his mind sharp and his senses keen. Success could breed complacency, and these mishaps provided him with a ball of knots that would be hard to untangle. In some perverse way, he enjoyed the sport. The drama, while worrying to a certain degree, gave him a blunt sense of excitement that his life had long since lacked. He had been a cautious man for many years, trading his gun for a laptop, swapping violence for Excel sheets. He no longer had to show his teeth to let people know they could be bitten, but from time to time, the mongrel in him had to make an appearance.

He raised his glasses, rubbed his eyes. He had been working on the accounts since the afternoon, and the daylight had melted away without him noticing. Of course, for the more legitimate areas of his car dealership business he had a couple of qualified accountants who took care of things. For the movements he made in secret, Dekkers preferred to keep track of the numbers himself, especially given that he would now have to plug a nine-hundred-grand deficit if they couldn't find Morley.

He blinked, yawned, and thought about pushing through for another half hour or so. He squinted at the screen but could no longer make sense of what he was looking at, and knew it was time to call it a night. He saved the worksheet, closed the laptop down, and then removed a bottle of Eagle Rare bourbon and a crystal tumbler from his desk drawer. Swivelling in his chair, he admired the winking city lights through the large rectangular window. The street sounds filtered in from below; a cacophony of car engines and garbled chatter. *Such a dirty, noisy city*, he thought.

He was just about to pour himself a small measure of Eagle when he felt his mobile vibrate in his inner breast pocket. When he removed the phone from his pocket and didn't recognise the number, he felt the faintest twinge of curiosity. For some reason, perhaps a subliminal sense of apprehension, Dekkers hesitated before answering. He didn't say hello. Just listened. After a few breaths rasped through the receiver, a voice said, 'Mr Dekkers? Are you there?'

'I am,' Dekkers replied, rising from his chair. He didn't immediately recognise the voice, and this agitated him like an itch he couldn't scratch.

'Mr Dekkers, this is Ralph Richmond.' When Dekkers didn't acknowledge the name, Richmond said, '*Sergeant* Ralph Richmond. Do you remember me?'

'Should I?' Dekkers asked, finally pouring the bourbon. He picked up the tumbler, swirled it, and sipped.

'Perhaps you should, but then again, probably not. I helped you about three years ago regarding a tip-off on a raid and—'

'Don't say anything more over the phone,' Dekkers said quickly, but calmly. In his mental database, Dekkers assigned Richmond's voice to the face of a tall, slump-shouldered man with gunmetal hair. Yes, now he remembered him. A sergeant at some pissant station who had been looking to get into Dekkers' good books as an internal informant. Dekkers, who had met Richmond once, briefly, preferred to let Mikkel liaise with him. Dekkers thought the man dirty in a way he couldn't rationally explain, and distrusted him deeply.

'I'm using a phone box, so don't worry,' Richmond said in a tone that suggested Dekkers should relax.

'What do you want?'

'I have some information for you.'

'Do you now?'

'Yes. Take this number down – it's the phone box I'm in.'

Dekkers picked up the fountain pen by his laptop and pressed the nib against the Post-it note pad. 'I'm listening.'

Richmond reeled off the number and added, 'I'll wait here. Call me back when you find a clean line.'

The phone went dead. Dekkers gulped the bourbon down and picked up his blazer.

In the dark reception area, Mikkel's stand-in sat sleeping in a leather armchair. Frans was only twenty-three but was built like a bull, his thick neck the width of an average-sized man's thigh.

'Wakey wakey, Mr Frans,' Dekkers said softly. Outside a car drove past, briefly illuminating the reception with its headlights.

Frans stirred and then snapped awake. He cleared his throat and, in French, asked Dekkers if everything was OK.

'Yes,' he replied in English. 'We're going for a walk.'

Frans escorted Dekkers to a road just off Soho where they found a red phone box littered with prostitute cards. The phone box smelled strongly of alcohol and one of the windowpanes was missing, letting in a cool breeze that he wasn't particularly annoyed about. Dekkers reached for the receiver, sighing when his palm made contact with the sticky plastic, and dialled the number that Sergeant Richmond had given him. Then, he removed his mobile from his jacket and held it up to the receiver, opened the voice memo app and pressed record.

Richmond answered after one ring. He began by saying, 'This young man that got kidnapped, the one with the eight keys of brown. He one of yours?'

Dekkers didn't answer the question. He wasn't dumb enough to openly admit something like that over the phone, especially to a fucking police sergeant.

'If he is,' Richmond continued, seeing the error in his questioning, 'I have something that might help you. Are you there?'

'Mmm.' Dekkers looked across the road, saw a tall, topless black man juggling while another man held out a flat cap for change.

'I didn't go to my usual guy on this because I thought you might want to hear it direct, especially given the scale of things. Before I say anything, I want you to know that I'm going above and beyond for you here. I shouldn't even touch this with a fucking barge pole given the amount of heat involved.'

'Mmm,' Dekkers murmured.

'OK. My spider senses tell me you're gonna want the people that took your man from Frazier Avenue. Well, one of my men has just told me something that might prove to be very useful in that endeavour, if you catch my drift. Do you still have that pen?'

'Mmm.'

'Then write down this address.'

Chapter Forty-One

Dillon only realised he was walking funny when he left the petrol station bathroom. He had gone in to check his wounds in the privacy of one of the cubicles, and woken up some time later, unsure of where he was. Gradually, he realised that he had passed out on the toilet seat, although in the first minute or so, as he regained consciousness, he thought he was dead.

By some divine intervention, he hadn't injured himself too badly, which really was a fucking miracle if his memory of the crash was anything to go by. He still didn't feel much pain, although through his anaesthetised muscles he was vaguely aware that something hurt. He fingered more coke into his nostrils before sheepishly wandering out of the cubicle.

He spent very little time dwelling on Tara, only mourning the link he had lost to the people that kidnapped Craig. The car was stolen, so it couldn't be traced back to him. She was dead, so she couldn't talk. She was as helpful to him dead as she had been alive.

His reflection in the mirror depicted a bloodless phantom. He barely recognised the large, skittish eyes staring back at him. He washed his nose to rid it of the crusted blood, and then splashed some cold water on a knot that had developed on his forehead. Then, quite suddenly, he burst into tears. He stood bent over the sink, his hands badly shaking, the haunting sobs sailing out of his throat. He indulged in the misery a little while longer before the despair evolved into anger.

In the privacy of a petrol station toilet cubicle, Dillon checked the phone that the golem had given him. There was a missed call and a voicemail. His stomach filled with acid at the thought of what he might hear. He took a sip of Evian – purchased legitimately in the petrol station shop, so as not to arouse suspicion when he staggered into the toilets – and then listened to the voicemail. It was twelve seconds of his daughter crying. He hung up, fighting the urge to smash the phone against the mirror with every molecule of strength left in his body. A low, primal roar revved in his chest, and then he was seeing stars. He stumbled to the door and placed a hand against it for support, waiting for the dizziness and nausea to pass.

Now he had no car and no idea what to do next. Perhaps he should just kill himself. That seemed to be the most reasonable thought to have entered his head in a very long time. He could walk out of the station, find a bridge and throw himself off. What would that Dutch bastard do then? Dillon doubted he would really murder his family. He would probably just write the whole debt off as a loss and move onto the next bit of business.

His sinuses were stinging madly and he felt hot and itchy all over. His brain was a scratched record, skipping every time he had a coherent thought.

Dillon pulled open the door and was heading toward the petrol station exit when the phone began to vibrate in his hand. A groan escaped his lips, and his saliva turned to ash in his mouth.

He thumbed the button to accept the call and placed the phone up to his sweaty face. 'Yeah,' he breathed.

'Christmas has come early for you,' Mikkel said. In the background, Dillon could hear *Peppa Pig* being played on the iPad.

'I don't know what that means,' Dillon said, his arid tongue lapping his lips.

'It means Mr Dekkers has a gift for you. He has the name and address of the woman that took your friend.'

'What?'

'Shut up and listen,' Mikkel ordered. In the background, Dillon's daughter giggled and garbled something in baby talk. Mikkel said, 'Your daughter is very cute. She likes the cartoons.'

'I know,' Dillon said, his voice sounding very far away in his own ears.

'This is probably your only chance, so pay very careful attention. And Dillon?'

Dillon closed his eyes. A lance of pain shot through his head, as though Mikkel's voice had chased away the high that kept him numb. 'Yes?'

'No more games. Your family are depending on you.'

Dillon listened to everything the golem said and then hung up. He palmed sweat from his face and stepped outside.

Beneath the white lights of the petrol station's roof, Dillon saw a woman filling up her car. She was staring at the scrolling numbers, ghostly vapour escaping her mouth in the cold night air. Dillon bent his head, squinting to see if there was anyone else in her car, and saw that she was all alone. He began to laugh softly to himself. He couldn't help it. He uncapped the water, took a large swig, and peeled the Evian sticker from the bottle.

Dillon hung back, watching as the woman went off to pay for her petrol. As she did, Dillon casually opened the back door of her car and sat directly behind the driver's seat, scooting down so she wouldn't see him upon her return. He listened to his ragged breathing, could feel the constant bounce of his heart. Sweat broke through his pores and trickled down his face.

Then he heard the woman's approaching footsteps and all other thoughts scattered from his mind. He uncapped the Evian bottle again.

The door opened, and the woman got in with a grunt and closed the door. She was humming something under her breath. Dillon sat up and said, 'Listen to me carefully because I'm only going to say this once.' He slapped a hand across her mouth when she opened it to scream. 'Don't make a fucking sound. Look here' – he held up the Evian bottle – 'I've got acid, do you understand? Nod your head if you understand.'

He could feel her lips trembling against his hand, her chest hitching, the scream still tangled in her throat. She nodded erratically.

'If you don't do exactly as I say, I'm going to pour this over your face and melt it right off.' At this, the woman squeaked and stiffened. 'Shut up. I'm gonna take my hand off your face, but don't make a fucking peep or I'll burn you.' Slowly he took his hand away from her mouth, and added, 'Start the car.'

He listened to the keys jangle in her hand and then the soft purr of the motor.

'Please… please don't…' she said, panting.

'I'm not going to do anything to hurt you if you do what I say. And I said not to speak, didn't I?'

'I'm sorry… I'm sorry.'

'Drive.'

She nodded, put the car in gear, and stalled the car. Dillon lurched forward. A sprinkle of water fell on the woman's arm, but thankfully she didn't feel it.

'I didn't mean t-to,' she said, her voice almost reaching falsetto.

'Do you want to lose your face? Do you think I'm playing with you? Start the car and get out of here. Now.'

'OK.' She started the car up again and this time, when she put it in gear, the car rolled forward.

'That's good. Take this left here,' he said as she reached the exit onto the main road. He glanced through the window and could see the traffic clogging the motorway in the distance. Overhead, the burr of a low-flying heli-copter, undoubtedly an air ambulance for his dearly departed friend, Tara.

He had an address and that's all he cared about. Soon, this whole thing would be over.

Chapter Forty-Two

When Jack returned to the warehouse shortly before seven in the morning, Emily was sitting on a plastic chair just outside the oiling room, waiting for him.

'What's going on?' he asked, striding across the warehouse.

When he got near her, she caught the strong, oppressive smell of perfume clinging to his shirt. She thought about asking him where he'd been, because he was all dressed up and had a woman's scent all over him, but she couldn't be bothered.

'He's in a bad way,' Emily said, pointing to the oiling room.

'You opened the door?' he asked gruffly and walked inside to check on their prisoner. Morley was asleep on the floor, shivering, with his teeth chattering madly.

'I changed his dressing,' Emily said. 'He was banging his head against the pipe there.'

Jack looked at the pipe, saw the blood smears, and then glared over at her. 'What did he say?'

She put her finger up to her lips and gestured for him to follow her. Jack left the room, locking the door behind him, and they went upstairs.

Limping, Jack said, 'What happened while I was gone?'

'He said he didn't do it.'

'Yeah, I gathered that. What's all this about headbutting the pipe?'

'He was trying to get my attention. It worked.' She stopped and inhaled. The intake of air hurt her lungs.

Jack shook his head, a joker's grin stretching across his lips. 'I told you not to listen to anything he said. And the reason I warned you is because I knew he would try and turn you against me.'

'Jack…'

'Enough.' Jack waved a hand across the air between them as though rubbing away her words. 'Fine, my word as an eyewitness isn't good enough for you. But how much more proof do you need? He's got an arrest record a mile long. He's got a song mocking us, Emily. He's making fun of the murder right there on the internet, bragging 'cos he got away with it.'

'But Jack…' She could barely muster the energy to speak, and here she was using her last reserves of strength to defend Morley. Is that what she was about to do? 'We could be wrong.'

'I'm not wrong,' he shouted and stuck a finger in her face, an inch from her nose. 'I'm not wrong and fuck you for even suggesting it. I was there with Kate when she was dying. I saw it all. And you have the nerve to tell me different? How dare you? How fucking DARE you?'

'Don't blow your lid. I'm just saying…'

'Don't say. Just don't say anything. It's too late for you to voice your concerns now, Emily. We've done it, we've taken him off the street. And look what's happening out there. Are you seriously trying to tell me that's an innocent man?'

He isn't innocent, she thought, *but he might not be guilty of the crime we're accusing him of.*

Jack stood before her, his wide shoulders heaving, his eyes bulging with intensity, his fingers curling and uncurling.

'You're right,' she said.

Perhaps it was her weary mind that felt like an overheated car engine, smoking through the bonnet from sleep deprivation, but she would be damned if he didn't seem… *crazy* was the wrong word. But it was almost as if he had stepped offstage and discarded a disguise. He was not the meek man that had called her out of the blue, detailing a plan of dignified retribution. He was something else, and she felt deceived.

'You said you wanted to talk to me about something.' He stomped over to the kitchen and hunted for a bottle. Finding none, he swatted the box of PG Tips, scattering teabags onto the concrete. She watched his jerky, erratic movement from across the bare storage space and a fleeting thought infected her mind. *He tricked me. He's more dangerous than Morley.*

'So talk if you're going to talk.' He began furiously undoing the buttons of his shirt, revealing the puckered red puncture mark on his chest from where Morley had stabbed him. He tore the shirt off and let it drop from his hand before rooting through a bulging bin bag. He pulled out a crumpled blue jumper with the word 'STRIDENT' emblazoned across it and put it on.

She would not tell him about Bernard now, not while he was in this state.

'It's nothing,' she began cautiously. 'I just don't want to do anything too hasty.'

'Hasty?' he chuckled darkly. 'Hasty. What's too hasty then, Emily? Beating him over the head with a hammer? Kidnapping him?'

'Burning him with boiling water,' Emily interrupted. 'I'd say that's pretty fucking hasty.'

'Then you're an even bigger idiot than I thought you were.'

She recoiled and felt claustrophobia creeping up on her. The warehouse, which had seemed so large and cavernous before, was shrinking around her. Her lungs felt like they had about a thimbleful of air in them.

'I don't have to stay here and listen to this shit.' She had to get out of this warehouse, away from the gritty air and the toxic, oppressive atmosphere.

'Get back here, Emily.'

When she didn't obey his command, he stalked after her. He had to walk quicker than he was comfortable doing to catch her at the stairs. He saw her ponytail swaying and wanted to grab hold of it and pull her off her feet. He resisted the urge and took the support of the banister instead. 'Emily, will you just wait a second?' She continued gliding down the stairs. He waited until he had reached the last step before grabbing hold of her arm. 'I told you to stop.'

She spun and snatched her arm away. 'Don't you ever put your hands on me, Jack.'

A look of cold, hard anger touched his face like a passing shadow. Then he gave her a sheepish, apologetic grin.

'This is a stressful time, I know,' he began to say, each word like an obstacle course for him. He was struggling to catch his breath, and his forehead shone with sweat. 'A lot has happened in the last few days and we wouldn't be human if we weren't a bit on edge. I'm sorry.'

She said nothing.

'Look, I'm close to getting the truth out of him, I know it. I just need a bit more time and then we can be rid of him forever. We can wash our hands of the whole thing.'

He tried to reach out for her hand. She pulled it away before he could touch her.

'Just give me one more day with him,' Jack said, his face strained. 'One more day and I'll know why he did it. And then we can bury him and the past with him. What do you say?'

She bit her bottom lip, chewing it white. 'We could let him go,' she whispered.

She saw that shadow pass across his face again. He blinked rapidly and sputtered, 'W-what?'

'Hold your horses. I can see you're already getting angry.'

'I just want to make absolutely sure of what I'm hearing,' he said.

'We dump him somewhere. The police pick him up or somebody else does; either way he's out of our hair and he goes to jail or he gets killed.' The more she spoke, the better the plan sounded. 'It takes the onus off us to deal with his body. And this way, if the police get him, he goes down for a long time.'

'No,' he said firmly.

'Don't you even want to think about it? This gets us off the hook, Jack.'

'This isn't about him going to prison and it isn't about someone else killing him. This is about *our* revenge, not his punishment.'

She saw that he had turned into a brick wall and would not budge. She opened her mouth to say more, but by now, every word was a workout. She opened the door of the warehouse and stepped out.

'Do you want a lift?'

'No,' she said, and almost laughed at the absurdity of his offer. She thought about the hotel she had checked herself into and the dent it was putting in her credit card. Maybe if she called her boss and grovelled, explained that she'd had a family tragedy, then she'd be able to go back to work next week. She was about to walk off when she said, 'Will you at least do me one favour?'

'Name it.'

'Don't hurt him any more.' Even in the darkness, she could see his mouth opening to object, but she steamrollered ahead. 'I know you're trying to get a confession, but will you just wait until I get back here?'

'Why?'

'Because I think there's more than one way to skin a cat and it doesn't include mutilating him. He's already in a bad way. You do anything more to him and he's going to shut down completely, maybe go into shock. He could have a heart attack or something.'

'Fine. I'll just get him a nice fluffy pillow, make him some bacon and eggs and see if he's feeling better. How about that?'

'I'm not telling you to pamper him,' she said flatly. 'I just think we need to try another tactic. Beating him with hammers and scalding him with boiling water hasn't done much to change his tune, so maybe we can think of something better.'

'I'm not going to have him trying to confuse me,' Jack said indignantly. 'I don't care what he says, this time I know it's him for sure.'

This time?

Before she could ask for clarification, knowing it would spark off another argument that would frustrate Jack, he said, 'Your wish is my command. I won't touch him. I won't speak to him. After all, I think it's important that you're here when he confesses. I wouldn't want to rob you of that. Maybe when he gives up his reason, we'll both stop having nightmares about her.'

She could just about make out his impish grin. It was as though he had reached into the memory well at the back of her mind and stirred the pool with his finger. A collection of snapshots made a mosaic: Kate trying to stop a mouthful of tea from spilling out of her mouth while laughing at a rude joke; Kate's red face and frizzy hair as they argued about a ripped T-shirt that Emily had borrowed; Kate driving down the motorway singing along with a Cher song; Kate sitting at her breakfast table with a bloody scarf knotted around her neck...

Emily hoped he could keep his hands to himself until she got back.

Chapter Forty-Three

The warehouse sounds spooked Craig.

One of the few secrets he had left that he would, it seemed, take to the grave with him, was that he was ever so slightly afraid of the dark. The origin of that fear started from a young age, and while most children would have shrugged it off by the time they reached their adolescent years, it had always stayed with him. At night, he would curl into a tight ball in bed with the quilt covering every inch of him, burning up all the oxygen with steady, measured breaths. With his eyes tightly closed, a fork of tension would twist through his forehead, and as his skin grew hotter, an acute sense of claustrophobia would set in. He would always be tempted to throw the quilt back and gasp for air, emerging from his swaddling like a person who has just surfaced after nearly drowning. That was how he had fallen asleep most nights as a child: his whole body clenched like a fist, suffocating on his own breath, too petrified to move a muscle in case the bed springs whined and broke the silence.

He was not afraid of ghosts or goblins knocking around the house. He wasn't even bothered by the story he'd heard at school of the pigeon lady that sits on the end of boys' beds with an awful smile on her face (although it had creeped him out well enough). He knew that all these things were myths and vapours. However, he also understood that if he were to pull back the quilt and peek out into the darkness of his room, there was a chance he would see his brother standing there with that terrible, dead look on his face.

Maurice liked to creep around the house at night. He didn't sleep very well, and whether that was down to the noises in his pillow or a side effect of the medication he was taking, Craig never knew. Yet Maurice's wanderings would usually end with him standing next to Craig's bed, staring at him, whispering in a low voice, 'I've got to give you something.' More often than not, Maurice would have some obscure gift for him that never made much sense, but was always of the utmost importance to Maurice: a fuzzy keychain with goggle eyes that he had found at the side of the road; a book about Osama bin Laden; a pill bottle filled with ball bearings.

Other times, Maurice would just talk. He would enter Craig's room so silently that Craig wouldn't even know he was there until he heard the breathy incantations emanating from the corner. The conversations that Maurice conducted with himself always sounded like nonsense to Craig. Yet sometimes there would be a startling clarity in his voice that almost made him think Maurice was pulling some sort of joke on them all, that he was in fact just a regular guy with some irregular ideas.

He tried not to think about his brother so much because dredging up those memories made him cringe and run cold all over. He could be at a traffic light or withdrawing money from a cashpoint and Maurice's strange, flat voice would creep into his mind, pebbling his cheeks with goosebumps. Whenever that happened, Craig would scrunch his eyes closed until the breeze blew out of his system, weathering the chill as best he could.

Beyond the door, Craig could hear the heavy thump-drag of Jack's pacing. He was muttering to himself, and sometimes the muttering would grow louder and more intelligible as he neared the oiling room door. It seemed to Craig that Jack had been walking around for hours. He was agitated. Craig could hear it in the cadence and rhythm of Jack's speech, the way certain words would leap out of the darkness and ring through the warehouse.

He's going to kill me soon, he realised with a finality that was as close to peaceful as he could hope for. There was no way out of the ropes. He had resigned himself to death, welcoming the idea as the only reprieve he was likely to receive against the ungodly agony he had endured. He had hoped that the pain in his head would have killed him. He would have welcomed a death like that if it meant he robbed Jack of the opportunity to do it himself.

He listened to the pipe gurgling behind him and the echoes of Jack's footfall. He had neither the strength nor the enthusiasm to sit up. Even if, by some miracle, the ropes loosened and the door creaked open, Craig didn't think he would be physically capable of leaving. The pain owned him completely. Even breathing was an exercise in torture, each inhalation setting off a bomb in the minefield of his skull.

The door opened and Jack's silhouette filled the threshold, his frame haloed by the milky white warehouse lights. His shoulders heaved as though he had just finished jogging and was still trying to catch his breath.

'It's time now,' Jack said, steam rising from his mouth as he spoke.

'Just kill me,' Craig mewled.

'Yes, that's what I'm here to do.' He stepped into the room. In one hand he held a plastic bag, in the other a meat cleaver.

Craig's eyes met the gleam of the cleaver. Warm sweat dribbled over his cold skin and he shivered. The pain in his body was still enormous, but now it registered as some undefinable anomaly. He was floating, detached from himself, but the cleaver pulled him right back.

'I want to end your misery in a humane way,' Jack said tonelessly, standing like a monolith before Craig's broken and blistered body. 'Will you at least let me do that for you?'

'I just want to die,' Craig croaked. Every swallow was like a mouthful of sand forced down his throat. 'Just let me die. Please.'

'I can do that for you. I can give you a quick death.' Jack pulled a face and eased himself down onto one knee. 'I can make all your pain go away. Or, if you want to drag this out, I can suffocate you slowly, take you to the brink of death and pull you back again. But I don't want to do that.' He reached out and stroked Craig's knotted hair, one calloused thumb brushing his sweat-beaded nose. 'Confess to me.'

Craig gave him the slightest nod, his rough tongue probing the blisters that clustered his lips. 'I will.' He felt the warm breeze of Jack's breath on his face. 'Throat... dry... water?'

'You promise to confess your sins?'

'Yes,' he coughed out painfully.

'All right then.' Jack vanished and came back with a cup of lukewarm water. He placed the cup at Craig's lips.

'Open your mouth,' he said, and delicately poured the water into his mouth. 'Is that better?' Jack asked. Craig sighed. 'You know, Craig, I almost admire your spirit. I don't know how you held off for as long as you did, but now you can give it all up and go with God. Does that sound good?'

'Yes,' Craig said and smiled, involuntarily causing the corners of his mouth to split and bleed.

'Then tell me.'

'Will you do it quickly?'

'If you tell me the truth, then you have my word. If you lie, you get the bag.'

'All right then,' he said. 'I'll tell you why I did it.'

Chapter Forty-Four

It was time to go. She could feel the walls closing in, and speaking to Morley had set off a siren in her brain, shrilling for her to get out, get moving. She had to put as much distance between her and that warehouse as possible, erase all memory of what she had helped to do. Morley was right, she was a coward. She could not be there for the slaughter, but she knew it was close. She could sense Jack's lust for it increasing when they last spoke, and the more she questioned Morley's guilt, the more incensed he became. Jack was desperate for his blood.

The adrenaline boiled in Emily's veins, dissolving away her lethargy. Her body had been like a sandbag and now, as she jogged down the street, she was barely aware of any heaviness at all. She was in cruise control, all her muscles operating on memory, her feet slapping the pavement so fast she thought she might trip over. It was as though the wind were pushing her along, carrying her. Her mind was a crowded room, full of conversation. Through it she could hear snippets of thoughts, fragmented ideas, all of it lost beneath a haze of fear.

She had been running almost full speed since the train station, her lungs burning with every laboured breath. As she skidded up the path to her house and stopped at the front door, she became light-headed.

Roger opened the door, his face shuffling through expressions, unsure of how to look. 'Emily,' he said, his lips working overtime to find the right words. 'What do you want?'

'My stuff,' she said, combing her sweat-greasy hair away from her blotchy face. 'I need the rest of my stuff.'

'Oh,' he said, and his current expression seemed to collapse with disappointment. 'Um, sure.' He stepped back and held the door wider, allowing her passage.

She moved past him and into the silent house. 'I need to go to the shed and get the big suitcase.'

'The one with the broken wheels?'

'Yeah.' She nodded.

'That's *my* suitcase.'

She blinked, felt sweat sting her eyes. 'No it isn't.'

'Yes it is. I got it from TK Maxx before we went to Morocco.'

She cast her mind back, searching for the memory. In her head, she pushed through the crowded room, came to a jittery black-and-white TV screen and tried to tune the aerial. She remembered both of them being in TK Maxx that day, but couldn't recall who had paid for it.

'Look, either you let me have that suitcase or I'll have to make two or three trips to get all my stuff.'

'Or you could just buy another one,' he said with a shrug. He was back to being a petulant little boy.

'You know what? Fine. Keep the suitcase. I'm going to take a few of my things and you can do whatever you want with the rest of it. Take my clothes and burn them on the lawn if you want to. I don't give a shit any more.'

She charged up the stairs and headed to the bedroom. Upon opening the door, she was met with the pungent odour of food – what smelled like Pot Noodle and Chinese takeaway – and recoiled ever so slightly. It smelled like the room of a man who'd been holed up for days, bingeing miserably.

She opened the sock drawer and rifled through it until she found her passport. Then, with that safely tucked away in her pocket, she rooted through the dressing table, scooping up all her jewellery – tangled necklaces, rings, earrings, bangles. None of it was worth very much but the accumulation might fetch a few pounds if she found herself in a pinch. That thought almost made her laugh, because boy, oh boy, was she in a pinch now.

What else? She thought about whether it was worth taking any shoes, but decided against it. Her shoes were generally cheap and most of them needed resoling. Underwear? She could pick up some cheap items from Primark. She scanned the room frantically, knowing that she was forgetting something, but not quite sure what. Then she saw a photo of Kate wedged into the mirror and remembered the shoebox. Her old photos were the most precious things she owned, and there she was worrying about knickers and scuffed old shoes.

On all fours, she reached under the bed, shifting Roger's junk around in an effort to locate the shoebox. She moved the bag that contained his archery set – one of his expensive fads that had fizzled out almost as quickly as it had arrived – and brushed aside loose free weights and boxing gloves that had never been used.

The old shoebox wasn't where it should have been. Her first thought was that he had thrown them out in an effort to spite her, and a new wave of panic welled up. She reared back under the bed, bonking her head hard against the wooden slats, and shuffled out. She could hear him coming up the stairs. She stormed across the room to meet him on the landing.

'Roger? Where are my photos?' She flung the door back. It bounced off the wall and echoed through the house. She saw that he was carrying the broken-wheeled suitcase up the stairs for her. It was wrapped in a ragged bin bag that was covered in a coat of dust and probably housing a thousand spiders.

'I got the case,' he said quietly.

'Where are the photos?'

'What photos?'

'You know what photos. The ones of my sister. Where are they?'

He shook his head. 'I don't know.'

'They were under the bed! Don't tell me you don't know when they've always been under the bed.'

'I haven't touched them. Did you look properly?'

'Yes,' she snapped.

'I bet you didn't,' he grumbled, and got down on all fours to investigate. Grunting and shifting, he reappeared a moment later with an old Adidas shoebox. Emily exhaled and pressed a hand against her forehead. She fought the tears through a rolling tide of relief.

'Thank you,' she said, and carefully relieved him of the shoebox as though it might disintegrate at her touch. Like the bin bag covering the suitcase, the shoebox was coated with dust. When had been the last time she had looked at these photos? A year? Two years? More? She felt the strength disappear from her legs and sat down on the bed, cradling the box like a baby. Eventually she said, 'I'm sorry, Roger.'

'Don't apologise.' He sat down beside her, giving her about a foot of personal space.

Emily opened the box and selected a photo from the mound. It was a picture of her and Kate at Disneyland with matching Minnie Mouse ears on.

'God, you look young there,' Roger said gently.

'Yeah.' Emily cleared her throat and put the lid back on the box. 'Think we were eleven in that picture.'

'You look like you're having fun.'

'We were,' she said, and met his eyes. 'Thanks for bringing the suitcase up. If you really want it, I'll drop it back once I'm settled.'

'No, I don't want it back,' he said. 'I just wish you didn't have to go.'

'Well, I do.' She stood up and pulled the bin bag off the suitcase, coughing as the dust tickled her throat. She unzipped and opened it. Inside, there was a tag from a swimming costume she had worn on their last holiday together.

'I've been looking at houses in Bournemouth. You always said you wanted to retire there. And I found this one place I'm sure we can afford, and—'

'No, Roger,' she said painfully. They went to Bournemouth every year for Valentine's Day, always staying at the same hotel by the sea. She had loved that tradition.

'What is it, Em? What's going on?'

'There's nothing to tell. I'm leaving and that's the end of it.'

'I deserve a reason, Emily. Don't I deserve that much at least?'

She started to pack, vaguely glad that she could take some underwear after all. 'We haven't been working for a long time now. You know that and I know it. Why don't we just leave it there?'

He left her to pack in silence for half a minute or so, before saying, 'You're in trouble, aren't you?'

'No,' she replied, too quickly to sound casual.

'When you came back the other day, you know, that day you stayed out all night, I saw you had blood on your hand. I didn't really connect anything until I had time to think about it.'

'I didn't have any blood on me,' she said flatly.

'All this weird business with Jack just turning up out of the blue. And then this other guy.'

She froze. 'What other guy?'

'He knocked this morning looking for you. At first I thought he was a homeless man. He was pale as a sheet and had these scary bulging eyes. He was skinny too, like a rake. And before he started talking I thought he was some kind of cripple knocking around for money or something, because he walked funny and—'

'You spoke to him?' she asked, dropping a bundle of T-shirts to the floor.

'Yeah. He asked if you lived here and I said you used to, but now you didn't.'

'What else did you tell him?'

Roger grabbed the pillow, placed it on his lap. He looked down at the carpet and said, 'Nothing really.'

'Roger. What did you tell him?'

'I don't know,' Roger whined. 'I asked him why he was looking for you and he said he couldn't tell me. But he said it was a life or death situation. I almost laughed at that until I realised he was serious.' Roger tittered, hoping it would change the look on Emily's face, as though she might suddenly see the funny side in all this. 'The way you had been acting lately, I didn't know what you were up to. So I said if he wanted to speak to you he should try getting in touch with Jack.'

Emily thought she felt the room spin.

'What was I supposed to tell him?' Roger yelled defensively. 'I had this feeling that he was telling the truth, that this might actually be a life or death situation, and… look, I haven't done anything wrong, Emily. I'm not going to keep being your answering service and forward all your post. This is what happens when you break up. Sometimes there are loose ends and—'

Bernard's laughter cut through the noise in the crowded room of her mind. Bernard, who had been to the house once before for dinner and knew her address. Bernard, who she had used to get information on Morley and then taunted when he tried to turn it to his advantage. Surely she could have played him better, held him off for a little while until she had room to move, instead of firing off that text message. Had Bernard set the dogs on her? Had he paid someone to harm her, to—

Life or death situation.

—kill her?

'Shut up a second, will you? When you say you told him to get in touch with Jack, what do you mean?'

'I gave the guy Jack's business card. I found it in your jeans the other day when I went to do a load of washing. Don't know why I kept it really, but I suppose it came in handy.'

The blood drained from Emily's face.

'Em, are you all right?'

'No,' she whispered. 'I don't think I am.'

Chapter Forty-Five

Dillon hadn't been sure of how to approach the warehouse. The name on the business card said Jack Bracket, and that was all he knew about the man he assumed had helped kidnap Craig. It had all started to add up on the drive over. This woman Emily and this silly prick Jack had snatched Craig off the estate and they were keeping him at the warehouse. Why, Dillon didn't know, and so far as he was concerned, he didn't care.

He'd had quite a battle trying to wrestle the woman out of her car. Fearing that he was going to force her legs apart or maim her with acid, she kicked and clawed at him until, for one insane instant, he thought she was going to overpower him. He got behind the wheel and left her bawling and screaming by the side of the road, waving her arms to try and flag down help. Like everything else, it had been a mess. Now, he reached in his pocket for the polythene bag. There were a couple of grams left, enough to dust each nostril and give him a kick up the arse when he needed it, but now wasn't the time.

He could feel himself tumbling. He placed a hand on the wall to steady himself, his other hand coiled around the car jack. His heart flapped in his chest like an angry bird. His first thought had been to ring the buzzer and crack the head of the first person that opened the door. From there, he would sweep through the warehouse, swinging the car jack like a battleaxe until he found Craig and… and nothing. It was a ridiculous delusion. Even if he had a whole ounce of coke to throw him into a berserker frenzy, he knew it wouldn't work. His borrowed bravery was vanishing, and Dillon knew he couldn't rush into this. He had no idea what was on the other side of that warehouse door.

The twilight was deepening, the shadows stretching across the industrial estate. Dillon withdrew from the door and continued backing up until he reached a large commercial waste bin opposite the warehouse. If there was ever a time when he needed to think things through, to assess the situation and not go in there raging like a nutcase, it was now. Carefully he crouched down behind the bin, the car jack clanging noisily off the metal. He cringed away from the noise, expecting someone to come rushing out of the warehouse to investigate, but nobody did.

He watched and waited, and thought about his daughter.

Chapter Forty-Six

Emily jumped out of the Uber, grabbed her case from the boot, and raced up to the warehouse, the soles of her trainers kicking up pebbles from the uneven concrete. She stumbled to a halt and thumbed the intercom, before battering the door with her fists. She bent down, flicked the letterbox open with her fingers and shouted through. 'Open the door! It's Emily!' Her words echoed off the boxes and bays, ricocheting around the warehouse. For an awful moment, she thought Jack might not be there, but when she whirled and saw his van still parked by the side of the building, she unleashed another flurry of thumps on the door.

'Jack, open up!'

The lock turned and she barged through the door before he had it fully opened, the suitcase toppling over on its side.

'What's got into you? Are you soft in the head or something?' He followed her down the aisle, struggling to keep pace with her. He caught her by the elbow. 'Hey, I'm talking to you.'

'Has anyone been here today?'

'What do you mean?'

'What do you *think* I mean? Has anyone knocked on the door today?'

'No.' He shook his head. 'Why?'

'Were you here the whole day?'

'Yeah. What's the matter?'

She turned away and continued down the aisle. She reached the oiling room. The door was locked.

'Open it,' she snarled.

'Wait a minute. You can't just come kicking and screaming at that door. There are other people in those warehouses out there. Are you listening to me?'

'No, you listen to me,' she fired back, slapping the oiling room door. 'Open the door! Are you deaf?'

'Let me know when you've finished your little hissy fit.' His face was beet red and he was breathing heavily through his nostrils. He palmed his beard and said, 'Are you going to keep rabbiting on or…?'

'We need to get him out of here, drop him off somewhere, and… just smooth this whole mess over before it gets any worse.'

'What's with the suitcase? You planning on doing a runner?'

She swallowed. Her forehead burned and the veins in her temples throbbed. 'I'm leaving, Jack. Someone knows. I came here to warn you and that's it. I'm going.'

'Knows what?'

'About what we did.' She shook her head. 'I went back to my house today to get the rest of my stuff and Roger said someone had come looking for me. And Roger gave them your business card, so now they know I've been hanging round with you and could be on their way here right now.'

'Calm down,' he grunted.

'Fuck calming down! This is no time to be calm. We have to get Morley out of here. Someone is coming after me... *us!*'

Laughter tumbled out of Jack. It was high-pitched and erratic, a frightening, jagged sound. He rubbed his eyes with the heels of his hands, grabbed a nearby stepping stool and sat down on it. 'I'm not buying it. I've been here all day and nobody has come knocking. And if anyone does decide to turn up, we'll deal with it.' He stopped, his head cocking to the side. 'Why are you looking at me like that?'

'I don't know,' she said. Could she still trust him now, after everything that had happened between them, after all her doubts? 'Right now the only thing I know for sure is that I helped kidnap Morley, I helped hurt him, and he could be innocent.'

'He isn't innocent!' Jack bellowed, his face vibrating with rage. His complexion darkened and a thin white foam formed in the corners of his mouth. He began to rasp for breath, wheezing with the effort.

'What I'm saying is that I'm not a hundred percent sure any more. And I only ever wanted to do this if I was completely certain—'

'He confessed.'

Jack's words cut her sentence short. Her mouth snapped shut with an audible click.

'I don't understand,' she sputtered. 'When did this happen?'

'About an hour ago,' he said.

She looked at the oiling room door uncertainly. 'Open it. I want to ask him for myself.'

Jack shook his head. 'You can't.'

'Why?'

'Because he's dead.'

Chapter Forty-Seven

A plastic bag covered Morley's face, sucked in at the mouth from where he'd gasped for air. Emily stared at the body, stunned to silence. She expected to be able to think something, or to have some kind of emotional response, but she came up short in both departments. Instead, she just stood there, wavering on the spot like a tall blade of grass in the breeze.

It was all over.

'So that's it,' she said, barely aware that she was talking at all.

'Almost. We still have to bury him.'

Her stomach flip-flopped. She closed her eyes and tried to will the rising tide of panic to settle.

'I don't think…'

'You don't think you can?' Jack barged past her, picked up the hatchet from the windowsill, and hacked through the ropes. Without the bonds to support its weight, Morley's body flopped down and made a sickening slap on the concrete. 'You just want to leave me to do all the heavy lifting, is that it?'

For some reason her nostrils had only just scented the wretched aroma of bodily waste, and she gagged, covering her mouth. The stink got right into the back of her throat, coated her tongue.

Jack bent down, grabbed hold of Morley's ankles and began to drag him toward the doorway. About halfway across the room, he stopped and hissed, muttered something about his back through gritted teeth, and then continued dragging him. 'Get out of the way,' he said, and Emily moved. He brought the trolley over and with an effort that made the veins stand out in his head and neck, lifted Morley's carcass onto it. When he was done, he stood up and used the front of his jumper to mop the sweat from his brow.

'You think I'm going to bury him alone?' Jack said. 'You thought you were just going to pack a bag and leave me in the lurch to deal with it by myself? No chance. We're in this together until the end.'

'What did he say, Jack? Why did he do it?'

'I'll tell you in the van. We've got work to do.'

'I want to know *now*,' she said, almost screaming with frustration, her fingers raking through her greasy hair. 'I want to know why he killed Kate.'

He whirled on her, pupils ablaze. 'Keep your voice down,' he growled. 'Stop acting like a spoiled brat and let's get him in the van. We've got a long drive ahead of us. I can tell you everything on the way.'

'No. No more. I'm not going with you. I've done my part.'

'No, you haven't,' he countered. 'You haven't done anything.'

'Yeah? If it wasn't for me, Morley would have got away in the car park, and he would have escaped when *you* let him cut through the ropes. I saved you both times.'

'Yeah, bravo.' He clapped condescendingly. 'You hit him with a hammer after I'd already stunned him and fucked his head up so he didn't know up from down by the time I tried to question him. No wonder it took him so long to start talking sense.'

'You rushed into this. You went charging in without knowing the truth and you made me believe it. I was trying to help.'

'Yeah, big help you were too. And you can stop trying to pin this whole thing on me, making everything my fault. You're a grown woman. I didn't put a gun to your head and force you to do anything.'

'No,' she agreed. 'And you can't force me to do anything now.'

'You're absolutely right. But maybe you should think it over.' He gave her a mirthless grin and pointed to the corner of the warehouse. A CCTV camera was trained directly on the oiling room. 'You've been on camera the whole time. So you can go and jet off into the sunset and leave me to do the rest of the dirty work, but god forbid I don't get that grave dug by morning and someone sees me standing in the open with a dead body at my feet.'

Jack opened the warehouse door and walked out to the van. Beyond the bright glow cast by the motion-sensor spotlight, the industrial estate was a black void. He opened the passenger door and was about to climb in when he thought he heard something off to the right. It had sounded like the crunch of gravel underfoot. He stopped, turned his head and peered into the darkness. Had that been a fox? Had it been anything at all? No, perhaps not. Perhaps all the evening's excitement had his senses fuddled. He stood there a second longer, head slightly cocked in the direction from which the sound had come, and heard nothing except the gentle stirring of the wind. Now that the adrenaline was beginning to ebb, he was tired and feeling dopey. His mouth opened wide to accommodate a series of yawns, and then he got in the van. He began to reverse so that the back doors would lead directly to the warehouse entrance, which would make hoisting Morley's body aboard that much easier. He did not turn on his headlights as he reversed because he only had to move the van back about ten feet.

If he had turned on his headlights when he entered the van, they would have shone directly onto Dillon, who was waiting by a large commercial waste bin, wielding a car jack like a baseball bat.

Chapter Forty-Eight

Jack had one foot across the warehouse threshold when he heard the crunch of gravel again. This time, however, it was faster, like something running toward him. The shock of the sound set off a flashbang of panic inside him, but before he could fully turn around, something heavy struck him in the crook between his neck and shoulder. There was no immediate pain, only a whirlwind of confusion that gathered around his thoughts as he buckled awkwardly to the floor. His cheek slapped against the concrete and instinctively he began to roll onto his back so that he could see what had attacked him. Had he not reacted so quickly, the car jack would have come down even harder against his spine. Instead, it struck the floor with a loud metallic crescendo that rang through the warehouse.

'Wait, wait, wait,' Jack said, his hands coming up to cover his face. 'Wait a second, please!'

Dillon had the car jack raised over his head, gripping it with both hands. He was about to bring the thing home against Jack's skull when he saw the body. He stopped, lowered his arms, but did not let go of the jack.

'Oh Jesus above, help me now,' Dillon murmured, hardly aware that blood was dribbling from his left nostril and tracing over his top lip. In a daze, he walked over to the body piled atop the trolley. He exhaled long and hard, and his head began bobbing forward. At first, Jack thought the man was going to be sick, but Dillon was actually trying to swallow. 'What have you done to him?'

'Just wait a second, will you?' Jack said, pressing his palms against the floor to get up into a sitting position. A raw ache throbbed through his shoulder and he thought his arm might collapse beneath his weight. 'Can I explain? Will you give me that at least?'

'You killed him?' Dillon's voice was dull and lifeless, and now he was sucking in air, gasping for breath. He reached out to touch the bin liner that covered Morley's face, but retracted his hand. 'Is this him? Is it Craig?'

'You have to let me explain,' Jack panted.

'Is it *him*?' Dillon whacked the jack against a metal pillar.

'Yes,' Jack replied, patting his fleece pocket. Thank god above. He had his knife. 'But you need to let me explain.'

'Oh, you're going to explain,' Dillon said, nodding. 'You're going to explain it all. But not to me.' He removed a phone from his pocket and thumbed the buttons, glancing up every couple of seconds to check on Jack. Jack didn't move from the floor, but his hand crept toward the zip of his fleece pocket.

Dillon placed the phone up to his ear and wiped away the rogue tears that had begun to seep from his eyes.

In the silence of the warehouse, Jack could hear the phone ringing through the receiver.

'Hello,' Dillon said when he got an answer. 'Listen to me. I've found Craig, but you need to get here now. No, you don't understand.' He stopped, a look of pain tugging his features into a scowl. 'It isn't what you think... Do you really want me to say it over the phone? Just, please, come down.' He paused, pacing back and forth. 'The address? Yeah, hold on.' He cradled the phone between his ear and shoulder and reached into his pocket, removing the business card he had received from the man at the address that Mikkel had given him. 'You have a pen? All right, it's—'

Dillon dropped the phone and a scream ripped out of his mouth. His head jerked violently to the side and he spun around, flailing his arms, and then collapsed. He continued to scream as he rolled around on the floor, and the sound of his distress filled the warehouse.

Jack could not work out what had happened to the man. His screams only served to startle and bewilder him further. He could see blood now, some of it sprayed across the painted cinderblock wall, some of it dotting the floor. Jack hesitated, still unsure of the situation, and then he saw Emily off to the side, stepping out from behind a column of boxes. She was holding something, her complexion the colour of sour milk.

It was the nail gun.

Jack looked back at the man, but he was still rolling around so frantically that Jack couldn't quite see where the nail had struck him. He put it out of his mind for the moment and saw the green glow of the mobile phone's screen. Jack picked it up and held it to his ear.

'Dillon?' A deep, uninterested voice said down the receiver. The voice had an accent. Jack terminated the call, undid the back of the phone, removed the battery and snapped the SIM card in half.

'He was going to tell,' Emily said shakily. She sounded like a little girl. 'Here,' she extended the nail gun toward him like a gift. 'Take this. He… he was going to tell.'

The man was howling like an injured dog. He got onto all fours, cupping his mouth and chin with his hands. Blood spilled through the gaps in his fingers. When he pulled his hands away, a cupful of blood splashed onto the floor and the man's screams filled the warehouse.

'Take this, *please!*' Emily thrust the nail gun into Jack's chest. 'Take it, will you!'

'Yes,' he replied, accepting the nail gun. He placed it on the metal stairs that led up to the office, and rested his hands on Emily's shoulders. She flinched and backed away from his touch. 'You did the right thing. You did the right thing, Emily.'

'Can't you get him to be quiet?' She pressed her index fingers in her ears and screwed her face up. 'I can't bear it.'

'I know,' he said. 'Don't freak out. It had to be done.'

Jack turned and saw the man struggling to his knees, clawing at his face. The screaming had been replaced with high-pitched shrieks that came out with every breath. Jack saw that this whole time the door had been wide open. He strode across and went to close it with his right arm. There was an instant blossom of pain through his shoulder as he pressed against the door, so he barged it shut with his other shoulder. Then he saw the car jack on the floor and picked it up.

'Emily, are you still there?' Jack asked, without turning to see.

'Y-yes,' she said, almost choking on the word.

'I want you to turn away and press your hands over your ears. You're not going to want to see this.'

'What are you—?'

'Emily!' he bellowed. 'Do it.'

She turned away as she had been instructed, and stared at a stack of imitation marble countertops piled in six-foot towers.

Jack looked down at the man. A three-inch nail had pierced his cheek at an angle and appeared to be lodged in his soft palate. The blood pouring out of his mouth was black and thick as treacle.

'Look at me,' Jack said to the man. The man's eyes were wild with fear. His face had turned sickly pale from the blood loss. 'Is there anyone else on their way here?'

The man's eyelids fluttered. He gargled. His white hands trembled up to his face, his bloodstained fingers nearing the nail. He tried to pinch at the head of the nail and cried out in pain.

'I'll help you with that nail if you answer the question. Is there anyone else on their way over? Just nod yes or no.'

The man shook his head.

'You're not lying to me, are you?'

Again the man shook his head.

'Good,' Jack said, and then swung the car jack with all his strength.

Chapter Forty-Nine

The van's headlights carved a slice of the motorway out of the darkness. Emily sat up front and watched the white lines on the tarmac blur past as the road unfurled before them. She concentrated in an effort to keep her thoughts at bay and to try to stem the motion sickness that was slowly swishing in her stomach. Beyond the fusty, oily metallic smells that lived in the van, she picked up Morley's putrescence and wound down the window. The cool night air kissed her hot skin and she was dimly thankful for it.

Jack muttered under his breath as they clocked up the miles. She couldn't make out much of what he was saying, but it sounded as though he was planning out their next steps. She stole glimpses at him as the van passed beneath the overhead motorway lights, periodically washing the car in an amber glow. His eyes were wide and unblinking.

'Why did he do it?' she said, her words sounding odd as they broke the silence between them. 'You said he confessed. I need to know, Jack.'

Jack looked over at her for a long, hard moment. The van began to veer into the left lane and Emily's feet started to tingle. What was he thinking, taking his eyes off the road for that long while they were barrelling along at this speed? Then he returned his gaze to the road, righted the van's course, and said bluntly, 'She was having an affair.' His eyelids lowered until his eyes were nothing more than gleaming slits. 'Her boss.' There was a dull squeak as his grip tightened on the steering wheel. 'It was his baby, not mine.'

Emily looked at him.

'The man was already married with kids. Kate was trying to blackmail him, threatening to tell his wife, to tell people at work unless he kept paying her.' A low, dry laugh left his lips. 'I was wondering why she was buying all those designer shoes. She said that she got a pay rise and I believed her like a damn fool. Turns out it was hush money. Anyway, this man she was fucking' – he paused, cleared his throat – 'he used to buy coke from Morley, and one day he told him about the situation. Morley offered to get rid of her for five grand.' A tear ran down his face and he wiped it away. 'So there you go. Mystery solved.'

Emily rubbed her face. She sat there a moment, bent forward, one hand pressed firmly over her mouth.

Then she said, 'I don't believe it.'

Jack rolled his shoulders, blinked more tears. Drily, he said, 'Oh yeah? You seemed to believe everything else he said.'

'I don't believe it because I know she loved you.' As she said this, Jack bit down hard on his lower lip, the muscles in his cheeks twitching. 'I knew Kate as well as I knew myself, maybe even better. And one thing I knew beyond a shadow of a doubt was that she loved you, Jack. You remember how superstitious she was, how much she believed in karma. She would never do that to you, even if she wanted to.'

The tears rolled down his face freely now, each drop large and greasy.

'I'm telling you, Jack, she didn't do that.'

'Maybe you didn't know her as well as you thought you did.'

'You don't know how close we were…'

'I know you were close until university. Then you dropped out and she stayed on, got a new bunch of friends, got involved with me, became her own person and not just a twin any more.'

Emily didn't think there were any more tears left in her. She was wrong. 'So you really believe that, do you?' She wiped the tears away with the back of her hand. 'You believe she cheated on you and was murdered to keep it secret?'

'I don't *want* to believe it,' he said, 'but hearing him say it made sense. It was like I'd found the missing piece of a jigsaw and now I can see the whole picture.'

Emily made a disgusted, spitting sound. 'Morley was trying to make her the villain to get you on his side. He knew you were going to kill him no matter what, so he gave it a shot.'

Jack flicked the indicator on and pulled off the motorway. 'I think we will just have to agree to disagree. He's dead, and that's all I care about.'

Chapter Fifty

When they came off the motorway, Jack drove them through a series of country lanes. Emily could only make out their surroundings in the light from the van's full beams, and felt the road dipping and rising beneath the tyres. The van rumbled along on the rocky ground. The leafless tree branches flanking them on either side of the lane scraped the windscreen and roof with an eerie screech.

Jack deviated from the lane, continued on to a patch of field and shut off the engine.

'Where are we?' she asked.

'The middle of nowhere. The nearest building is a pub about four miles down the road. Come on.' He got out of the van and Emily quickly followed behind him.

'What if a car comes along?' She reached out and touched his arm, but could barely make out his silhouette.

'The hedgerows hide the van from the road. And anyway, I doubt a car will come by this time of night.' He opened up the back doors, releasing a backdraught of fetid, human odour. 'But if they do, they won't see the van.'

'Are you sure?'

He reached into the van and grabbed a shovel, a torch and a canvas bag. 'We'll dig the hole first and then come back for the bodies.'

'What's that?' Emily asked, just about able to make out the bag in the moonlight.

Jack switched the torch on and trained the beam inside the bag, showing her the gun and hammer.

Emily felt warm breath leave her cold lips. 'You… you went back?'

'No.'

'Then… how?'

'Does it matter? There's nothing else that can tie us to Morley now. We bury it all together.'

He led her to a patch of grass by the hedgerow. 'Here,' he said extending the shovel. 'Dig.'

She took the shovel. It felt weighty and cumbersome in her hands. She hadn't dug anything since she was little, playing with a bucket and spade on the beach with Kate.

'Maybe it'd be better if you…?'

'You're going to dig the hole,' he said. 'My back is giving me murder.'

She had been thinking that he would likely get the job done quicker and more efficiently, even with a bad back, but she said nothing. She placed her foot on the shovel head and pressed her weight down until it broke through the earth. She chipped off a small portion of the soil and heaved it to the side.

'Don't toss the soil so far,' he admonished. 'We need it to cover them up when they're inside the hole.'

She began to build up something of a rhythm. The friction from the shovel's metal handle was already blistering her palms, and the muscles in her forearms burned.

Her mind was almost completely blank as she worked, but every few minutes a thought did resonate: she was burying a pair of human beings. Their bodies would rot in the ground and the worms would feast on their flesh until nothing but bones and the fabric of their clothes remained. And while all this was happening, she would go on living her life, growing old and decaying in her own way, pushing the memory of this night further into the back of her mind until it became a dream.

The earth was hard, and after half an hour, she hadn't made much of a dent. She tossed another shovelful of soil to the side and paused to catch her breath. Her cheeks were hot with the effort of her labour, and she was sweating inside her clothes. The cold no longer bothered her, but she could feel the large blisters pulsing on the pads of her hands. She spared a thought for Morley, what it must have been like for his whole face to erupt with blisters like an outbreak of acne, and then went back to work. Her lower back was starting to seize up, and her forearms became as stiff as tree roots. She flexed her fingers, heard the percussion of her popping knuckles, and tested the hole with her foot.

'Hurry it up,' Jack said. 'You don't have time to admire your work. You haven't even dug a foot in the earth yet. We need to bury them deep so that nothing digs them up when we're gone.'

'I'm trying,' she said, sticking the shovel back in the soil.

'Try harder.'

She gritted her teeth and decided to plough through the pain. The muscles in her neck and upper back were knotting up and she could feel the perspiration dripping off her chin. Soon she was standing in the hole, and in the torch's beam saw that she had dug about a bathtub's depth in the earth. Her progress spurred her on, and she attacked the soil with a renewed sense of determination; the quicker she dug the grave, the quicker she could bury her old life with them.

'What do we do after this?' she asked, huffing through her task. Her palms felt wet and she thought she might have popped her blisters, but she didn't stop to check.

'We drive back to London and carry on like nothing ever happened.'

He shone the torch into the hole to gauge how the grave was coming along. Another couple of feet and they could chuck the bodies in it.

'Take that light out of my face,' she said. 'I can't see.'

'Want me to take over?'

She looked at him warily. He extended his hand. She took hold of it, seething as their palms made contact, and climbed out of the hole.

'I'll finish up,' he said. 'Why don't you wait in the van?'

'I'm not waiting in there with… *them*.'

He climbed into the hole, relieved her of the shovel and started digging. 'I'm sorry about everything I said back at the warehouse. I didn't want to do any of this. I don't want to hurt anyone. But this had to be done. I couldn't live with myself if I let him go.'

She watched the fluidity of his movement as he dug without respite or complaint.

'I'm just a man that loved his wife more than life itself, and without her I'm… I'm nothing. I've woken up feeling empty inside every day since she died. I hope you never…' He paused. 'I hope you never have to know what that's like.' He tossed earth over his shoulder, wincing, and said quietly, 'Even if she did cheat on me, she still didn't deserve what she got. And I still love her.'

She heard the anguish in his voice and turned away.

–

The sky was beginning to brighten by the time Jack was finished. Emily could just about make out the hills in the horizon, and had a better idea of how vast the surrounding fields were.

Jack got behind the wheel. He turned on the ignition and began to drive. Emily wanted to ask him if he thought the hole was deep enough, whether there was any chance of foxes or badgers unearthing them, but in the end, it didn't make much difference. Even if he reassured her she would still wonder about it, and maybe that constant paranoia would be the luggage she would have to carry with her for the rest of her life.

They drove through the growing dawn and watched the sun appear over the hills as a dull yellow smudge in the misty white sky. Their eyes were wild and bloodshot in their grubby, sweat-streaked faces.

They looked like two people that had spent all night digging a grave.

The sun was warm and the sky was blue when they arrived at Jack's house to get cleaned up. Emily thought she could smell the first signs of spring in the air, but could very well have imagined it. A thought fluttered through her mind like a butterfly: Kate was still alive and Emily was just arriving for a visit. They were going to have a girls' night in with white wine and crap romcom movies, and any time Jack tried to poke his head round the door he would be banished because this was sister time, no boys allowed. She wondered how Kate would've coped with getting old, how she would've dealt with grey hair. She wondered about the trips they would've taken to New York like they always said they would.

She wondered what Kate would say if she could see her now. Would she be happy that they had killed Morley? Would she pat Emily on the back and tell her that she had done the right thing, that *anything* done for love was the right thing?

She wondered a lot as she entered Jack's house. She went up to the bathroom and washed her hands and face, saw the purple crescents beneath her eyes. Her eyes didn't look the same to her any more. They were now as dull and lifeless as old coins.

When she came downstairs, Jack was waiting for her by the door. 'I suppose you want to be on your way,' he said, unable to look her in the face.

'Yeah. I think it would be for the best.'

'I want to give you something,' he said, and held out a bulging envelope.

'What's that?' she asked, without taking it from him.

'It's about three grand. I've got some savings here and I thought this would come in handy for you. Go on, take it.'

'No.' She shook her head.

'Emily, please,' he implored, gesturing to the envelope. 'I want you to have it. It isn't much but it will give you some breathing space. Go on.'

She shook her head firmly. 'I don't want any of your money, Jack. I just want… I just want to know that everything will be all right.'

'It was a deep hole. I packed the earth well and it didn't look too obvious.'

'I don't mean that. I mean, just in general.'

'If you're asking me whether I think we'll get found out for Morley, then the answer is no.'

She swallowed the obstruction in her throat and said, 'I don't know if that's what I was asking.'

She turned the door lock and stepped out. The birds were singing and the sun shone directly into her face, warming her skin. 'She didn't cheat on you. You know that as well as I do.'

'I'm not so sure any more,' Jack said. 'I didn't want to believe a word Morley said, but that rang a bell with me. Doesn't matter much now either way, does it?'

'No,' she replied quietly. 'Because I think we killed an innocent man. Two innocent men,' she quickly amended.

'Innocent,' he snorted. 'That's where you and I have a different opinion.'

'Seems so.' Emily shielded her eyes against the sun and scanned the street. She started to walk down his driveway, her shadow stretching long behind her.

'Where will you go?' he called from the doorstep.

'I don't know yet,' she replied. 'But I don't think we'll be seeing each other again.'

Jack nodded and watched her walk down the street. When she was out of sight, he closed the door.

He was glad to see the back of her.

Chapter Fifty-One

Later that evening, Jack stood among the weeds in the garden drinking a beer. He decided that tomorrow he would drive out to the local garden centre and get everything he needed to transform this jungle into a picturesque paradise. He was going to buy flowers, a bench, pull up the weeds, mow the grass and get the place looking respectable again, like how Kate would have wanted it. He was going to plant some carrots and some tomatoes, and he was going to tend to them every single day, monitoring their progress. He had made himself this promise many times before, but he thought he might finally keep it now. After all, he would need something to focus his efforts on, to stop him from getting bored and surly. Gardening was as good a hobby as any.

He closed his eyes and replayed the last moments of Morley's miserable life in his mind. A cool gust of wind blew through the garden, stirring the weeds and tickling his skin, carrying the heady scent of soil and flora. He exhaled and felt every knot in his body loosen, the tension melting out of his muscles, the worries dissolving in his mind.

He could almost hear the sucking gasps as the plastic bag suffocated Morley, and delighted at the way his violent bucking had weakened, until his thrashing was nothing more than a series of feeble jerks.

In the end, Morley had literally had the last laugh. Instead of explaining why he had killed Kate, as he had promised to, Morley chose to use his dying breaths to chuckle in Jack's face. The chuckling escalated into a hacking fit, bloody foam flying from his ruined lips. He barked out a series of guttural coughs, drawing blood from his lungs, and then he spat a wad of phlegm in Jack's face.

'I hope you never find him,' Morley had said, with a bead of bloody saliva dangling from his smiling lips. 'Fuck your wife and fuck you. I hope you never find who did it.'

Those were his final words before the plastic bag encased his head and stole the last of his breath.

There had never been a confession about an affair. There hadn't been an explanation of any kind, but he supposed it no longer mattered. The main thing was that Jack knew he had caught the culprit. He had succeeded where the police had failed. He had avenged his wife, his dear sweet, beautiful Kate. She was smiling down on him from heaven, no doubt about it.

'Now we're even,' he said aloud, thinking about the way Morley's bowels had loosened right after his pathetic mewling dwindled to silence.

He drank the beer down to the dregs. He almost tossed the bottle among the weeds but caught himself at the last instant.

He waded through the tall grass and went back inside. By the time he was in bed, Craig Morley was nothing more than a distant memory.

Chapter Fifty-Two

On the other side of London, Bernard stood at his living-room window, holding a kitchen knife. Through the curtain, he watched the black boys playing football in the road, yelping and laughing like the animals they were. They seemed to be making a game of how high they could kick the ball; so far they had got it up past the telephone lines. Each time the ball came down with an echoing thud that shuddered through Bernard's rapidly tightening chest. A couple of times, the ball had gone into someone's front garden, and the boys had scrambled over the wall to reclaim it without a second's thought to the flowers and plants that might lie there.

Bernard had had enough. He had been watching them for the best part of an hour, his palm callousing from the grip around the knife's handle. He was sure that, at any moment, one of them would kick the ball into *his* garden, and when they did he was going to make the only stand he could. He was going to stab their ball with his knife and hurl it back across the road to where their mother sat listening to music on her phone. Of course, the ball would be the consolation prize, but he could always imagine that he was driving the knife into their eyes. In fact, he would look directly at them as he ruined their game, would savour their shocked expressions. He would laugh at them, maybe ask how high they could kick their ball now that it was flat as a fucking pancake. And if their mother piped up, well, perhaps he could give her a few home truths. He would tell her that he worked for the police and he had friends in high places. He could get hold of immigration, put a stop to her benefits, get her kicked out of her council house on an ASBO order. How would she like sleeping in the park with all her kids? That would be ideal, wouldn't it? Then they could kick the ball as high as they wanted.

He watched the boys separate as a Bentley crept along the tarmac before parking outside Bernard's house. A large man got out of the car and said something to the boy holding the football. The boy laughed and handed the ball over and the large man began to do kick-ups. He did about six or seven, and then headed the ball away. He went into his pocket and... was he giving those little bastards money? The boys' mother grew curious and looked over, before giving the large man a stupidly wide grin. She obviously approved of strangers paying her children for doing nothing; they learned from the best. The boys ran off whooping excitedly, their game forgotten.

The large man went around to the back door of the Bentley and opened it to allow an older but sharply dressed man out. The older man's white hair fell down past his shoulders and reminded Bernard of a wizard.

Who were these two? Property developers? Estate agents?

Bernard watched as the two men scanned the houses searching for something, before the larger man pointed directly at Bernard's front door. Bernard took a step back from the window, disturbed. Had they seen his silhouette? What were they looking for?

And then, as they started toward his doorstep, Bernard knew exactly who they were and what they wanted.

When the doorbell rang, Bernard dropped the kitchen knife. He slapped a hand over his mouth and stood completely still.

'Bernard, we know you're in there,' a deep, accented voice said from outside the door. 'If you don't open this door, my colleague will be very insulted. This will not be good for you.'

Bernard panted softly. His forehead became incredibly hot and moist. He waited a second longer before saying, 'Hold on a second, please.'

He looked down at the knife. Then he thought better of it. Hesitantly, he opened the door and was greeted by two very grim faces. The large man placed a meaty hand on Bernard's chest and pushed him back into the house, before they invited themselves in. When the door was closed, the older man with the white hair said, 'By now you have probably worked out who I am, yes?'

Bernard nodded. The tip of his penis began to throb with the sudden urge to urinate.

'Good. You are going to tell me everything you know about Emily Matthews and then you are going to take me to her house so we can speak with her boyfriend. And please, for everyone's sake, don't lie. My friend here has had a long week and is not in the best of moods.'

Epilogue

Three weeks later

The Seagull Café didn't see many regulars in the spring. In truth, it no longer saw many regulars at all, but still maintained a steady, if not sleepy, stream of custom. Today, however, marked the fifth day in a row that the woman had come in, choosing to sit at a table near the back, facing the wall.

This time, when Barbara took the woman her tea and toast, she said, 'There's a much better view of the sea if you face the other way.'

'Hmm?' Emily looked up at Barbara as though the waitress had just roused her from a very deep daydream.

Barbara pointed to the window. 'I've noticed that you keep coming in and sitting facing the wall. I was just saying that the sea is much nicer to look at.' Having spent longer than the usual five seconds it took to bring the woman her food, Barbara noticed just how ill she looked. The skin on her face was waxy and appeared as though it was pulled too tightly over her skull. Far more worrying, however, was the woman's vacant gaze that seemed to be looking directly through Barbara. Barbara had seen that look many times before. The seafront was no stranger to the junkies that shuffled around like the walking dead.

Some mornings it was like running an obstacle course, trying to avoid their outstretched hands as they harassed her for spare change. Barbara couldn't tell if the woman was a user or not. She seemed far too clean and articulate, without any of the jittery mannerisms that Barbara had come to identify. In fact, the woman was incredibly still, a waxwork that occasionally nibbled at her toast and made a cup of tea last for hours.

'Oh, sorry,' Emily said. 'Should I move?'

'No. You sit where you like, my love.' Barbara was about to go back to the counter and continue with her crossword, but said, 'Are you OK?'

'Yeah.' Emily pushed a strand of hair behind her ear. 'Yes. Fine, thank you.'

'Not from around here, are you?'

Barbara saw the woman's face grow wary. 'No.'

'You're a Londoner, aren't you? I can tell by the accent.'

Emily lifted the cup and took a long sip. 'Yes.'

'I can't blame you for wanting a break from that place.' Barbara watched the woman shift in her seat, knocking the table with her knees and jingling the teaspoon on the saucer.

'Yeah, I know,' she said quietly. 'I'm thinking of trying to settle down here for a while.'

'Oh yeah? Bournemouth's lovely, isn't it?' Barbara pointed to the sea view, her hands pink and puffy from years of ferrying hot plates about the place. 'Nothing like the sea air to clear the head. I'll warn you, though, it's a completely different pace to London, as I'm sure you can imagine. Life moves a lot slower down here. We don't go around stabbing each other if we can help it.'

For the first time in five days, Barbara saw the woman smile. 'Good. That's just what I'm after.'

Barbara gave the café a cursory glance, saw that the only other patron was eating his omelette by the window, and invited herself to sit down at the woman's table.

'What's your name, love?'

'Emily.'

'Barbara.' She offered her hand and Emily shook it. 'Where are you staying?'

Emily pointed vaguely and said, 'A bed and breakfast a few streets away.'

'I don't mean to pry,' Barbara began, knowing that prying was exactly what she meant to do. 'You can tell me to piss off if you want, I won't be offended. It's just, you don't seem very well.'

'I…' Emily lowered her gaze to her lap. 'I've just come out of a bad break-up.'

'I see. Were you with him long… or her, if it's a *her*.' Barbara shrugged emphatically in an effort to show that lesbianism wasn't going to be a problem for her.

'I was with him a long time, yes.' She sipped the tea again and then wrapped her hands around the cup to warm them. 'I've left everything behind in London. I just want to make a clean break.'

Barbara nodded. 'You looking for work?'

Emily considered the question. She was on the brink of bursting the credit card's limit and then she would really be up the proverbial creek. 'Yes,' she replied, although she was still unsure as to whether she was in the right frame of mind to commit.

'Well, there's none here,' Barbara said. 'I mean not in this café. But you know the Anchor, the pub down off the pier there?' Emily nodded, even though she had no idea where it was. 'The landlord, Callum Murray, he's got a few businesses along the promenade. His son owns the gym, and they have a little restaurant called La Cocina, you know, Portuguese food and that. Anyway, if you go and ask Callum, I'm sure he could slot you in somewhere, depending on what your experience is, I mean.'

'Thanks for the tip,' Emily said. 'It's really nice of you to do that.'

Barbara patted Emily's hand and stood up. 'No guarantees, of course, but it can't hurt to ask, can it? Drop my name if you like. Don't know if it will do you much good but I've known his family going on thirty years now so, you know, can't hurt.'

Barbara went back to the counter to greet a young couple that had come giggling in, full of life and optimism.

Emily turned in her chair and looked out toward the front of the café. She watched the sea crash against the sand in the distance, the seagulls wheeling in the air, squawking for scraps.

When she'd finished her tea and toast, Emily left the café, shielding her eyes from the sun. She breathed in a deep lungful of the sea air and began strolling down the seafront.

Since the burial three weeks ago, Emily had only had one dream about Kate. In the dream, Kate was waiting for Emily on a bench in Hyde Park. It was summer, the sun streaming through the dappled branches, the air alive with laughter and conversation.

As Emily neared, Kate looked up from the book she was reading and waved emphatically. She was smiling, the sunlight painting her skin gold.

'Hurry up, slowcoach!' Kate cried across a knot of inline skaters. 'I've been waiting ages. What took you so long?'

'I don't know,' Emily called back. 'I don't know!' she began to laugh, her feet gliding down the path, her arms open wide.

Kate met her halfway and they crashed into each other, hugging and spinning, cackling wildly like two naughty schoolgirls, not really sure what was so funny, it was just that intuitive twin telepathy.

'I love you so much,' Emily said, appraising her sister, and upon seeing no hideous markings on her neck, pulled her close and hugged her tighter.

'I love you too. I love you so much.'

Emily had woken to the sound of her own laughter and the memory of Kate's voice fading in her ears. She had laughed some more, and then she had cried, and then she had decided that maybe, just maybe, she might be OK.

–

In the café, the man sitting by the window finished his omelette and approached the counter.

'How was it, my love?' Barbara asked with a pleasant smile, vaguely surprised at how large he was.

'Delicious,' the man said, removing his wallet before picking out a ten from the fold of notes.

'Ooh, that's a nice accent you have there,' Barbara said as she rang up the cost of his breakfast and handed over his three pounds' change. 'I have an ear for accents, you know. Let me guess. German.'

The man received his change and then placed the coins in the coffee cup labelled 'tips' atop the counter. 'Dutch,' he said, returning her smile.

He wished her good day, and then headed out into the sunshine.

–

'Jackie, we need to be at the venue for four o'clock, OK?' May said rapidly. 'If we're late they're not going to wait.'

'I know.' Jack sighed.

'So we need to be there on time because otherwise we'll miss the six o'clock appointment as well, and I *really* like the look of that venue, so please, *please*, don't be late.'

'I'll be there, hun.'

'Please be on time.'

'I will,' he said. 'Calm down.'

'OK, sorry, sorry. I'll let you get back on with your lunch. What are you having anyway?'

'A sandwich,' he lied. 'Look, I'd better shoot off.' He could hear her gearing up for more conversation so he gave her the magic words. 'Love you.'

She giggled. 'Love you. Husband-to-be.'

He ended the call. He still didn't like using these damn mobile phones, but May had surprised him with a new one and he was not in a position to refuse her. It was one of the terms in their revised, unspoken contract. They did not talk about what had happened on Frazier Avenue, and she had never asked any follow-up questions. Although there were times, if they were relaxing on the sofa watching TV or in the middle of eating dinner, where he could almost hear her thinking about it. He could sense that it took every bit of discipline and self-restraint she had not to bring it up, for fear that it might rock their new-found stability. She had everything she ever wanted: she was living at his place full-time and had put her house on the market. He had relented to her request for an exotic honeymoon. And why not? He needed a decent holiday, and maybe two weeks lying on a sun lounger without any heavy lifting would help his back.

So he would keep her sweet, get another ring put on his finger, listen to her ramblings and carry on as the big, quiet dummy he had always been. Because he never knew when he might need her again.

He pulled up at a traffic light and heard his stomach growl. He had been on his way to the Cheshunt warehouse to shift some stock and remembered a new steakhouse that had opened nearby. The almost porno-graphic poster of perfectly pink meat in the window had stayed with him. Today was as good a day as any for a T-bone.

It had been three weeks since he dumped Morley into that hole. He was due a treat.

He pulled into the car park and was happy to see that, despite it being lunchtime, the steakhouse was still relatively empty.

A tiny, smiling brunette greeted him eagerly at the door.

'Hi,' Jack said jovially. 'Table for one, please.'

'Sure thing. Right this way.' She walked him through the restaurant and gestured to a series of empty tables next to the window. 'Somewhere here, sir?'

'I think this'll do fine, thank you.' She placed the menu on the table as he sat down and asked if she could get him a drink to start with. 'I'd love a pint of your local ale, please.'

'Sure,' she beamed at him as though genuinely happy for his custom, and then skipped off. She returned a moment later with a pint glass on a tray. He took a long, luxurious sip and smacked his lips. He couldn't say that it was the nicest beer he had ever tasted, but it had to be in the top five, maybe even the top three.

He was feeling very good about the beer and the steak he would order when his waitress returned. He looked over the dessert menu with great interest. He was quite sure about the chocolate brownie, but the apple pie looked pretty fantastic too. You know what? He was seriously considering getting both. Why worry?

He heard his waitress greet a new customer and briefly looked up from the menu, ready to grab her attention when she was done.

And that's when he saw him.

Jack's back arched against the chair. He gripped the edge of the table, his throat slowly closing until it felt like he was trying to breathe through a straw.

A man stood by the doorway with his young son. The waitress was asking him where he wanted to sit and the man looked down at his son and said, 'What do you think, Oliver? The booth over there looks good, doesn't it?'

Jack dug his nails into the table. His heart palpitated painfully. He grabbed his beer, gulped, and rolled the glass across his forehead in an effort to cool his flaming skin. He plunged his hand into his pocket and touched the folding knife. Thank god he hadn't forgotten it.

His appetite, which had been ravenous just a couple of minutes ago, had vanished. He had to do something quickly. He watched the waitress take their drinks order and disappear off to the kitchen.

I hope you never find him.

Jack's scalp prickled. His scrotum tightened around his testicles, sending a ticklish, almost unbearable sensation crawling through his thighs. The beer swished sickeningly in his stomach and the aftertaste was like battery acid in his mouth.

He eased the chair back and stood up. His legs felt like he had drunk five pints instead of half of one. He watched the man talking to his son as they looked over the menu, and slowly began walking toward their booth.

Upon noticing him approach, the man gradually looked up from the menu to see Jack standing there, sweating and shaking before him.

The man's green eyes flashed at him. Jack cringed and looked at his son, who also had the same reptilian eyes.

'Can I help you?' the man asked, his brow creasing with concern.

Jack forced his face to smile, but felt the grin twitch unnaturally on his lips.

'Yes,' Jack said. 'I feel like I know you from somewhere.'

The man considered it for less than a second before shaking his head. 'No, I don't think so.'

'You don't recognise me?' Jack asked.

'No,' the man replied, firmer this time.

'I see.' He glanced at little Oliver, who was staring up at Jack with a queer sort of nervous curiosity. 'This your son?'

'Yes,' the man said sharply.

'You look too young to have a son this age. What are you now, thirty? Thirty-one?'

'I'm sorry,' the man began warily. 'Is there something wrong?'

343

'Wrong?' *What could possibly be wrong?* Jack thought. He put his hand in his pocket and held the knife. 'Nothing wrong. I just feel like I know you from somewhere.'

'Well, like I said—'

'You've got unmistakeable eyes. I bet lots of people tell you that.'

'No, not really. We're actually trying to order our food, so if you wouldn't mind…' His green eyes narrowed.

This time I know it's you, Jack thought.

'Of course,' Jack said, the words wobbling out of his mouth. 'I'm sorry to have disturbed you.'

Jack made his way over to where the waitress was standing. He apologised, said he wasn't feeling very well, and asked if he could settle up for the beer.

Then he left the restaurant, headed back to his van, and waited for the man to finish his meal. He would follow the man, find out where he lived, where his son went to school. He would learn the man's routine, and then, when the time was right, he would take him. Maybe he would get May involved. Yes, he thought she might be ready for it, would probably even get a kick out of it. And he'd need the help too, if he was going to pull it off without a hitch. It wasn't like the old days when his back was stronger.

So he had been wrong about Craig Morley. Jack rewound the tape in his mind, thought back to when he had first spotted him that day in the supermarket, and then began to laugh. He shook his head, thought the laughter had subsided, and then began cracking up again, his stomach muscles tightening painfully. When was the last time he had laughed like this? He couldn't remember.

Poor Craig Morley. Well, Jack had made a mistake; what else could he say? It wasn't the first time he had got it wrong, but practice made perfect. He was only human.

He supposed he owed Emily an apology.

The last giggles slithered out of him, and he turned his mind to more serious business: the man in the steakhouse. The man who, twelve years ago, shattered Jack's life into a million pieces. He had grown up to be quite the respectable gentleman, hadn't he? The fancy clothes, the almost unbearable politeness, and he had a handsome young son. He'd had twelve years to perfect his act, denying all recognition of Jack right to his face.

The audacity and cunning of the man amazed Jack as much as it upset him.

But Jack knew the truth. It was all a veneer and he could see right through it.

Because the eyes never lie.

Acknowledgements

A big thank you to my agent Tom Witcomb and all the team at Canelo for your invaluable guidance and support throughout the whole publishing process.